Books by Carolyn Slaughter

THE STORY OF THE WEASEL
COLUMBA
MAGDALENE
THE HEART OF THE RIVER
DREAMS OF THE KALAHARI
THE BANQUET
A PERFECT WOMAN

The INNOCENTS

The INNOCENTS

CAROLYN SLAUGHTER

CHARLES SCRIBNER'S SONS

New York • *1986*

Johnson

This novel is a work of fiction. Names, characters, places and incidents are either the product of the author's imagination or are used fictitiously. Any resemblance to actual persons, living or dead, events or locales is entirely coincidental.

Copyright © 1986 Carolyn Slaughter

Library of Congress Cataloging-in-Publication Data

Slaughter, Carolyn.
The innocents.

I. Title.
PR6069.L37I56   1986   823'.914   85-30269
ISBN 0-684-18643-8

1 3 5 7 9 11 13 15 17 19   F/C   20 18 16 14 12 10 8 6 4 2

Printed in the United States of America.

For my husband,
Kemp Battle

PART ONE

I, *a stranger and afraid*
in a world I never made.
A. E. HOUSMAN

One

"I'M BEING BURIED ALIVE."

Her lips drawn back, her teeth clenched, she snarled it at no one. For the room was empty apart from the fly, which had stopped for a moment on the window pane as if to gaze at what was out there: heat, dust, emptiness—mid-afternoon heat, dust, and emptiness. No movement. Even the glare was static.

She lay on the bed, naked but for short white socks and tennis shoes. Slowly, seductively, she began to arrange her body in the pose that she adopted each night before falling asleep: her left leg flat, the other bent provocatively at the knee; her hips at a slight angle, nestling into the bunched sheet; her arms above her head in the coil she'd copied from the calendar picture of a movie queen once found in the attic.

The fly marched its silver-and-green body up and down the window, making an angry, drilling sound. She sat up to watch it with fury, the plumpness of her arms hardening into muscle, a little ribbon of fat furrowing her belly. Immediately she flopped back again, rubbing sweat into the rough pile of her hair with her hands. An elephant-hair bracelet slipped up her arm to lodge in the flesh, denting it. She snarled again, pushing her face into the pillows as if to suffocate herself.

In the yard outside, Willie was watching her. Or, what he could see of her: the incomplete soles of her shoes, the tip of one knee, tousled hair thrown back on a mound of pillows. There was no harm in watching, the boy thought, when he could see nothing. A hose pipe hung limply in his hand, the stream of water making holes in the earth between the rows of dusty geraniums. When he noticed the damage, he shrugged: it was only a Thursday job. By Thursday he was so tired out with his schoolwork and the work on the lands that his energy was gone.

He pushed back the wooly cap so that it sat on his head at a cocky angle. This hat was a private joke—when he wore it he assumed the guise of a garden boy.

He glanced back at the window and knew that in a short time the sun would move around and turn the pane into a mirror. He thought of her lying there and it brought out a brief smile of compassion. From where he stood he felt he could read her mood, but when she was like this he could not approach her. He yanked the hose pipe along to the flower beds near the mulberry tree. The ground under the tree was stained purple and he rubbed the soles of his shoes into the sand to dislodge the splattered fruit. He hated the ground when it was like this. And he was careful about his shoes, did not like a mark on them. But then neither would he go barefoot.

She too hated the ground like this: "It's like when Boykie squashes the ticks from the dogs under his feet—it looks like blood in the dirt. It's disgusting." He smiled: to him she was still that same little girl he used to play with, his head and hers close together as they peered into the shoe box punctured with holes where they kept the silkworms, feeding them on mulberry leaves. "Look, Willie, just look, man, how the sun makes water on the silk." He would bend toward the iridescent sheen. "No, don't touch, just look." He would also have liked to touch, but in some delicate things, he would do as she said.

By now the water from the pipe had made such a deep trench in the mud that he was forced to put it down, stoop, and push the roots of some ugly pink flowers back into the earth. He did it carelessly, breaking the limp leaves.

She was standing by the mirror in her room. When he straightened up he could see her. It wasn't right that he should see her like that, being neither her husband nor her lover. He turned away and moved backward so that the window should not attract him again.

She returned to her bed, lay down on it, and picked up a fat, padded book. It was her diary. She unlocked the small gilt lock with a key hung on a chain around her neck. And began to write, quickly and furiously with a biro, making round looped characters.

I hate this ugly name they gave me: Ruth. Ruthie. It stinks. It's a dark name, like Rebecca, Rachel, those black ugly Bible names, names of people who had dreadful things happen to them. I should be an Anna-Marie, Mariana, Gloria. My mother was blond and very beautiful, true as God. My pa also. It doesn't matter I never saw them, or pictures even. That old bitch burnt everything. Ja, every single thing. Made a funeral pyre of my mother's things the day after, all the stuff that should have come to me. Every thing of hers and his burnt to nothing. Don't tell me it's because she went mad with grief. She hasn't a sad feeling in her whole body, that one. She did it to spite me, that's why. She blames me for being alive, for being in my carry-cot safe when the car crashed. I wish I had died. What would it matter? The only thing they gave me I hate. My name. Nothing else to pick up and look at and say: This was given to me by my mother. If I could just see her picture, maybe she'd be smiling out of it and I could pretend it was at me. Burnt. By my aunt who hates everyone. They tell me nothing. Not even Hannah will talk about my parents. She shrugs. She looks sort of peculiar. When I ask questions now, they don't even bother to look at one another like they used to. Sometimes I scream: Aren't you ever going to tell me *anything*? I've a right. A right. They just look at me as if I'm making them tired, then Hannah will say, "There's nothing more to tell, Ruthie, your ma and pa were killed on the road outside the old farm." But that's not all there is to tell, I just know, I've always known, since I was tiny. They're lying.

You could die here, you know that? Nothing for bloody miles, except that burnt farm. So why doesn't someone pull it down? Hey? Why not? Not even the blacks will go in there. They say it's full of bad spirits. I've been in there and it gives me the creeps. It was part of our land once. But it's another thing we don't talk about, that burnt farm. Willie said it was something to do with our family, but he doesn't know what. He looks shifty, so that sometimes I think Willie also is hiding things from me. And he's the only one I can trust. I think the bitch burnt it. She's that way inclined after all, and once . . .

A noise in the corridor outside caused her to snap the diary to and stuff it under her pillow. The door was opened and Hannah walked in.

"Why don't you bloody knock, hey?"

Hannah hated swearing, but only a flicker around her eyes betrayed her. "The door was not closed." The calmness of the woman infuriated Ruth.

"I'm so bloody bored I could die," she said.

"Don't talk like that."

'*Don't talk like that.*' Ruth aped the other's patience, screwing up her face at the same time, "Don't think like that, don't make like that, don't do like that." She threw her legs off the bed. "What do you want anyway?"

Then she saw the towel in Hannah's hand and she backed away without realizing it.

"We have to do it," Hannah said, pleading.

"No, I won't." Surly, her mouth twisted, her beauty gone, "You can't make me," she said.

At the corner of Hannah's mouth a muscle began to throb.

"Don't make trouble, hey? It won't take long, I promise you."

"What's it to do with you?" Her mouth trembled as it had when she was a little girl.

"Let's just get it over with." Hannah moved forward.

The girl began to wheedle, "Ag, please, Hannah, not today. Okay? Tomorrow, I promise you. I mean it, true as God."

Hannah did not reply; instead she moved to the basin in the corner of the room and began to fill it with water. She drew up a covered stool, put down the towel, turned and waited.

"No, I'd rather the bath," Ruth snapped in a low, beaten voice, "not here."

Hannah followed her down the dark corridor into the bathroom at the end. She went in and turned on the taps loud and fast. Ruth perched herself on the edge of the bath, nonchalant. Hannah drew up the faded wicker chair and made a cushion with towels draped across its back.

Ruth darted from the room. Hannah stopped. Her eyes glazed with weariness. She walked slowly to the door. The girl stood in the corridor, furious, her hands on her hips, her voice harsh and loud.

"Why must I listen to you, anyway? You're not my mother."

Hannah watched her quietly, saying nothing.

"What are you, anyway?" Ruth yelled. "You're just a kaffir. A kaffir with a spit of white in you. That's all, that's all you are, isn't it? Isn't it?"

She saw Hannah's face stiffen, then turn pitying. She screamed, "Don't you pretend with me, don't pretend you're white. Just because we let you live here with us, don't act like you're one of us." Her voice became spiteful. "I could tell on you, I could." Then it descended into a wail. "I could change everything around here."

Hannah controlled the shudder that went through her. She could feel the vibrations in each vertebra—like shot hitting the separate bones.

"Don't be ugly," she whispered, "don't say things that we can't forget."

She was angry, but she forgave Ruth at once: it was fear that made her like this; she was a good child. Sometimes she said things like that because she couldn't help it. It wasn't her fault. But the words would never go.

Hannah waited with dignity for the girl to recover, to become again the sweet person she loved. But then the tears broke. Hannah waited for their intensity to pass before she moved forward and took Ruth in her arms to comfort her. "Hush now, hush, it's all right."

Presently she lifted Ruth's chin and smiled ruefully. "You're so wet with crying now, that you won't even notice the water."

She felt the body stiffen against hers, but knew that it was over. They walked slowly back into the bathroom.

And Ruth suffered her hair to be washed.

Two

HANNAH WATCHED RUTH AS SHE SAT IN THE SUN. HER LONG hair was spread thickly over her shoulders; she was calm now, but withdrawn. Watching her, Hannah relived all those dreadful times in the past when Ruth's hair had to be washed. When Ruth was tiny, her Aunt Zelda would drag the child to the bathroom and hold her down. The little face grew quite savage with fear as the water ran down her cheeks and into her eyes. And, since Zelda would tolerate nothing she did not understand, she would persevere, not with cruelty exactly, but with diligence, ignoring the screams.

One day, unable to bear it another moment, Hannah walked into the bathroom, placed her hand on Zelda's shoulder and said, "Please, let me do it." Zelda looked up sharply at her, but allowed it. From then on, Hannah's relationship, not only with the small child but also with the mistress of the house, altered. She took responsibility for Ruth, and Zelda stepped back.

Hannah tried to get Ruth over her fear of water, and began by finding new ways of washing her hair, but nothing helped, not even the plastic shield wrapped around the child's forehead, which kept the water off her face. It was as if Ruth knew what it was to drown. She never ventured near water; she kept away from it the way the Africans hid from thunder and lightning. She dreamt of drowning, time and again, and Hannah would comfort her in the night, whispering to her, as if an explanation might take away the fear: "Perhaps you were scared when you swam in your mother's stomach, or maybe you remember when the waters burst and pushed you out?" She didn't make Ruth swim, or allow anyone else to do so. She protected the child fiercely—for who else was there to do it?

But now Ruth sat in the sun, drying her hair. She would only stay there as long as it took to dry. Her skin was pale, she would have it that way. From the time she'd grown vain, at puberty, her skin had never had a tan; she protected its bloom the way a gardener nurses a prize orchid. She took a bath only once a month; on other days she merely sponged her body, but for Hannah's sake she filled the bath, then let the water run out again.

Hannah was watching Ruth the way she always did, with love and with fear. She saw how the girl's hand moved to her right temple and fretted there, as if to remove something stubborn and ugly. How she hated that birthmark. Whenever she sat so, apparently unobserved, she would chafe at the dark mark on her forehead. Once she said, "I'll take a knife to it one day, I promise you, and cut it away." And Hannah had said, "No, no, don't think that way. It's where the spirits of your ancestors kissed you when you were born, it's the mark of love."

Hannah put down her book; she felt she must go in, check on the kitchen girl and see that supper was begun before Zelda came back from the lands. But she went on sitting, watching Ruth with a particular concentration. It was something spiritual, something almost removed from the world, even from God, quite total. She shifted on her chair and laid her feet flat on the polished stone floor of the stoep. The dogs, lolling and listless, moved from one place to another, trying to cool their flanks in the afternoon heat.

She was remembering herself at Ruth's age. It was then, at sixteen, that her life seemed to come to a halt. All she could do was to pick it up and carry it like a load upon her back. Better not to think of that time, better to remember before that.

ON THE OLD FARM, YEARS BACK, WHEN THE OUBAAS WAS ALIVE and before his wife moved to that little flat in the Cape, Hannah led an enchanted life. She'd been taken in by the children at the old farm: Zelda and her twin brother Dawie. In many ways, indifference had brought it about, that and the isolation of the place. Mrs. de Valera, the mother of the twins, had suffered a tragedy which made her careless of everything except the events of that tragedy. She let her children run wild, doing as they pleased without even really noticing.

She was away a lot; she said the farm tormented her, brought back the memories, so she spent her time visiting her relatives living on similar farms or in towns far away. Her husband moved between his large and remote farms, spending a month or so at each—"Collecting land," his wife sneered, "the way a Jew collected money." Soon he had more land than anyone in the district, but he was not liked, being unsociable and cold to his neighbors. He and his wife had little in common. ("It was not for me to be a farmer's wife, God meant me for better things." And he: "If God meant for you better things, why then aren't you doing them?")

The farm was set in a vast, flat country with a monotonous grandeur and beauty discernible only to those bred to it. The land was broken up by rocky koppies and shallow valleys over which vultures swooped looking for dead things on the thin gray roads. There was a certain fertility to the earth—crops grew, cattle and sheep grazed the tough veld grass, keeping close to the brown rivers with their fringes of willow and poplar. There were orchards in some parts, and in springtime the peach blossom was beautiful, bringing softness to a land as gruff and inflexible as the Afrikaners who worked and loved it.

This land seemed to have got the God it deserved: He had little forgiveness and he was peculiarly indifferent to suffering. In some ways, the land and the life still echoed the Old Testament. On Sundays, the dominees, in white churches up and down the country, sent out their warnings and read to the people the only real literature their forbears had known: the Bible, the Lord's Word. Black and colored people, who had once prayed at the back of the church, taking the Sacrament after pink mouths had sipped and passed, now preferred to keep their own happier celebrations separate from their employers. These employers, in spite of their simplicity (some said backwardness), were often fabulously wealthy, owning vast tracts of land and thousands of head of sheep.

Zelda de Valera, who, at the age of eight, scorned all of the above and proclaimed herself a free spirit, had been the person most responsible for drawing Hannah into this singular world and out of her own. It was Zelda who insisted on Hannah's participation in their life and it was her brother, Dawie, who cajoled their mother, always more susceptible to him, to allow it.

So began an unusual friendship. The three got on so closely that soon they seemed as similar as three prongs on a fork. They went into the bush with guns to shoot hares and birds. They took lumps of dark bread, yellow cheese and oranges, and made their camps. They held an initiation ceremony closely resembling that of the adolescent black boys. They were the same age almost to the month and they felt they were the same sex. From the time they were nine, you never saw one without the other two.

Dawie showed them how to trap birds and to shoot the way his father had taught him. Zelda was soon as fast and as accurate as he was, but Hannah held back. She hated it when Dawie crouched down in the dirt to skin the hares, pulling back the pelt to leave the naked, veined body, small and still. But he would squint up at her, his face in the sunlight radiant with wonder. The hares, the little shiny birds he shot, he was tender with them. Zelda was the hard one. The other two gave way to her unless they united against her.

These days, when Hannah and Zelda sat on the stoep and talked of the old farm, how it had been—the planting of the trees and crops, the years of drought or illness—harmless, finished things that connected their history—it was as if they had always been together. So much of their lives had been shared. They were like sisters, one could not imagine being without the other, and yet neither would admit it. So much was unspoken between them now, and they tried never to talk about Dawie. That last time he'd come back—oh, years ago—it had been so terrible.

But at nine years old, life was simple and good. The old homestead, with its beautiful gables that threw tall shadows across the lawn, the trees that shut out the glare and hid them from the outside world with its strange ways—this was more than sufficient. There were few visitors. They went to church once a year. An Indian trader came weekly with his truck to deliver groceries and give lollipops to the children. The nearest dorp was several hours away and they had no interest in it. The farm was theirs, their own country, a complete, sealed world in which Hannah was allowed to play indoors like a white child, to romp on the beds, sit on the chairs, eat at the same table, go to the lavatory, even take a bath in the shiny white tub with feet like lion's claws. Sometimes the kitchen woman, Ilsa, would take Zelda aside and say, "No, missy, this is not right, the missus she would not like this." But the missus didn't seem aware of what went on outside her bedroom. Sometimes she would shout at them through her closed door and tell them to be quiet. Mostly the missus just walked heavily up and down her bedroom in the long, dead afternoons and drank many transparent drinks that sent her to sleep or caused her to weep in the room of the old spinster auntie, her sister, Ethel. Ethel was a birdlike woman, a bit mad for the love of God, who took her meals alone and seemed to have no purpose but to listen to her sister's sorrows. She took little notice of the three children either.

And Zelda, steadily more stubborn and wild, took no notice of anyone. The world spun on her axis. At the end of the day, when Ilsa chased the twins to bed and sent Hannah home to her mother's hut on the other side of the dam, they would separate and smile. Later, as the old woman spat on her iron, stamping it down on damp clothes in a kitchen loud with music from a local African station, Zelda opened the dining-room window and Hannah crept back in. She usually slept in Zelda's bed while Zelda slept on the floor with an arm flung around the neck of one of her dogs.

The two didn't talk a lot in the night, not as Zelda did when she visited her cousins in the Transvaal or the Free State—whispering all night, making up fantasies and gruesome tales to frighten and impress them. Her cousins seldom made return journeys; Zelda discouraged it because it meant keeping Hannah away. With Hannah it was quiet, it was understood between them: they planned the next day, they shouted goodnight to Dawie across the hall, and slept. Life was so full it exhausted them.

At dawn, Dawie would come in and wake Hannah with hot sweet tea and rusks. He sat on her bed and told her his dreams in minute detail. It was a time precious to them both, Zelda powerless with sleep. The minute she was awake she must exert herself, and if she had no one to dominate she became hostile. So Dawie loved to sit on the end of Hannah's bed or get in with her on cold winter mornings and talk without his sister's interruptions. He loved to hear Hannah say, "Ja, ja," nodding her head gravely, sipping her tea, dipping in her rusk, listening to every word he said and dreading the moment she would have to leave.

For when she left, she must take off the beautiful lawn nightdress with its pink rosebud and put on an old secondhand dress of Zelda's. In the big house—at home, as Hannah thought of it—Zelda would dress her up in the party dresses her mother brought back from Cape Town. Zelda never wore them, only shorts and jeans, the older the better, but these dresses were quite delicious to Hannah, so delicate, so infinitely superior were they to the nylon frocks her mother made for her to wear to church. She had come to despise the crisp cloth that stuck out around her legs and was covered with white dots on a blue or yellow ground. And once, once she had loved these dresses with all her heart, and begged for one, had cried when her ma brought the cloth from the store and sat up all night sewing it. It had caused her mother worry and sadness to see the change in her child, but when it was your child, how could you deprive it of what it wanted most—even if in the end it brought sorrow? And besides, Hannah had never been as the other children—and that was not her fault.

Hannah's mother was a Xhosa woman who had been with a white man, having one child by him before marrying a man from her own tribe. They had a Christian marriage in Mossel Bay and, when she got pregnant, he brought her back to live with his clan in the country. He did not mind the colored child, but then the Xhosas always got on well with the coloreds and often married them. He did not mind that the girl was so pale—after all, her mother too was pale. He rather liked it. But he was gone now, with the other men from the land, working in a fish factory and living on a compound. They were not allowed their wives and families with them. But Hannah could remember a time when

they had all lived together in a pondokkie made of tin and cor-
rugated iron. It was on the outskirts of some town, and those were
happy days. She had liked the city life, the noise, the different people all crowded together happily with a shack each could call his
own.

Later, the bulldozers came and the trucks, but she could remember this less well. What she did remember was the way her mother
cried when parted from her husband. She was sent away, back to
the raw land, to a country she'd never seen, to strangers she feared.
There had been many moves since then, trying to get back to her
husband, looking for work so that she could feed and educate the
children. And what Hannah had come to hate was her mother's
Christian patience, her acceptance of her lot, her humility to God—
who seemed always remarkably absent when all these things
happened.

And perhaps she too would have grown like her mother, would
have bent her back and her pride simply to exist. It was startling
to look back to that one day in her life and to see how completely
it had altered everything.

She had been sitting by the dam, plaiting grass, when a strange
girl, standing above the rocks, had called out to her, "Hey, you,
can you do what I'm going to do?"

With this, Zelda stood there poised, and then dived straight into
the deep water. She had not surfaced.

Hannah was afraid, knowing about the submerged rocks and
how only the bravest would plunge from that height and find
the cleft between the rocks. Zelda didn't reappear. The ripples on
the water flashed.

Hannah ran over to the rocks, climbed them to a point above
Zelda's dive and peered into the water, seeing nothing below. She
dived in herself, never having done so before: something com-
pelled her—it was as if the other's will had wiped out her fear.

It was a moment of exhilaration—falling through the air,
plunging down to the depths like a fish. When she surfaced, shaken,
amazed to be alive, she saw far, far away in the center of the dam,
a laughing face, and then an arm, waving triumphantly, beckon-
ing her.

"That was our baptism of courage," Zelda announced later,

lying on the bank, while Hannah sat awkwardly a little distance away. "Ja, you'll see, this is just the beginning. You come with me now, we'll be friends, we'll do everything together. Don't look like that, who's to stop us? Hey? Nobody. Come over to my house, now—now—I want you to meet my boetie. We were born just minutes apart from one another. Him first, then me. His name is Dawie and there is no one like him in the whole world. He's the best. Come. Quick now. You don't need anything. Just come."

Three

THEY WERE NOT IDENTICAL TWINS. ZELDA WAS A LITTLE
taller than Dawie and he was thinner, but they shared many man-
nerisms and they had the same flaxen hair, high forehead, and
deep-set eyes. Dawie was more good-natured and he put up with
his sister's bossiness, saying, "Ag ja, she's like she is because I got
out into the world ahead of her. Now she's always trying to catch
up with me." He, like his sister, did entirely as he pleased on the
farm, but he was better at getting his own way than she, with her
tantrums. He did it by being reasonable, logical, and quiet. And it
was Dawie who decided that Hannah must do her lessons with
them.

A retired schoolmaster came to the farm each day to teach them.
Dawie took him to one side and said, "Now look, meneer, how
would you like a nice, bright pupil for a change?"

"Are you thinking then of working a little bit?" the meneer
asked sarcastically.

"Ag no, man, I'm not talking about me, or Zelda. No, we have
a brand-new pupil for you. No, don't look like that. It's okay,
we've got permission from ma, you can ask her when she gets back
next week. How about it?"

Hannah stood at the door, a little defiant, a little afraid, waiting for the dismissive toss of the head, that look that would separate her from them. Meneer stared at her, then at Dawie, then at
Zelda, who flashed him her brittle, mocking smile. Then back to

the tall, thin child with her apricot skin, her hair pulled back into a ponytail but frizzing about her temples, her full Xhosa mouth and broad, pretty nose.

"Get a chair—ja, from there," he said curtly. "Quick now, don't hold up the class."

Meneer's instinct about her intelligence was immediately rewarded. Not only was she brighter, but she worked harder than the other two put together. She was determined to catch up on all the school she'd missed taking care of her siblings while her mother went away to look after other people's children, instead of her own.

One day, Hannah heard Zelda's mother say, "Zelda, who cares if she learns or not, hey? What good will it do her? For what is she learning? In the end she must just work with her hands, isn't it?"

As the anger rose in her, Hannah heard her ally say, "Now look here, Ma, if we opened your head and took a look inside a bit, we'd see nothing. Inside Hannah's head there's all sorts of things, there's knowledge you never even dreamed of. That room full of oupa's books that we never go in, she reads them. Oh ja, I'm telling you, if ever you can't find her, she's in there." Then she laughed and whispered, "And she knows what's going to happen, too. There's witch doctors in her family. She has strong powers, so you mustn't mess her around. It's true, I'm telling you, even Dawie doesn't dare. She's clever, man. She can say the whole of the Song of Solomon by heart, and if you pick out a bit from Isaiah, she'll tell you where it's from, honest to God."

Her mother snorted. "So what's so clever about that?"

"It's clever, ja, it's clever," Zelda said simply, smiling, infuriating her mother.

"Don't look at me with that cheek on your face, you hear now? You cut that cheek or I'll tell your father."

Zelda laughed. "What'll you do then, Ma? Write him a letter? Send him a telegram? Where is he, ma? Tell us, then. Where?"

HANNAH LOOKED UP, CLOSING HER EYES TO THE PAST AND TO the present glare that seemed to beat at her eyes. She thought it

must be Zelda's truck making that cloud of dust in the distance—
but it was taking the left curve, away from the farm. How distant
even the road was.

She got up and went to the kitchen and ordered salads for dinner; slices off the beef they'd had hot at the big midday meal; lots
of young corn because Ruth liked it; and fat tomatoes from the
garden, with those griddle cakes.

She went from the kitchen across the backyard to the vegetable
garden to pick the tomatoes, and saw that Willie had not watered
today as he was supposed to. When she had done everything, she
went back to the front porch and there she saw Willie. He'd just
driven up in the old bakkie, which he was forbidden to use because he drove it as if he was trying to kill people. It was a wonder he'd only mown down chickens so far. And perhaps, knowing
Willie, there was a reason for that too, because the flattened
chickens weren't wanted at the farm kitchen. Willie's family ate
his accidents.

Hannah smiled with affection, and disapproval, as she saw him
leap from the van, slam the door, and dance over to where Ruth
sat in the shade, pulling a brush lazily through her hair. Look at
the way he walked: as though some melody pulsed through his
head that made his feet skim over the sand, and his shoulders and
hips roll as provocatively as a girl's, but *not* like a girl's—something bold and virile, manly and proud—something coming
directly from the rites of the bush that he'd recently been through.

He stood before Ruth, still swaying a little. She slowly looked
up at him.

"How goes it?" he asked.

"Fine." She turned her head downward and the hair fell, shield-
ing her face. Then she added, "Shouldn't you be watering?"

"Finished," he said, stemming his annoyance that she liked to
pull him back from his happiness.

He began to strut around her in a way he had, a way that made
her say with a laugh, "Ag, you think yourself so smart, Willie."

"That's what I am," he crooned, "the Marlon Brando of the
bush." And then he became that man: he pushed his shoulders
back in his immaculate white t-shirt, he pouted his mouth and

let his head rock gently as he began to walk in the way of the actor. Ruth laughed, shoving at him with her hands.

"Hey, but listen now, I'm forgetting myself. There's someone I've brought to see you. Wait a minute, now."

"Who?" Ruth asked with pleasure, pushing up the sand into a mound with her bare feet, her toes curling into the warmth of it.

Willie ran back to the bakkie, opened the door, and lifted down a plump little girl of three, his sister, Hettie. She clutched a doll tightly to her side; a doll with a white plastic face, one of Ruth's. The doll still wore her pink taffeta dress, her gold hair curly but matted, and her mouth open in a tight circle to take a bottle— long lost now.

Ruth got up and moved toward the little girl. "Ag, shame, isn't she sweet!"

She picked her up and began to talk to her affectionately in Afrikaans. Neither Willie nor his parents spoke their own language; the children had never known Xhosa apart from occasional words. Only the older people spoke it.

"Are you hungry?" Ruth urged the child. "Of course you are." And she shifted Hettie onto the saddle of her hip and strode off toward the kitchen, where Ilsa began her customary grumble, "Not now, don't come with your messing. I'm busy with the cooking here."

Ruth took up a crusty loaf of bread, still warm from the oven, and carried it to the table. She plonked Hettie down on the table next to the bread.

"This is not hygienic," Ilsa said furiously. "How do we know where this child has been sitting?" She whisked her off the table and put her in a chair by the fire. "Now you be quick, Ruth, I'm working here. It's late already."

Ruth cut a wedge of bread, spread it first with butter and then thickly with golden syrup. Then, taking a teaspoon, she plunged it into the tin, twirled the golden skeins, and popped it into Hettie's mouth. The brown eyes widened, the cheeks sucked in as her small mouth puckered with pleasure. Ruth laughed and tickled her chin. Hettie was given the lump of bread, and sat, munching, looking with no trace of alarm at the scowling Ilsa in her crisp white doek, who was sniffing crossly, knowing the sticky spoon would be left on the table, together with the butter and bread, for her to clean up later.

She chased them from her kitchen and got on with her cooking. Ruth walked outside, carrying Hettie over to the shade of the peach trees, letting her sit on the ground until she'd finished her bread.

"Lekker, hey?" Ruth said, watching small bites diminish the doorstep. Then, impulsively, she snatched up the child's hand and licked the syrup off her fingers.

From the stoep, seeing this, Hannah flinched a little: the child was a raw, kraal kid, it was not right, it was not . . . She shook her head.

Willie had gone to water some seedlings he'd planted in the vegetable garden for Hannah. And when he returned he saw Ruth with that strange, forlorn look about her. She stared off into the distance at the long throbbing horizon. It made him feel helpless. Even his happiness was fading; he could feel it go as he watched her.

The heat was so oppressive, the dust made a haze all around. The shadows from the trees hadn't yet moved across the stoep to where Hannah sat, with that stiff watchful gaze that made Willie feel she was in some way on guard. Ruth seemed to torment her, the boy thought, perhaps that was what came of bringing up children, even other people's. But with Hannah and Ruth it was different—it was not that Hannah had been a servant or a nanny, it was simply that Hannah had been allowed to bring Ruth up. This was the strange thing, this was the strange position that the colored woman held in the house.

But then, glancing back at Ruth, he thought he must be crazy. From what should he, or Hannah, be trying to protect or save her? Just look at her, delicately poised on her haunches, her arms outstretched to Hettie, who was crying over some small hurt. Ruth's dress—tiny pink roses scattered on lilac cotton—see the way it billowed out behind her, the way the fabric clung to her thighs and pulled itself into little ripples across her ribcage and then swelled out across her breasts. It was so moving to him—her womanliness, her beauty. He was awed by it. She could need nothing from him, ever, with such beauty. But now the child moved away from her embrace and, as she did so, the wind went out of the pink-sprigged dress, the fullness from Ruth's body. The dress now was no longer that proud, heavy sail, but simply a length of cloth from the Indian store trailing limp in the sand. And just now— how sad it was—he could almost have felt that the dress was cut from a piece of the morning sky.

How she pulled at his heart. He pitied her and this was a feeling that made him very uneasy. It was like looking at her naked. It was forbidden. He cared too much for and about her. How sad she made him feel on long summer evenings when he would see her dressing up, putting on high-heeled shoes and makeup and then walking up and down her room. Up and down, up and down, so lovely, so alone. Nowhere to go, no one to flirt or dance with. It was wrong, surely it was wrong to live like that? But he could not say what had gone wrong for her, he only knew that she blamed the place she lived in, that and her aunt. But it was not the place. On other farms, throughout the district, there were parties and the young people traveled miles to go to them. She did not go. She was not invited. You could not ask her why without making her vicious. Why was it? Always, since she was a little child, it had been so. She was an outcast.

Four

THE TWO OF THEM, RUTH AND WILLIE, SAT ON THE DOORSTEP
out at the back. The earth in front of the step was hard and bare,
polished by many feet, looking much like the patina on an old
table. White-washed stones were carefully laid along the length
of a path leading to the vegetable patch. There was a chicken coop,
where a cock shook his great wings and strutted off to the water
trough. Behind the mimosa trees the sun was setting.

"You haven't come by for a bit, Willie," she said reproachfully.

"No, my friend, but I've been busy these last weeks. I have to
work hard now. Not just here, but also at old Mrs. Swanepoel's,
and for her I have to make the long train journey at night, and
this after starting work on the lands at six. "Ag," he laughed, "all
these jobs, they'll kill me with work, and at the end, so little
money."

"But I thought you were going back to school," she said, turning her face away with that characteristic shame.

This way he could look at her more openly: her face had a
slumbrous quality—to him she seemed unawakened. Her voice
was the same, it was slow and deep, as if it lay curled up far inside
her like some dormant animal.

He shifted uncomfortably and brought his knees up. "School
I must leave for a bit. But it's all right, I'll get back to it. I'll finish my Matric, no problems. I can go back next year."

"You must be clever," she said vaguely, "to miss so much, a year or more, and then go back and pass."

"Ag no, man, there's just no other way. I can work at night sometimes, or on the train. The money I was making, I set some aside for the school fees, but most I must give to my ma for her and the children."

She knew that his father was dead, had been killed not long ago by the skollies in East London. Willie had to earn the money to keep them all now. That's how it was with them—he was the eldest son. His family was very poor, so she gave him food to take home, mealies and pumpkins, sweet potatoes and squash. And often she would find that Hannah put other things in the box: sugar and coffee and bread. They hid these things from Ilsa, who would not have approved. Ruth worried about his family because sometimes children came from those places and they looked half-starved, sick, almost too scared to beg.

"Is it true?" she whispered, "that people are really starving over there?" She pointed to the tribal lands across the blue koppies.

"It's true, ja. The drought has made it worse—bad, bad." He shook his head. "But always there is starving there." He jerked his shoulder savagely in that direction. "Those people are put there, they put them there to do nothing, to have nothing, to wait quietly till they die."

"Will you go there, Willie?" she asked in the same breathless tone, as if she was thrilled by the notion of suffering.

He laughed with all the courage of his youth. "Me? Never, man. Never." Then the long lines of his face hardened and he said gravely, "No, I'm a city-born. They won't get me. I'll go back to the location that my mother and us children were thrown out of when they would not give us papers, made us come back here to this kaffirland. Only my pa, he could stay because of his job, that contract job that means death. No, I'm not fooling you, you sign on and they own you, body and soul. But not me. I'll not live like that." He was quiet for a bit, so that she thought it must be his father's death he was thinking of.

"Ja," he said softly, "my folks, they were married twenty-two years and never once did they live together in the same house more than the two weeks he got off a year. And when he came home"—his face lit up—"we children were so happy, we would run all the way to the train station to greet him. He bought meat, clothes, and a scent in a blue bottle for our ma." He added quietly, "He was our pa, but we never knew him. We just loved him. My ma, she cried when he had to go back, she cried many, many nights. Sometimes she went to stay with him, but they always caught her and threw her back."

Rubbing her bare foot on the earth and flexing her toes, Ruth said, "Hannah used to tell me things like that, about when she was small. When I asked her who does those bad things to people, she would just say, 'It's the law.' Is it true, Willie?"

"Ja, it's true. You break it until it breaks you, that's all."

But she was untouched by any law, so she asked, "But if you are hungry, why can't you grow mealies and kaffir beans, pumpkins and stuff?"

"Ah!" he cried in amazement. "Why you never look, hey? Why do none of you people come and see? That land they give us when they steal ours, it's dead land, I'm telling you. They give you a tiny piece, for which you pay, and not even weeds come up. My ma, she can't grow any food. So you work hard to make money for food and rent and school fees and when you've finished school, there's no work. Nothing. No, man. That's why I'm going back to East London. They won't kill me quietly like a dog."

Then he stood up and pulled himself to his full, lean height. A smile came to his face, it grew and grew; it was the smile of someone who was sure of himself and of his place in his world. "Me," he announced proudly, "I'm an Afrikaner, ja, and I'm proud to be. I don't speak Xhosa, I don't know it. No, I'm an Afrikaner from East London, the place where I was born and my father before me. That's where I will go, because that's what I am and there I will take my place and earn money."

With amazement, with amusement, and a little disdain, she whispered, "An Afrikaner? But you're black!"

He looked at her, shaken, but still convinced. "That also is my pride." He kicked a stone in the direction of the cock, who was allowed to wander where he willed in the backyard. "That I can't change, but other things, those I can change."

"Ag, who can change anything?" she sighed, sinking, letting her hands fall between her knees.

Everything she did was sensuous, yielding, and he wanted to shake her hard, even to hit her for this weakness. But always these feelings were mixed up with the desire to hold and protect her.

His voice was strong and determined. "Those fat Dutch girls, they messed up your spirit the short time you went to that school. They have spoilt you, made you lazy, my friend." He bent down in front of her and took her hands in his. "You had a bad time there, ja, I know it, but you did not fight. What's the matter with you that you don't fight? Always you must fight or you'll die, one way or the other. Ruthie, I'm telling you, listen now. When I was just small, I ran with the children in the township, we were fighting about the school and we made a lot of trouble. Ja, we fought the police—not just us children, but my pa and my oompie too. He got killed, but not for nothing. We did something, see? You can't just lie under the boot, or down it will come, again and again."

He began to stroke her limp hands tenderly. "There's trouble for you too, I know it, always has been. I don't know why or what, that's not my business, but you have your trouble as we have ours. And also I know that your tant, she makes her own kind of trouble for the police and the authority people. But you—what is it with you, Ruthie, that you are suffering so bad?"

She pulled roughly away from him; any talk of her troubles was forbidden. If, in the house, someone—a visitor or a cousin maybe—asked a question, then Tant Zelda would go rigid. She would not answer, never had. She'd made it clear years ago there were things that must never be brought up. Ruth was scared of what she didn't know. She had run away from this same thing at the school. Girls leering and whispering about her. And the worst thing was that they never spoke one word that led to her enlightenment. Or perhaps they knew as little as she did? Either way, they seemed to hate her, they wanted to torment her the way chickens will peck the different one, the gold among the black, the small among the big—they kept on with their beaks the same way they would tease her about the birthmark on her face, until she felt it was pecked all raw and bloody.

One night she found a piece of paper on her bed. On it was written, in ugly Sarie's writing: "What happened to your pa then? Where is your ma? Where did the orphan child creep from? Ask your auntie. Ask your auntie what she did. Ask about the shotgun. Ask her what she did." And then later, when they came to bed, they began to chant these things at her, dancing around her like savages, round and round, pulling at her hair till she thought she would go mad.

She had run away from school that night after lights-out. She had taken a lift early the next morning on the main road, from a man with a cattle truck, arriving home at dawn the day after. All she could do when she got there was to run straight to Hannah's room, shaking her, flinging herself at her. She couldn't speak about it. Her shame and confusion was overshadowed only by her ignorance—and now she meant to keep it that way.

"Willie," she said calmly, "I have no trouble, true as God, there's nothing." She believed it too.

"But you have left the school, Ruthie, and without education there's also nothing."

"I don't need school" she said, tossing her golden head, "that's for poor people, for black people. I have money of my own, shares in de Beers . . ."

"Stop that rubbish now." He shook her arm. "You too, like me, have nothing. We don't pretend to each other. Now, you must tell me: What happened in that school, what happened? Hey? It can't be so bad that you can't tell me."

"Ag, it was nothing," she said vaguely, pulling up her hair with both hands and then letting it slide through her fingers. "What school do you mean anyway?" It all seemed so long ago.

"You know, at Bergen High. For a little bit, a few weeks, you were okay there, isn't it? So then what happened?"

His face was filled with anxiety and concern for her, but she looked at him mockingly.

"They made up a story about me," she spat out angrily. "I don't know what. Hannah says when a new girl comes to a place they pick on her and invent stories. That's all. Okay?" She glared at him.

"So what was the story, then?" She infuriated him the way she circled everything, peered around it but never at it, like someone trying to find light looking through the chinks of her fingers. She was such a child still. And scared too.

"I don't know," she shrugged. "When I told them up at the house, they said I must not go back there again, they didn't want to know the story. So that very day I left." She was triumphant, thinking of it.

"You must have told them more than that, to make them keep you away," he insisted.

She was patient, without interest. "No, just that there were rumors about me. . . . Then I said about the shotgun—and that really got to the bitch." She laughed cruelly, "That really made her scared, man, you'd think it was the police. And that was it. Now I'm finished with the place, and good riddance to bad rubbish." Her face looked worn suddenly.

He moved closer to her and they sat so, not quite touching.

"Ruth, you must stop with this messing about. You must come right. I'm your friend, for me you don't have to play these bloody fool games. If there are things you must know, then find them out."

"There's nothing to know," she said sweetly, opening her eyes wide. "What is it with you, Willie, that you must always be thinking there's something wrong with me? I'm sick of it, I'm telling you."

Behind her smile he could see the small scared child he used to find crying down by the dam when she came home from the dorp-school, her bottom lip bitten and a bewildered despair in her eyes. He had no power to help her. All he could do now was to let her creep back into that silence she had come to protect herself with.

"Okay, he said, "let's forget it, then."

To distract her, he began to tell her things he had done in East London. He wanted to make her laugh and he succeeded. He was a fine mimic—now he became a colored man selling fish or reeling about drunk, or one of those white madams who were so high-and-mighty because they had a black woman in their house whose very right to exist there depended on them. He could chant like the old witch doctors who still robbed the gullible with their failing magic; or shout like a boss man who has had a bad morning.

She laughed at him and it made him happy. He couldn't bear for her to be sad, he felt somehow he was responsible. He wanted to protect her like a brother and be as intimate with her as a sister. He wanted to give her the family she did not have. He tried to nurture her happiness in the same careful way you cupped your hands around a small flame when the wind blew. He must get for her those little glass beads and pearly necklaces from the Greek woman's store—she loved things like that. He would work extra hard to get them for her, ja, that was his plan and he was pleased with it.

But when he looked at her again, he could see that she was still unhappy. When she spoke it was in a hoarse whisper. "Willie, what happened?" She breathed so hard he thought she was sick. "What happened? What happened to my pa? Tell me, Willie? Please."

His heart was in pandemonium again and he dreaded to look at her. "Ag," he said sadly, "you know. You know he's dead." He turned away. "They're both dead, man. You know."

Her face was bent low, buried by her hair; he couldn't hear her without straining. "They said at school my pa wasn't dead. And if . . ." Her face lifted, becoming tender as it filled with hope. "If I had a pa, then, ag, Willie, then everything would be different."

"No," he said loudly, "don't begin with that, you know the truth, you know he's dead; hoping can't make him come back. He's dead, you know it." He was too close to his own father's death, and to his own refusal at first to believe it, to be gentle with her now.

She flew up in a rage, and turned on him. How could he obliterate it all like that—this secret she had nursed in her heart these last weeks? How could he be so vicious?

"What do you know?" she shouted. "You know nothing. No, get back, get away, don't touch me." She struck at him. "*Voetsak!*"

He went for her, grabbing her arms furiously, his white teeth glinting. "You—you never speak to me that way, you hear? You hear now? You never say voetsak to me."

"Don't you touch me," she said in a low, warning voice, "don't you, don't you put your black hands on me."

Then she stared at him, aghast. That it was so easy, after all, to come to this. So quick, so easy. All the time, easier. She wanted to cry, she wanted to run to Hannah and bury her face in her lap as she had as a little child.

"You want to play that low, dirty game?" he said, quivering, his hands in fists. "You make *yourself* low. You want to smash everything, hey? You want to pull everything to pieces because you hate the world. Don't pick on me," he sneered, "because I'm the nearest, the easiest. Don't start on me or you'll have no one."

Silence: the dust swirled where he had turned, the air pumped out heat, the lizards slid under the leaves and lay still.

Her head fell into her hands and she wept: *No one, no one.* Her hair trailed in the dust, the lilac-and-pink-sprigged dress pulled across her back as she heaved, as the small ribcage shook and her tears fell fast.

He watched her for a while and then he left her. She wanted desperately to call him back, to beg forgiveness. He wanted to be called. Neither moved or spoke.

Five

THE CLOCK STRUCK SIX. FROM THE KITCHEN WINDOW THE
stony koppies turned pink, lilac, and gray; the air blowing the curtains back was sharp and invigorating. Hannah stood by the old
stove waiting for the coffee to come to the boil, her face in the
morning light soft and rested.

Her face had not always looked this way: the calm exterior was
entirely the result of control and self-discipline—the burying of
passion beneath patience, the bearing of suffering by resistance to
it. Over the years, she had come to feel that what had happened
to her was simply inevitable, the result of her time and place. Her
life could not be judged, it was something in its own right. She
accepted it as such and took whatever God meted out to her. For
how could the sand resist the might of the wind, or the crops the
blight of drought? These things were sent by God and, as such,
must be endured.

How much she had once scorned such thinking. Now time had
taught her to bow beneath its weight. And, staring out of the
window again, surely nowhere on God's earth could a human feel
so insignificant as on this endless dusty plain where the farm and
everything on it lay seared and humbled by the sun.

She stood there and watched the morning unfold, the same, the
exact same way that it always did. The men and boys were
straggling into the yard, some sleepy and slow if they were lucky
enough to have their quarters behind the storeroom; others, hav-

ing walked an hour already from the village, chirpy and brisk, chucking jokes about. They gathered under the trees, sitting with their knees up and their backs to the tree trunks. When they'd had their coffee and mealie meal—which Ilsa prepared the night before in great vats—the lorries would come to take them to the lands.

Hannah could remember a time, when Zelda and Dawie's father ran the old farm, when the backyard was literally crammed with men, particularly when the animals needed dipping and shearing. But the new machines had changed all that, reducing their work force considerably. Zelda was the one who had made the biggest changes in the district, buying expensive, imported machinery and teaching new methods, trying new crops.

Hannah drew back from the window as the coffeepot began to hum. She took one last look at the flat mountains in the distance, the little brown bushes running across the veld to the sky. No place was so lovely or so dear to her as this farm at sunrise.

She took a cup of strong black coffee down the corridor to Zelda's room, as she did each morning. There was no servitude in this. She worked in the house as once she'd played in the old farmhouse; she loved and tended it as any woman would; it was her home. Her room was not an outside room, made up of discarded old furniture—it was a large, airy bedroom next door to the room that had been Ruth's as a baby.

Hannah tapped lightly on Zelda's door and walked in to put the coffee down on the table beside the iron bed. Zelda, just woken from sleep, had a vulnerable, startled look. Her pale brown-gold hair was severely drawn back from her brows, but it was plaited, not knotted. The plaits reminded Hannah of Zelda as a stubborn schoolgirl being sent away to school for the first time—bitter and complaining to the last minute. Hannah had watched her go, and felt a great sadness; she even felt that there was sadness in Zelda's eyes, too, as she waved and turned quickly away.

"Are the boys here yet?" was all Zelda said, pulling herself up against the pillows.

"Nearly all. But Ilsa's late this morning. She's getting old. We should get someone to help her."

[31]

"Hm, maybe. She's not up to the carrying anymore, but she's known us so long, I'd hate to have to get someone new."

They spoke in English, a habit Zelda had begun after an English-speaking boarding school had altered her opinion of her mother tongue.

"I'll leave you to suggest it to Ilsa," Hannah said with a grimace.

"Are the lorries here yet?"

"Not yet."

There was that sharp click of disapproval from the back of Zelda's throat; then she took up her coffee and began to drink it. Her face had a brooding, almost hostile quality. "I'd better hurry up," she said. "I must go to town to get the wages today."

Hannah heard her, but barely; she was staring at a particular place on the bureau, on which a brush, a mirror, and a round glass bowl were laid out. Where Hannah fixed her eyes there had once been a framed photograph of Dawie in his army uniform. Looking up, Zelda saw her staring, and knew precisely why she stared.

"Is this the same coffee, then?" she demanded.

"Yes, why?"

"It tastes peculiar."

"It's the same." Hannah would not be drawn, but her voice had stiffened as if to protect itself. But as she moved away to the door, she could feel her compassion for Zelda returning. Whenever she felt angry with her, she made herself remember Zelda as she had been before all the bad things had happened. It was the only way to forgive her.

How easy it had been to love her when she was young. She made everything look so easy. "Watch me, watch me," she would yell as she flew from one high roof to another like an Icarus who could never fall. She had no fear, no hesitation, was fueled entirely by her will—and her will, then, was a beautiful, proud thing, undented by disappointment or bitterness. Until one person had resisted her. Dawie had always said, "Zelda must be hurt, be made humble, before she will understand anyone else." But when she had been resisted, it had not been in her brother's way, with grace and the courage to show her where she went too far. This resistance had humiliated her, killing all that was bright in her.

And now, as Hannah saw the tall woman who had once been so stately rise from her bed and move across the room, she was seeing a sad replica of what Zelda had once been. It was this, always, that made you forgive her: this loss of her true self. Her body had lost all lightness; it was no longer that life-giving form it once had been. Her face was lean and harsh; like her body, it had become asexual. It had lost the capacity for love or passion. Looking at her, you felt no part of her could be touched. Some experience had altered her so dramatically that her youth, her beauty, and her sex had all gone from her. And watching her, Hannah was aware, as she always was, of her own part in Zelda's decline.

As the door closed behind her, Hannah heard Zelda's voice. "I won't be back at lunchtime. I'm going to be at Bester all afternoon. Okay?" In that last enquiry, there was something, just some small thing in her voice, that seemed to ask to be missed.

Six

BUT YOU SEE, FOR US, WHEN WE WERE CHILDREN, ZELDA WAS like a bright candle that we would follow anywhere, even into the dark. The dark drew Zelda, and where she was drawn I had to follow. And where I went, Dawie went too, because to him I was a bright candle. By this time we were becoming that way to each other; we had begun to illuminate the other's heart.

Zelda couldn't know about this—innocent though it was—because it would have crushed her. She couldn't share in the same way she could never, can never, understand loneliness. For her, Dawie had always been there, she had never been alone, not from their birth. And she wanted to possess those she loved absolutely, the way she felt she did her brother. We in turn did love her, so powerfully that we couldn't bear to crush her. Perhaps we were a bit afraid of her too. She could be dangerous. It was as if she had come to believe that the only way to control people was by wounding them. She liked people weak. I have come to believe that the best thing you can do for those you love is to make them strong. But that would have frightened her.

Because I owed her everything, I was prepared to shield her from her own tyranny. When Dawie swiped at her as I knew he must, I remained silent. I could not hurt her. You see, she had lifted me out of the narrow world I was born into, and freely, magnificently, had given me her own world: herself, the farm, her brother—everything she cherished. Her price was my submission. Well, it was easy enough for me to pretend. There was so much I didn't know, hadn't experienced, even in that enclosed little place. I wanted to learn, and she loved to teach, to tell, to assert. I let her.

Also, it was quite simply a pleasure for me to be with her, even, strange as it may seem, as it's a pleasure for me to be with her now. How could she manage without me—she who hates solitude and silence? We have always needed one another; like the opposite ends of a seesaw, we have our moments of ascendancy and decline.

The farm in those days was a secret place and our life there a half-imaginary one that seemed invisible to anyone outside our magic circle of three. Isolation of the kind we knew wasn't only possible then, it wasn't even unusual. I began to think that even God couldn't see us. I didn't want Him to see us. I wanted everyone out. When Dawie wrote for me on a piece of paper, *"Man is distant but God is near,"* I refused to believe it, but it was, I see now, like a finger pointing to our lives.

In order to understand Zelda now, I often have to remind myself of how she was then. And of life too, how it was then. And how I actually believed—no, I really did—that it was possible to stride off the path one was born to and go your own way. I was that innocent. But to be innocent that way is perhaps the only way to be happy.

I wish it was all intact somewhere, the old place, so that we could go back and look at it. The kitchen is the place where I remember Zelda best: sitting in the big chair strung with leather, her arms resting on the scrubbed table; she was always so languid unless she moved. I loved the half-door that looked out on the yard, which then led down to the stream with its line of orange trees. Their family had lived there so long, generation after generation, that they'd forced the dust and desolation back and made a little oasis. It had fruit orchards and old trees watered by the river, bougainvillea that covered the whitewashed walls, fig trees that gave us fat juicy fruit, and even a grapevine hung with small, sweet grapes as good as you get in the Cape.

Here, in a place that was like paradise, I learned, I watched, and I grew up. Everything I know now I think I learned in the years between nine and thirteen. I studied with such fervor, absorbing everything around me so hungrily, as if I knew even then that it couldn't last.

After Dawie and Zelda left me to go to school—how could I still go on believing I could live in their world after that sharp division was made? After Meneer had gone, still I struggled to study on my own, using their books and using the library in the house for a bit, before things changed. Dawie was good, he taught me when he came home in the holidays. But by then I had given up the idea of passing exams the way he and Zelda were doing. I persuaded myself that it didn't matter, that I must still learn what I could.

Zelda had been sent to an English-speaking school because it was the best school available, and she taught me English; before then I'd spoken Afrikaans all the time. She gave me her textbooks, some Shakespeare and some Bernard Shaw and poetry—and romantic novels, which I read avidly. She then convinced me that I ought to write a diary of my thoughts and leave it locked in her room. She was trustworthy then, but I was too stupid and trusting myself to see when she stopped being so. I paid for that. But I wrote the diary in English to practice and I began to love it and never stopped writing, though not so often now.

Dawie and I went on speaking Afrikaans together, I don't know why. Perhaps it was because we had begun to do so when we were younger; we were creatures of habit, and hated change. Now I hate the language, not just because it's ugly, but also because an ugliness has come to the Afrikaans people. They aren't what they were when I was a kid. And the officials who come here and try to force us to bend to their laws, they're all Afrikaners. They are mostly the ones who have made me come to hate the race.

Dawie speaking Afrikaans didn't sound ugly. If Dawie taught me most of what I know, then he certainly taught me everything that I came to feel. When he was away he didn't forget me. He wrote me letters and sent me money for things he thought I needed. Once, he sent me a silk scarf so sheer I could see my hand right through it. It was so beautiful I had to hide it from my mother.

Zelda would help me when she was there, but she didn't write.

When she was gone, she forgot you. When she came home she would scoop me up like a neglected puppy and then make me jealous with stories about her girlfriends and the fine things they all had. She made me know my poverty, my place in the world: she knew she did it. But then, when she had hurt me, she'd shower me with presents, bringing out of her trunk lovely under-things and soft jerseys, a pair of shoes with high heels, a lipstick that tasted of cinnamon. At first I was cold and I wouldn't take them, but she worked me round; she hugged me and said she was sorry, and I always forgave her.

But all this was later, when she was fifteen or so. When they first came back after being away, they were like gods to me, twin gods who held my fate in their hands and juggled it back and forth between them. Only I didn't know it then, I just lived for their coming back and I lived for the sound of Dawie's voice, for the deep security of his presence.

Such memories! Zelda, by the dam, naked in bright moonlight. She came up from the water having drowned her black satin swimming costume and stood in front of us challengingly—so tall and lovely, like a statue. She wanted us to follow her lead, but I was shy. Dawie was always cool with Zelda, as if she was another side of him that he must indulge sometimes, and some-times discipline. He too took off his costume and chucked it away into the bushes. He didn't look at me as if to taunt me, not like she did. And whatever he did, he did because he wanted to, not because she made him. But when he did that, and stood naked there for a minute, just as tall and beautiful as Zelda, I knew that it was only for me. He seemed to say to me, look at my body, re-member it. I remembered it, night after night. I remembered every line of it. As I remember it still.

Seven

RUTH PUSHED OPEN THE SCREEN DOOR AND CROSSED THE porch with her hips swinging. She was wearing a dress that she'd taken in at the sides so that it fitted like a clamp around her backside and thighs. Her mouth was hard and wide with its thick smear of red lipstick and a midnight-blue line circled her eyes. In the dining room behind her she could hear an occasional murmur as Hannah and Zelda spoke. They were going over the farm accounts and putting the wages in brown packets; as a little girl, she had liked to do this herself. Hannah did the figures each month and then she and Zelda went through things and planned ahead.

Ruth had deigned to sit with them for a moment as they drank their coffee, but she'd become so unutterably bored that she'd left and gone to her room. There she'd sat at the kidney-shaped dressing table and begun, with total absorption, the application of her makeup. She did this for an hour or more. She saw the mark and tried to cover it, looking into the glass with a face made humble, as if she begged the mirror to change its mind, to show her a face without a dark stain.

Now she sat on the stoep in a fixed, peculiar way. It was dark, but no cooler than the day. Insects whirred around the lamp outside the porch, hitting and sizzling as they struck the bulb. Far in the distance she could hear the roar of a car or a motorbike—whatever it was, the engine had a stutter of some kind. She looked up and listened; the sound petered out. Her body slumped forward in disappointment. She closed her eyes. And waited. Dreaming. Of no one she knew, but of someone she could most perfectly imagine.

The silence had become absolute, but slowly the soft song of the cicadas pushed through it. She heard the engine rev up; the roar seemed to be coming closer, until she could make out the beam of a single headlight moving steadily along the road to the farm. Nearer and nearer it came—but oh, so slowly.

It was indeed a motorbike. It turned the curve of the road, coming so fast that it almost lay flat against the ground. Then it sped up the drive at breakneck speed, skidding in the gravel as it came to a stop.

"Ag, Willie," she laughed, with pleasure but disappointment. "What you making such a bleddy din for?"

But Willie, flinging himself off the bike and kicking the kickstand down, strode toward her with all the magnificence of the prince she'd been expecting. He wore tight black trousers and white leather shoes without a crease and he smelt of pine and shaving soap. He knew his good looks and how the well-cut clothes became him: he was a man, an Afrikaner, the best. He had never worn a garment with a patch, and the splayed and cracked feet of his childhood had vanished forever beneath beautifully kept shoes. His mother, seeing him go out at night, especially on Saturday night when he took a good hour dressing, used to laugh with pleasure: "Our Willie, he's that sharp, you people, come and look at him!" She never begrudged his extravagance. After all, he worked hard and he only spent when he had the money. Then he would come home and shower them with gifts, and his sister would sit there with her cross Church face and click her tongue.

He walked to where she sat and let the door whang-to behind him.

"How goes it?" From his pocket he drew a packet of cigarettes, offered one to Ruth, and then lit both with a flourish. His body still seemed to move, lightly, rhythmically, as if he was dancing with himself. "I was going in for a beer, but came first to see you," he said, sitting on the chair next to hers. "You okay?"

"Ja."

He looked at what she wore with a sadness that turned to lust and then back to pity: she looked like a tart outside a shebeen. She shouldn't look so, it offended him; and yet she knew no better. His mother now, she would take a cloth, scrub her face for her and get all that muck off; she'd probably make her start Bible classes too.

"Whose bike, then?" Ruth asked, puffing at her cigarette and holding it awkwardly between forefinger and thumb.

"It's his bike, my cousin, Machine Mike. He brought it down from Port Elizabeth. He's a good job there, on the docks. Ja, makes plenty of money. But this thing here is a shit machine. He's fixing it up, he can fix up anything, that boy, he pulls things off the tip and fixes them up good as new. But"—he made a spitting sound— "this thing's shit." Then his face lit up and he smiled at her, teasing. "If *you* were to sit on her, now, she'll fly, I'm telling you. I'll make her fly for you— Ag, don't look like that, Ruthie, you're not still cross, hey? You were talking like a rubbish that last time and you know it. Ja, well, we won't worry about it. Just get on this bike here and I'll make it purr for you, I'll make it grow wings. Come on now, take off those stupid shoes and let's go, man."

Ruth jumped up, flung off her shoes, and ran—Willie pulling her—through the door and down the steps. Hannah, standing at the window, watching, felt the pain return between her ribs. She wanted to call out, "Come back. Don't go." She was aware of Zelda at the table behind her, observing, knowing it all, bitterly, and without comment.

Hannah looked at the motorbike with reproach. The man she had loved, he too had had a motorbike. Very like the one that Ruth now sat astride, skirt yanked up, holding Willie tightly by the waist as he kicked down at the starter pedal. She remembered how he had taken it apart, oiling it, adjusting, tightening, always working on it as she watched him in silence. He didn't see, as she did, that his passion for his motorbike had nothing to do with machines and everything to do with the fact that it would take him away. It was the same with Willie.

And then—astoundingly, as though she'd read Hannah's thoughts—Zelda spoke. "He was a coward," she said, her voice without emotion, still looking at the ledgers in front of her.

Hannah, startled, and then furious, spun toward the woman who sat so still at the dining-room table, the light full on her head, her expression, as she now raised her face to Hannah's glare, for once quite clear in its judgment.

"What?" Hannah breathed, not knowing now if she could bear the silence and secrecy, so long hoarded by both of them, broken into. But she longed at the same time to have it out with her.

But it was only for a moment. And now it was gone.

"Something will have to be done about Ruth," Zelda said shortly. "We must send her away. There's nothing for her here, and now her education can go no further."

"Where to? Where can we send her?"

"Maybe to Cape Town."

"There's trouble."

"There's trouble all over the place!" Zelda shrugged impatiently. "Besides, it's under control now, quiet on the streets again."

"It won't last."

"You mean you don't want it to last!"

"Do you?"

Now there was anger in both their voices. "You're not my conscience, Hannah."

They both knew this wasn't true; it was precisely what Hannah had always been. Just as, Hannah now thought bitterly, she had been to Dawie, too.

"I just want us to be left in peace here, I don't want more trouble."

"There will always be trouble," Hannah said quietly, "and it will spread here too. Nothing we do can stop that."

"When it does, we'll deal with it," Zelda snapped. "But Ruth must go. You know it."

"Yes, I know."

"If you keep her here, it will be your fault."

Zelda lifted the pile of books in one hand and took the empty cup in the other. Hannah moved forward, her face already darkening with the guilt of keeping Ruth here as long as she had. But she couldn't do it, she couldn't throw Ruth out, not unless she wanted to go.

"Not now, Zelda," she pleaded. "It's too soon. There are still patrols, rioting. Not now, please." She bent her head. "So many people have died."

"It's your decision." Zelda moved toward the door.

"Next month," Hannah said with determination, "next month, then. And I can ask her what she wants."

The door opened and Zelda strode through it, saying, "She doesn't know what she wants. And she never will."

Before the doctor closed, Hannah said, roughly, "Zelda, he was *not* a coward."

Zelda stopped, sniffed deeply: Oh, she thought, you were always so weak, so loyal, so trusting. You were always such a *fool!* Even now you can't bear me to tell the truth. Even now you'd forgive everyone every damn thing. "A coward is a man who does not stand by his feelings," she said brutally, feeling a certain pleasure in hurting her.

Hannah walked back to the window and with her finger began to trace a letter on the surface of the glass. Even Zelda's spite was dear to her because it meant speaking of him. She felt the pain flow out of her and her love return. She closed her eyes, she allowed it.

But not for long. She was a woman of discipline, and quickly now she put him away from her. She did it because it was essential. Her belief in one man, like her belief in God, was unshakeable. Neither would ever entirely forsake her and she would keep faith to the end. With such faith, one expected to pay the price.

Eight

WHEN HE HAD FIRST GONE, WHEN IT COULD BE SAID THAT THE worst was over, then, on those nights when the moonlight came out and flooded the veld, rippling the sand and making it soft and luminous—the moon round, not flat but round, globular and golden, rolling on a black sky—she would stand out there, waiting between the stones, waiting, watching and waiting, walking from moonlight into shadow and into moonlight again, breathless with the sky and the land's beauty, with her beauty, the pallor of her hands, the heaviness of her breasts, her state of grace, her closeness to God. And He was there, most surely He stood there with her. He held her close and took from her a small portion of her grief.

And when the intoxication passed, she stood quite still. She waited for her muscles to unbend, her skin to feel again, her blood to flow and rush. Then she raised her head, she opened her mouth and she howled, like a wolf, like a dog screaming at the moon— a high shriek from the very depths of her, echoing and resounding between the stones.

The sound was gone, lost in the emptiness, in the flat nothingness out there in the veld, in the shadow and the mad moonlight. But still she waited.

Nine

"WILLIE, STOP—STOP, PLEASE." RUTH DUG HER CLAWS INTO the sides of his body.

He did not stop.

"Willie," she yelled against the wind, "stop, we can't, stop PLEASE."

He brought the motorbike viciously to a halt and then sat, his feet planted square in the dirt, hands on handlebars, body rigid, the bike quivering as he looked straight ahead of him.

She lowered her voice. "Ag, Willie, what's the point?"

After a moment, very slowly, his head turned toward her so that now she could at least see his profile and not just the back of his head.

"The point," he said tightly, "the point is—only that I want to go down the fucking street, walk into the café and buy us two Cokes after this long drive. Ja, that's the point, that's all."

She was silent. It was as if—because of the row they'd had last time—he now blamed her for the fact that he could not go into the café. She was one of them.

"Ag, Willie," she whispered again, touching his shoulder and then moving her hand away, "we were so happy just now on the road."

He nodded his head soberly, remembering—the speed, the feeling of freedom, her cheek against his shoulder, the wind wrapping her hair around his neck like a silk scarf. "Come on, let's go," he said, determined again. "I'm not letting those little pip-squeaks stop me, come on, let's go."

She pulled herself off the motorbike with a jerky, hurried movement. "No, Willie, don't. They'll just beat you up again. Honest to God. Why do you want to go on with it? It's crazy! What's the good? Just for two Cokes? For what?"

"Just because there's no reason why I mustn't," he said stubbornly. "Why must I not walk in there? Hey?" He jutted his head aggressively at her. "Why not, hey? Do you want to tell me?"

"Because," she said wearily, "they will beat you up like last time and then throw you out."

"Then," he said slowly, "then that's what they must do. Are you coming?"

She shook her head.

"Scared, hey? Or ashamed of me perhaps, not want to be seen with me?"

She felt a long way from him, in age and in wisdom. She said slowly, "If I go in, Willie, they won't beat me up, I don't think, but they'll, they'll—you know, like last time, Willie, like every time—you know what they do to me. Sometimes"—her voice was so low that even she wasn't sure that she said it—"sometimes, I feel, I feel like I'm . . . like I'm black, too." The only emphasis came on the word black."

"Ja," he said, tenderly now, "ja, it must feel the same—to be hated for nothing you did, for nothing you can help." He coaxed her, "So come with me then, Ruthie, come. We have nothing to lose, isn't it?"

Still she hung back, almost in tears. "I'm not like you, Willie, I don't like to be hurt. I'm scared."

"Okay, so you wait here, it's better. I don't like you to be hurt either. I'll go and get us the Cokes."

He got on the motorbike, gripped the handlebars, and pushed back on the seat. But she pulled at him frantically, "Don't go, don't go to the café, Willie, I'm begging you. Can't you just go to the other place?"

"To the place for blacks only, hey? Out of town. To that place?"

"So—what's wrong? At least they won't give you a hard time. I'll come with you if you go there, I'm not scared of those people."

"Wait for me," he said firmly, "just a little bit. I'll be back soon. Don't be scared now, you promise me? Good. Now you stay there by that tree. Don't wander off into the bush with the snakes." He made a quick, darting movement with his head to make her laugh. "Pick up that stick and stay here." He gave her his brightest smile. "Come on now, you know me, I can beat them off with one hand tied behind my back!"

In spite of her fear, she laughed.

"Oh ja, laugh, man, that's right, laugh at me," he teased, as if he cared. "Soon you'll be crying with laughter when you see me torn to bits!"

After he'd roared off, she called softly after him, "Willie, please come back, please come back quick now, don't leave me here."

She walked away to the mimosa tree set back a little from the road. It was dark. She crouched down in the sand behind it and huddled there, rocking on her heels a little, thinking of him walking in there, into the bright café with the jukebox and the noise, and how those apes would look up, look at one another, nod, stand, move arrogantly toward him with their shorn heads, their flat faces, their hands beginning to move into fists: "Did you want something, kaffir? Or looking for someone? Maybe he wants a job washing the floor, hey? How about it? Let's see what you can do, then. Down on your knees, boy." And he: "I have come to buy two Cokes. Who's going to stop me?"

Ten

I WAS SMALL, JA, VERY SMALL, I CAN'T REALLY REMEMBER, BUT I was still small enough to feel that the dorp was very big. It was the first time that Hannah took me there; I had only known the farm till then. Nowhere else. So I'm walking down that street with Hannah and I'm feeling very important. There was a place where people were coming out with ice creams and cool drinks, and I wanted some. I said to Hannah, "Get me an ice cream, get one of those for me, please." She looked at me and then away, took my hand and made me walk on. "No, I can't, Ruth," she said.

So I began screaming like anything, and when a fat Boere vrou came by and asked me what the matter was, I screamed all the harder that I wanted an ice cream.

"Go round the back, girl," she said to Hannah, "and get for her an ice cream. Ask them for a cone for the missy or she'll deafen us all. Quick now."

Hannah did not move; she stood there with her head held up for a bit, then she pulled at my hand and made me walk with her. I remember the pain where she was twisting my fingers in hers. There was something about her that made me shut my mouth and drag along behind her, turning though to get the woman's sympathy.

We walked on past de Waal's butchery and the bread store that used to be there then, and on past the little shop full of bright things in the window—rubbish of course, but to me then they were jewels. Hannah bought buttons and a length of cloth there; she went to one side to be served. And still she said not one word. As we were coming out of that store, another woman looked at me with my pretty curls, that have now all gone, and my blue eyes and she said, "Ag, shame, isn't she sweet?"

I remember feeling so pleased and then so confused because her friend whispered something and pulled at her arm so that they walked on quickly. Hannah was wearing that horrible look, as though someone was hitting her, and she was pretending not to notice: her neck goes hard and long and her mouth is thin and all the color rubs out and when you speak to her she won't answer.

I didn't go there again for a long time, not until Zelda thought that it was time for me to go to school. I had been learning how to read and write at home a bit; Hannah taught me. But when I was seven, Zelda took me in with her. And I remember that— and all the other times—because they were the same, identical.

The school was a one-room building with lavs at the back. It was away from the dorp a little bit and it had a dusty yard all round it with a swing and a tree with red flowers on it. The teacher, Miss Klopper, came out onto the stoep to talk with Zelda. I was told to go play at the back, but I hung around just out of sight, behind the wall.

Miss Klopper was a very fat woman with false teeth that moved up and down in her mouth and curly brown hair. She was ugly, and for that I didn't like her. But her voice was soft when she spoke, in English, to Zelda, who was busy explaining that she wanted me to go to school there.

"Well, this is a bit difficult," Miss Klopper said. She seemed shy and turned her shoes over like a child.

"Why?" asked Zelda. "It's a simple matter, it's just time she was at school. She can read and make her letters, but she needs to be with other children." She talked fast. She wanted it settled fast.

"Ja, well, the problem is, you see, Miss de Valera, it's the others I must think of, the children and their parents." She shuffled a bit. "And of course there are the regulations. I have to follow the regulations." There was relief in her voice about this word, "regulations," which was a word I didn't understand then.

"What regulations?" Zelda snapped.

Miss Klopper hesitated, gave her silly laugh, said, "You know what I mean. You know how people are. And I can't just go over their wishes." Her voice started to run away. "Your farm now, Miss de Valera, it's out of my area, you see, I can't take a child out of my area. And you see how small the space is that we have here."

"As it happens," Zelda said, "my farm falls into no specific educational district—but yours does happen to be the nearest."

"That may be so," Miss Klopper said, losing her nerve now, "but I don't want trouble. Exceptions to the regulations, Miss de Valera, they don't go down so well in a little place."

I remember only being yanked away very quickly and how we almost ran to the bakkie. Zelda's face was blazing with anger. I don't know what she did, but she overcame those regulations somehow, because I did go to Miss Klopper's school.

It was all wrong though, like it had started. I hated it. Miss Klopper had it in for me before I even got there. The other kids hated me because she treated me differently. It was because of the trouble that Zelda had made, going over her head. When they began to pick on me, she ignored it.

At home, when I cried about it and didn't want to go to school, Zelda was a bitch. "You show the little bastards!" she said. "Don't you ever let anyone make you run. Where's your nerve?" She made me keep on going. I didn't complain after that, not even to Hannah, because when I did it made her so sad I couldn't stand it. She got so sad about things in those days. But after what seemed ages, there was one boy there who was kind to me. His name was Norman and he was bigger than the others, so when he waited outside with me till the car came to collect me, I was okay.

But though she made me go to that rough school, Zelda hated it when I spoke like those farm kids. She'd slap me if I said "ag," or "sis," or if any Afrikaans word passed my lips. It drove her crazy. The only exception was, she didn't object to me calling her Tant Zelda rather than Aunt. I did it at first to see if it'd annoy her, but she didn't seem to notice. But Zelda's like that, you never know where you are with her. Anyway, I suppose to her it always seemed like I was making problems and she didn't like me because of that. I used to imagine that my mother, her sister, couldn't have been anything like her. I used to comfort myself with that.

But she wouldn't talk about my ma. Only once she said anything about her. I was having a row with her and I said to her that my mother wouldn't treat me like she did, my mother wouldn't be like that to me, wasn't vile like she was. Then she laughed a revolting laugh and she said: "Your mother, my God, your mother was a fool, a damn fool, always was—don't tell me about your mother!"

The bitch, the bitch, the bitch. I'd still like to kill her for that.

She made me stay at Miss Klopper's till I was nearly eleven. Then I was sick a long time and couldn't start at a new school. That was a good time. Hannah taught me again, getting books from Kimberly. We had good times, Hannah and me; she taught me a lot. I had no idea she was so clever, she was always quiet and you didn't know what was going on inside her—but she really knew things, she was smart as hell. But then Zelda said it must stop—she seemed annoyed that I was happy. It was she who decided I must go to another school, far away, the boarding school near the coast. But God, man, that was really the worst! The worst ever! I thought I must die there. It wasn't too bad at first, in fact it was okay until Lorraine Fouché came there. She'd been at Miss Klopper's too, and then it started all over again.

All over again—that stuff about my pa, about the accident with the shotgun, about our family and how Zelda was, and about some man who'd died. It was never clear, it was all whispers. At least now I know that if ever Zelda tries to get rid of me again, all I must do is remind her about that shotgun and she will shut her mouth quick as that.

Anyway, now I've made a decision. I don't intend to go anywhere. Not for a bit, not until I've found out what it is I want to know. Then I'm going to look for my pa, that's what. You see, when my cousin Andries was here for a bit, passing through on his way to Cape Town, he said some funny things, things that made me think. He made me feel that maybe my pa wasn't dead after all. And when he'd gone, I went over what he said, many times, and I began to be certain that my pa wasn't dead. He's waiting somewhere for me to find him. It's because of Zelda that he can't come here. That's all I know, that it's her fault. She's kept him away and one day I'm going to get my own back for that.

She's evil, ja, that's what she is. She could easily kill a man. And I want to find out who, because if I know who, then I'll know for sure whether it was my pa or not. And I'm going to stay right here until I've found out.

Now, this is what I'm going to do. I'm going to try and remember all I can from the very beginning and I'm going to see if I can get anything out of Hannah too. And I'm going to watch Zelda, and when she's away I'm going to go through all her things. She never throws anything away, that one, but she locks everything up. I have to be very clever about it so that no one knows. And no one must think anything has changed.

But it did all change, everything changed that one night under the tree waiting for Willie to come back from the café. I suddenly saw myself, you know, as if from the outside, a miserable scared little thing crouching under a tree—always waiting, always scared. And then Willie came back, bleeding all over the place, his clothes all ripped, in pain—but there he came, laughing, I'm telling you, no word of a lie, LAUGHING.

He was my hero. He tossed me a Coke, and seeing him like that, well, I just knew. I too must fight back, everyone has to. You can't be afraid forever. You have to have a go. You have to be like Willie even if they do beat you to death one day.

I loved Willie that night.

Eleven

ZELDA SAT IN THE OLD ROCKING CHAIR THAT HAD ONCE belonged to her mother, jerking it quickly back and forth. She was gazing out across her land, her head held erect as if she were something carved, like a figurehead on a great sea vessel. Knowing this was when she was at her most dangerous, Ruth kept away, but such was her courage now that she played her records very loud, one in particular, letting it repeat in a way certain to annoy Zelda. Only the two of them were in the house and it was very hot. Hannah was away on one of her errands—or this was how Zelda sarcastically referred to her absences. No one knew where she went, but Ruth noticed that she took food with her and always came back rather withdrawn.

Zelda stared out across her one weakness, her one love: her land. The wind was blowing; every day now it seemed to blow, scattering sand and twigs all over the stoep. Some days it blew so hard that sand piled up smoothly in every corner. When you sat, or went to work at a table, you had first to take your hand and rub off the dust there.

Her land was all she possessed. And now there was trouble again and she did not know what to do. She wished her father was still alive.

Sometimes, when these things happened, she felt so alone. He had been a good farmer, conservative of course. She didn't know what he would think of her new breed of sheep—the good old

Karoo bred with a hardy Spanish strain, making better wool and meat. Even now she was a little intimidated by his judgment: a dour man with a hard Christianity. He, like the God he worshipped, had no weakness and no understanding of fear. "Break it, break yourself of fear," he had said to his children. "Without it you can do what you like." But could you, she wondered furiously, could you, with these pigs tramping all over the place?

The bougainvillea was beautiful in the soft evening light and the ripe scent of the peaches came to her with the wind, moving her in spite of herself. It was when she thought of losing the farm, or of it changing—that was what unbalanced her. There was no other home for her heart now.

She knew how much she'd changed, but she'd had to. She had simply become another kind of woman: bought new land with the proceeds from the old, staked it out, fenced it. She'd started all over again, building a new house, moving her stock, adding to it and altering it over the years. She'd done it all boldly, unaided by any man, making her neighbors nervous and critical. Just she and Hannah, year after year, getting the best yield, making good money, buying more land and animals and becoming prosperous. But it had made them old before their time, she now felt; they were women in their thirties but seldom felt it.

Hannah was walking steadily on the path from the direction of the dam. Zelda watched her moodily, remembering how she had walked a narrow dirt path like that a thousand times, with that same slow stride—patient, as if she could go on walking that way for ever. Remembering too the mornings that Dawie had crept out to meet her at the dam and how the two of them had walked back, talking urgently, their bodies close together.

Something about that closeness should have warned Zelda, but didn't. Not until that dawn when she'd woken for some reason and gone in search of him and not found him in his room. And had waited just like this, sitting in the same chair, and seen them come up together, their heads wet, their faces flushed and happy. Then she knew. She was excluded; they had a world of their own, which she could not enter. She'd lost both of them—a brother and a sister all at once.

Hannah, seeing Zelda sitting on the stoep, came round to the front of the house. She put down her old basket and drew a hand across her forehead, making a smear where the dust ran into her sweat. She smiled in a tired way and waited, reading the face in front of her as if it were her own.

"They've been here again," Zelda said shortly. "That van Reenen's been trying to lay down the law to me all afternoon."

"The same as before?" Hannah asked, feeling utterly weary now.

"Yes, but now they've nearly finished building the camp, so they're pushing me harder."

Zelda's head was down, dejected, and it was more difficult for Hannah to see her this way than any other. She went to sit down. "I've not seen anything being built."

"Well, you wouldn't, would you? They've built it out of sight, as usual, on the old road leading to the Plettenburg farm, miles from anywhere."

Hannah folded her hands together and locked her fingers. "So what did they say, then?" she asked dully.

"You're tired. Get a drink first at least."

"No, I will afterwards. Tell me."

"Well, this time they've made it quite clear. It's all down in writing, officially, from the Bureau in P.E. Our men who work the lands can no longer live here, none of them—they say it's too dangerous to have people on farms anymore. They thought they were being generous when they said maybe old Samson can stay on as night watchman. The men who come in from the village will go too, because the village is being broken up. All our protests have come to sweet f.a. about that. The women and children are to go to the Transkei. All men must go to labor camps, no exceptions."

"And if we refuse?"

Zelda laughed. "Then they'll just take their labor permits away and they won't work again." Zelda got up and walked to the end of the stoep and gazed through the netting like an animal in a trap.

"There will be some way round it," Hannah said, sitting very still.

Zelda turned and looked curiously at her friend. She was

touched by her nature, anchored as it was in some private faith that would not be broken.

"We just won't do it!" Hannah said quietly.

"No, we won't," Zelda agreed. "I'm not going to turn them off. These people worked for my father and they've worked hard for us since we came here. This is *their* home too. We'll just refuse."

They were both unaffected by the enormity of their decision.

"Have you discussed it with Boysie and Mr. Mantagisa?" Hannah asked.

"Not yet, but of course I will. They must know straightaway. I know what they'll say: that it's too dangerous for us, that they'll close us down. But to hell with it."

Hannah moved forward in her chair. "Perhaps we can be clever," she said. "Did he leave papers—regulations and documents that we can go through?" She was looking, as always, for little loopholes in the law, little ambivalences that had bought them time before.

Zelda jerked her head in the direction of the table, where some forms lay, but before Hannah could get to them, Zelda had begun to speak angrily again.

"I hate that bastard," she said. "I hate the way he always talks to me in Afrikaans—and he even has the cheek to lecture me when I talk back in English: 'These are times when we must stick together, isn't it?' I told him where he could stick his language. Then he kept saying he couldn't understand me, didn't get me, didn't I see how much easier it would be for me to have the blacks off my land?

" 'Now, they'll just come in the morning and leave at night. You don't have to see where they go or get mixed up with their problems. They just work and vanish, like little goblins. What could be better, hey? What's up with you people that you want to make trouble when we're trying to help you?'

"I said we had no problems here."

" 'But you will, Miss de Valera, you will, and it's worse for a woman with no man to handle the guns, hey? Things are hotting up. Terrorists all over the place, hiding in the hills, in the bush. We have to clear everyone out, give them no place for shelter or food.'

[55]

"I said he would have done it anyway, even if there wasn't trouble, and doing it was what made the trouble. Then I asked him how far it was to the camp, since you can't make even a dent on a steel brain like his.

" 'Ag, it's just down the road, man, a stone's throw.'

" 'How come I haven't seen it then? Who's building it?'

" 'Convicts.'

" 'How far?'

"He got surly. 'An hour or two, maybe, on the buses.'

" 'Who pays the fares?'

" 'They do, of course. We're not a bleddy charity, man.'

" 'So you make them leave and then you make them pay for it?'

" 'It's the law. I don't make it, I just make it work.'

"Then I asked him what was going to happen to the village."

"Was he specific this time?" Hannah asked. "Usually, the first thing you know, the bulldozers are there and that's it."

"Well," Zelda said, "then he got pretty angry."

" 'Now look here, Miss de Valera, you know as well as I that they've had it easy here. We've been lenient, patient. The cleaning-up schedule round here is way behind schedule. Those little letters and stuff that you sent to your friend tangled things up for me, I can tell you, so I'm not likely to have much patience anymore, is it? You can't hold it up any longer just because you own most of the land around here. You break the law selling land to blacks anyway. You can't go on doing what you want.'

"I told him I'd get an extension. But he said I couldn't, that that was over with because he now had greater authority than my 'clever friend in his big office in P.E.' When I told him we'd see, he started swearing and calling me names. But he ended up saying it was the end of the line, that when the labor camp was finished, then our people here would be finished too. That was the system, and I shouldn't make trouble trying to fight it because they had ways also of dealing with people like me. Then I kicked him out. But now, I don't know, I just don't know . . ."

Hannah thought about Dawie. He could help, he dealt with situations like this in Cape Town. Sometimes they read about it in the newspaper, but when Zelda saw it, she sniffed and said, "Well, that's one way of easing your conscience, I suppose." She wouldn't ask for his help. And Mr. Williams wasn't going to be able to help them anymore. Everytime Zelda went up to see him, the extensions got shorter. There wasn't anything he could do now. Van Reenen was right.

Hannah stood up. She took charge. "We'll find a way around this, don't worry. It'll come right. Come and eat now, you're tired. We'll think about it tomorrow and talk to the men a bit."

They walked slowly together into the house. Ruth, standing in the darkened room behind them, where she'd been listening, shivered in the heat.

Twelve

FOR THE FIRST TIME IN THIS ROOM I DON'T FEEL SAFE. EVERY
time they come I panic, and Zelda and I pretend it doesn't affect
me, that all this talk of moving people into camps somehow doesn't
have anything to do with me. We don't talk about it, but we both
wonder: How much longer? And then my life seems to me quite
mad—pretending, hiding, being someone that my color doesn't
allow me to be. And yet, who has the *right* to say how I shall live
my life? No one but God. This is a country of petty white gods,
millions of them, but they're not my God and I won't be bound
by them.

For so many years, I've lived in this room with its white walls
and green curtains. The little dried-out palm cross above my bed
that my mother gave me. That soft chair over there that Dawie
let me have from his room; I sat on it when I talked to him.
Miraculously, the fire only charred it, though the smell took years
to go. The Bible with its gold edges that I got when I was confirmed. The small bed. The shelves of books, each one read many
times. The china plate with pansies on it. All these things are
precious to me, as the country out there is precious too. But they
could exile me from all this tomorrow and I couldn't do a thing.

When Ruth was little, she used to come in here and sleep in my
bed and I'd read her stories. When she was ill and those night-
mares about water and drowning frightened her so much, she

spent all her time in here. I think of that time—we were so young, Zelda and I, trying to manage a farm, and a child, and not knowing anything about either. I miss it, though: all the things that went wrong, all the experiments we tried. We were alive then, even happy.

I used to take Ruth to the dam, try to make her touch the water, get over her horror of it. But there was no point, and now I don't think she'll ever recover from that dark night when she was sucked down into the water. Now, when I look at her, I am filled with so many different feelings. I like it that she's beautiful because it will help her to be loved and I want her to know love and see if someday she can learn it to the limits of her capacity. Other times when I look at her I want to cry. I see that birthmark, and sometimes when I watch it it seems to grow, even to fester there on her face. But then, on other days, when my own blood doesn't torment me, when I'm happy to be my mother's child, then that mark on Ruth's face seems to me like a little island, like the ones you see in the Pacific Ocean when you look on a globe.

We had one once, long ago, in the schoolroom. Dawie and I used to spin it round and round. He used to get me to choose a place where I'd like to live when I grew up; he used to say he'd take me anywhere I wanted to go. If Zelda came in and saw us playing that game, she'd get angry and say, "We don't want to go to any of those places. Everything we want is here. This is our place. (Only in those days she said it in Afrikaans: "onse plek.")

But Dawie did want to go. And I wanted to go, wanted to do everything he said he was going to do when he grew up. He let me think I could. When he spun the globe it was as though he were offering me the world.

We pretended too much. We're still doing it. In this house it's become a habit. So when Zelda talks about putting people into labor camps, we don't talk about me. But one day they'll find me. Something in me also says, "Let it be, I should go back to where I belong, to my own people—who I can't live with now that I've been spoilt by white people's ways."

If I wasn't a coward, I'd make Zelda discuss it, but I'm scared of what she might say. She's the one who decided long ago that we would never pretend to outsiders that I was a servant here. So officially I'm not here, I don't exist.

Years ago, Zelda was sitting at the table writing, and I asked her what it was; she said she was writing her will. I laughed because the idea of her dying seemed so preposterous—as if God would dare. But she looked up and said, "I'll go before you do, Hannah, I know these things. I want you to have this place when I'm gone. But of course I can't do that, can I?" She laughed roughly. "You're not allowed to own land, not even a little piece. It's things like this," she whispered angrily, "that make you know they're all mad."

We didn't talk about politics—what use were they in a world of your own making? We felt we could do just as we chose. That's what made her so mad, because when it came to putting things on paper—and Zelda knew the importance of that—when it came down to it, we couldn't do what we wanted. She couldn't leave me the land. When the outside world touched us, we were jolted back to reality; we couldn't bear it because it was so inhuman.

She often said, "What will happen to you when I die? Where will you go?"

The last time I got angry. I wanted to slap her: Zelda, you too, even you, you can't see me straight. I'm not your possession or property, I'm not yours to do with as you choose. You fall into the same trap as those you despise: you think you can control my destiny—that if you say "Stay," I must stay, or "Go," and I must do that also. You people all think the same: that you own us and can do what you please with us. Sometimes you do it with kindness, but it's the same.

And Dawie, weren't you the same too? When you abandoned me that day out in the veld, when you tried to treat me like a stranger and said, "It was something that happened when we were children, part of our childhood, that's all." Deciding everything so that you could go after what you wanted so bad; things you couldn't have if you had me. You too tried to put me in my place and leave me there.

"I have no choice," you said.

I knew after that you would shrink—your pride was gone, your decency, all the things that made you a man to me and to yourself. I often wonder if I've ever forgiven you.

For a long time I used to think you were no better than the Afrikaans farmers who take the black and colored girls and make them lie with them quickly, then wipe themselves and say, "That didn't count, that wasn't doing anything. It was only a black, just a colored. *Niks.*"

PART TWO

I have married my hands to perpetual agitation.
THEODORE ROETHKE

One

DAWIE, SITTING UNDER THE TREES, WATCHING THE BROAD leaves move like fans, heard his daughter cry at the bottom of the garden. It was a lovely garden, with sweeping lawns, hibiscus trees, and long beds of lilies and roses carefully tended by hands other than his. At the end of the garden, the pine trees began and strode up the green sides of the mountains. When you climbed them, you could see the ocean; always you could smell it. It was never unbearably hot here and it had none of the bleakness and isolation of his childhood terrain. It was beautiful, probably one of the most lovely places on earth—but it did not hold him. Coming here, long ago, had been an attempt at peace, a bid for forgetfulness.

He smiled an odd private smile that made him young again, his hair still blond and thick and the long, broad forehead smooth and unlined. There was something about him that made him seem more like eighteen than thirty-four, but it was hard to define: something arrested perhaps in his development, as though no real living had gone on in that face since his adolescence.

The colored girl who worked at the house went to see why the child cried and he watched her walk past him, wiping her hands. Somewhere in a neighbor's garden his wife, Sara, was playing tennis. Or maybe she was not—she could just as easily be with her lover. He didn't bother, these days, to check on her stories; it was a relief that she seemed happier. He didn't have affairs with other women: "Too busy," his wife sneered. "Work, work, work, looking after his conscience, reserving himself a place in heaven by defending politicals."

It was too late for a conscience, that had gone away, had had to. It was the little things that wouldn't go away.

The little things. He could remember the way Zelda screamed that night, but it didn't touch him, even though at the time it felt as though the world was toppling and could not be righted. As the words she'd screamed came back to him—"Who're you going to blame, Dawie? Who?"—he knew now that there was no one to blame ever, for anything. Nor could you blame society or circumstance. His father had turned on his God when blights or droughts came, turned on Him with the same vengeance he felt he was being meted out. He got relief from his rage. For Dawie, there had been a time when he could blame his country. But politics were too slippery; a true man couldn't let them warp his own morality. Individual conscience was all that counted.

He had failed. Every day was a new reckoning of that failure. All he could strive for now was to ensure that the bitterness of his defeat didn't eat into the last reserves of his honor. You could not repair a life, but you had an obligation not to let it degenerate further. His had not been a failure of love, but of nerve, courage, integrity—the values he held most dear. It was as if he was at the lower slopes of the mountain behind him, knowing that he could never reach the top, and that heady, clean air again. But he must never lose his foothold at the bottom either. Or he'd be damned. He knew the seduction of damnation. He had seen it in his sister.

In his law practice he was considered a good man, even an honorable one. He took on the difficult and hopeless cases: people being crushed by the system so that the only way left was to try to beat it with a legal system that still had its teeth. There were so many political prisoners now, though of course most never got near a lawyer. He did what he could with a compulsion that did not escape him. Only in his work could he maintain the illusion of a man making a stand against the tide. He knew it was hypocrisy, because he had failed his own heart. But at least others benefited from his sense of shame. This was what he meant by holding the lower slopes.

It was the little things.

Not Zelda's unforgiving, not even her hatred could touch him. It was the memories of Hannah. Of Hannah as a child, when it was permissible to play with her—all those free, easy years before adolescence. After that, in an unspoken way, it should have stopped, as she should have begun to call him baasie. It was not that they refused those traditions, purposefully broke the rituals and taboos of centuries, it was just that it never occurred to any of them that they were anything but equals.

The pain of discoveries to the contrary. Walking into that dark hut of clear sunlight and taking in the smell of it, airless and earthy. He had never been to the place where she lived: that circle of huts with the old women sitting in the sun minding the children while their mothers worked in the mealie lands, swatting the flies, clicking their tongues, shooing the fowls from the pots on the fire. He had to ask which was her hut and endure a certain suspicion that fell on him, and would fall on her, because of the visit. In her hut he saw the rough blankets on the floor, an old striped pillow, tin mugs, a straw mat, a coir mattress set upon the dung floor, magazines, a broken radio, saucepans, an old dress of Zelda's. And three small children crouched at the far end, backing away from his authority as he stood there, sunlight from the door cutting between his white legs.

He was awed, feeling, for all his height, somehow small and petty, unfamiliar with the world. A little boy was asleep, mucus cracked around his nose and mouth, and a small girl of about six was rocking a two-year-old. The six-year-old, clearly in charge, said with a directness that reminded him of Hannah: "We are waiting for our sister, she has gone to get us food."

The small ones were afraid of him. He tried to reassure them but could not. He sat just outside the hut, feeling very conspicuous and uncomfortable, but determined to wait for her return. The baby stopped screaming and crawled out to stare at him; he took the plump brown hand and held it until he became embarrassed. The old women laughed indulgently at him, one offered him tea from a tin, which he took and drank, if a little cautiously.

He had gone back into the hut and had given the baby his keys to play with when Hannah entered. It was hard to recognize her in this setting; it was as if she'd become someone else. She was nearly thirteen, his age, but she seemed more like thirty. It was the weariness with which she put down the paper bag with the bread in it, the way she took off her shoes. The baby began to cry. She looked around her for the first time. She saw him, but her expression did not change. It was dull, lifeless.

Picking up the baby, she asked, "What are you doing here?"

She sounded angry, but he knew anger was not what she felt, it was the only way she could talk to him in this place.

"We came back this morning, early," he said.

"What a lovely color from the sun!" she mocked. "How was the sea?" (He had told her about it so many times, but she felt she would never see it.) "Good weather, hey?"

He had nothing to say. In his pocket, his fingers curled around the little flat box with the gold chain in it that he'd bought for her in Cape Town and some shells he'd picked up on the beach for her.

She busied herself hushing the crying baby; the child clung to her and she moved it across her belly to her hip as she went about gathering up the tin cups, shaking the blankets, tidying up. Her movements were sharp and he could see she wanted to cry.

"I must feed my mother's children now," she said, as if dismissing him.

When she looked at him, he thought that her face was old: steady and patient. Not like Hannah, not like the laughing girl who sat on his bed with her knees pulled up listening to music and his stories about school. She whisked her hand across the baby's face to chase away the babble of flies around his mouth. All of it disgusted her so much she wanted to vomit. He could see this so clearly.

"Where's your mother? Is she working?" he asked.

"Her sister is ill, she is gone to her sister's." She sat and began to hack the bread into lumps. From the same bag she took out some cold meat and placed it on the bread. She said to the little girl in Afrikaans, "Boil water for the tea."

"You've been working?" he asked, sadly, knowing it meant she could not study. "I've been waiting for you for a long time," he said softly.

"Ag, shame," she said sarcastically, her eyes thickening all the same with tears. Then she said flatly, "In the morning I clean."

She handed the bread around to the children, who began to eat hungrily. She ate nothing and offered him nothing. He wondered if she'd been given the meat, it was probably leftovers from her employer's lunch.

He had seen her only once before in the presence of white people other than himself and Zelda and, very occasionally, his parents. He'd gone to the Vorsters' farm to collect some shearing equipment for his pa. She had been in the kitchen, on her knees, a cloth folded up beneath them, scrubbing the floor. She'd looked up at him when he walked in, then down, slowly.

They did not greet one another. This had shocked him so that he said, "Hullo, Hannah?" quietly, but not surreptitiously. She did not respond; she was keeping all her will to stop herself running from the room.

"Come, sit," Mrs. Vorster said. "The girl will make you coffee. Quick now, Hannah, coffee for the baas."

She had risen from the floor in a most curious manner, drawing herself up very tall, looking at them as if from the brow of a hill.

He had been proud of her that day, as she wiped her wet hands on her apron and went to the stove, taking a cup from the dresser with the plastic flowers on it.

Mrs. Vorster gave him a look which meant she did not like Hannah's manner, it was "cheeky"; but he would not collude with her. He took the cup when Hannah passed it and thanked her. He had been proud of her dignity as she returned to her cloth on the floor.

She had always been the same: there was no cringe in her. She was hard, she was strong, she would never grow supple enough to call anyone missus. Sometimes he thought of her as a little cockroach; she was as indestructible as that. When he'd told her so, she had laughed: "We cockroaches, we will inherit the earth. When all you people have gone, we will still be here."

The last time Dawie had seen her, before they had gone on that holiday, she was sitting on Zelda's bed, painting her toenails with Zelda's new pink polish with iridescent colors in it. The latest thing. And she was wearing a blue dress that made her look so beautiful. It was the color of her skin when it was wet. She'd adjusted the dress to show the cut between her breasts, the smooth slopes of her neck and throat. She had become full-breasted and womanly very fast—in a matter of months it seemed to him—while he was away at school, getting into the first team at football.

Now, seeing her wipe the baby's hands, she was neither child nor woman. She was something eternal, womanly only in the way her dress pulled across her breasts and in her weariness, but childlike and afraid in her shame, her wanting him gone. Pushing the mug to the child's mouth, her hand shook a little. He wanted to cry too.

He stared miserably at her thighs as she crouched to lay the baby down, her face held away from him. He remembered lying very quietly with her on his bed in the early mornings, holding her hand and watching how her heart beat under the light cotton nightdress and how hard his own heart had beaten with feelings he'd never known before. How he'd touched her breast and been amazed when she rolled over to face him, her dark eyes very quiet, very close to his own.

Trying, he now said, "Do you remember how we went into the bush? And I caught the bird for you? Made a pen with the long feather. Remember?" He wanted to make her happy, he wanted to give her the gold chain in the plush box, to say that he had thought of her and missed her every day. She would not look at him, so he walked outside, where he waited.

When she had finished with the children, Hannah came out and stood at the doorway of the hut. She folded her arms. He could see her legs through the threadbare frock. She went over to the fire and took up a black pot that stood near it. With a handful of sand she began scrubbing the inside to get the pap off.

"Hannatjie," he whispered, "don't be mad. I'll wait until you can come. I'll tell Zelda you can't come now. We'll wait for you, man. However long, I promise you." He wanted to reassure her, to at least take her hand or touch her a little to apologize somehow. "Nothing has changed," he begged. "It's happened before. We must just wait, isn't it? It'll get better. We'll wait."

"No," she shouted, "no, I'm not coming back." She had turned away from him entirely, so that all he could see was her back hunched, the muscles of her arms hardening in the effort of scouring the pot. "I'm not coming back, *ever.*" She screamed the word at him and ran inside.

Two

IT WAS OVER A YEAR BEFORE SHE CAME BACK, AND IN A REAL sense she never came back—not to enter the house again as home, spend the night, bathe in the bath, sit on the beds, sleep there, go to the lavatory. She was a colored girl. Now she knew it. She was too old for dreams. The house was closed to her and with it a whole world had to be relinquished. She felt that her girlhood was over and she put it away from her, as she did Dawie and Zelda, with terrible determination.

Dawie pined for her. He went off alone into the bush and sometimes he saw her in the distance. Quickly, she went in the opposite direction. She looked very thin, her clothes were ragged and he couldn't bear to see her and not help her, not touch her. Zelda pretended not to care; she was brutal sometimes about it. Other times she would plead with him: "Go and get her back, *make* her come back, Dawie." But he knew her pride too well to humiliate her further. He waited; he believed things would get better. He returned to school, and when the boys in his form went to the flicks with girls at the sister boarding school, he did not do so. When they went to parties and began fondling and kissing when the lights went out, he did not do so. His sexual pride would not allow it. He had touched Hannah that way and would no one else.

She had gone back to her own school, had passed Standard Seven and then she'd thrown it all up. Too much time had to be spent away from school, looking after the children. It angered her also that she was taught so badly; much as her teachers tried, they did not have the books or equipment. She did not have money for the fees, or the blazer. This second relinquishment made her more bitter. It was too much all at once. She noticed that her stomach had shrunk with less food; she hoped that her heart and head would do so also.

But Dawie was persistent, and when he felt that the time was right, he approached her again. She was sitting by the dam and he came and sat beside her. He could see the bones of her knees, and her skin had lost some of its luster, but he could smell that the anger had gone out of her.

"How have you been?" he asked. "It's been so long and I've missed you. Zelda too, she misses you, though you know her, she won't admit it."

For a minute Hannah felt she was there again, on the bed in his room, having conversations about Zelda. "Ag, I'm fine," she said, but she wouldn't tell him that she'd left school. It was painful to hear about his school and how far he'd got.

Noticing this, he began to talk about what he was reading, and he offered to bring some books to her. She didn't refuse. Soon Zelda came too, and the three of them began to do things together again. But never inside the house. It was understood: their discussions and walks went on outside. Nor would she wear Zelda's clothes or try on her makeup.

Dawie was proud of her; he said so. He also said that he loved her. He was patient with her sharpness, as if he took the blame on himself for what had happened to her. Because of this, she began to feel that there was something just a little penitent in the way he came to her. It was as if she had become his conscience. And she wanted things to be as they had been before—simple, equal, untarnished. But, as he returned each holiday, unchanged and devoted, she slowly grew more certain of him.

They began to create a new secret world, and what had once been a hunger to learn became a different hunger—one that excluded Zelda. Excluding Zelda was like smashing a taboo. It felt a far closer step toward guilt and calamity than either felt in the other's arms.

Hannah felt, on dizzy ecstatic afternoons as they moved closer and closer to it, that she must throw herself recklessly toward her fate. He felt no such fear: to him it was merely a natural consequence of their feelings. Soon they had gone so far that there was no point in drawing back. Soon they had learned how to lose all restraint. Now they were bound together as allies against the world, as partners in passion, as sharers of a single country more precious even than the country of their childhood.

Three

DAWIE ALWAYS REMEMBERED THE FIRST TIME AND HOW DIF-
ferent it was, how much deeper in feeling it took him, so that the
casual romances of his boyhood seemed absurd in comparison. It
was like being in the cool and quiet of a church, their two bodies
lying in the damp sand that ran smooth to the edge of the dam.
He put his hands behind him, stretching his spine, pressing his
fingers into the dirt and feeling the sharpness of the willow roots
making patterns on his palms. Looking over the dam, he could
see the sun breaking the surface of the horizon.

"Don't touch me," she whispered, and shivered. The ducks rose
up and flew across the water. She took his hand and pressed it hard
against her throat so that he could feel her heartbeat there. "See,
it's moved," she breathed. "Can you feel it, my heart, how it's
beating?"

"Ja, I feel it."

His own heart was stretched painfully. His hand circled her
throat. She looked afraid. Then, with her finger, she touched his
cheek, moving down to his neck, his shoulders. It was as if, for the
first time, she touched white skin. It was not the same as her hands
and his making a dam as they used to do; it was not like their
bodies rolling and fighting in the bush that day because they were
both so happy and had not known how to express it. This was new
touch, new awareness of skin, texture, color. And now, because
of her touch, his skin went different colors: pink, then back to

brown, then very pale. Hers, she felt, remained the same, sand-colored, unalterable.

"Touch me, touch me now," she whispered. It was so innocent, the way she spoke, an offering of herself with reverence and tenderness. Her eyes were wide, clear brown, her body the first he had entered or ever wished to.

He said quietly, "I have hurt you."

"No," she said, turning her face away.

"Ja, I did," he said softly.

"It's done now," she said, seeing the blood. Slowly, almost dreamily, she took up some sand from the dam and began to smooth it across his cheeks and down his naked body, rubbing it on so that his skin was dark brown all over.

"We will never betray one another," he said.

It was like that child's vow made with the blood from the pigeon's throat. It was Dawie who made the rituals, who put their wishes into words, who would say: "Remember when we did that, and what it meant." He would never let anyone forget the significance of an act; he was a chronicler, one who understood and marked each stage of their history.

She said nothing, but it was a covenant for her, too. "I must go home now." She took up her clothes.

"Not yet."

"I must. Are you going to stay?"

"Ja, for a bit." He felt no shyness with her as she looked at him, lying naked there.

But seeing her preparing to leave made him panic; he reached for her hand and held it fast. "Come back later, Hannah, come back for a bit?"

"Maybe." She seemed withdrawn, but he felt completely at one with her.

She went down to the water and walked into it. The sky looked ominous now. They both lifted their heads and looked at it. Then she stooped and began splashing water onto her body. As she bent a little, her back to him, he saw a tiny triangle of light through the top of her thighs. Then she turned to look at him, as if she did not know who he was, as if she were held in a dream or mood he could not enter.

He caught his breath: she was so beautiful, so pure. Her hands moved quickly, splashing up the water lapping against her legs. Her skin shone like a ripe fruit, pale blue lights and a sheen his could never achieve. He went down into the water too and they stopped and looked at one another. The mud had dried on his skin and now it was splintering into little cracks. She touched it and didn't like how it felt. She began to wash him, slowly and carefully, until he was clean again.

"Come and lie down," he said.

"It's too light. The cattle will be coming."

With a sense of loneliness, he watched her dress. She did not speak to him and when she was finished, she turned to go, without touching or kissing him again.

"Please come back," he said.

"I will try."

He closed his eyes and when he opened them again he saw her walking steadily across the veld, a tall erect figure made small suddenly by the flatness of the landscape. When she reached the scruffy trees at the outskirt of her village, she stopped, she looked around her, and, as if bewildered, let out a high-pitched keening sound. Then she stood quite still. It was a sound he had last heard when his grandfather was being put in the ground; the Africans had gathered around, some singing, some rocking their bodies, some making that same shriek of grief.

By the time he had flung on his clothes and run after her, she had disappeared between the mud walls and entered her own domain.

Four

SHE HAD ALWAYS KNOWN THAT THERE WOULD BE THINGS SHE must hide from him. And there were many times when she could not come to their place under the willow trees in the early morning. He noticed that she seemed troubled, but would not tell him why. Her stepfather had not sent them money for two months now. Her mother could not work, her legs were swollen up so badly and the medicine she walked so painfully to collect did not help. Hannah could find no work, and to take a live-in job at the nearest dorp was impossible because then there would be no one to look after her mother and the children and collect the food and water. She was the eldest child, there were many burdens on her.

There were only a few coins left in the tin and Hannah was growing desperate. She had planted some mealies and beans in their scrap of soil, but they were weak and slow. The three fowls needed to be fed; it was a question of keeping them alive in case they had to be sold. There was no thought of eating them—they had not eaten meat for months. Hannah's mother complained that now the chickens were fatter than they were; she tried to make jokes about it to cheer up the children. Her mother spent her days sitting outside, sewing patches on the clothes the children ripped running about in the bush.

Hannah looked many times at the gold chain that Dawie had

given her. She couldn't sell it because no one could afford to buy it and she dreaded the day when she would have to part with it for a couple of coins at the Indian store. She kept the chain in the cleft of a tree and wore it when she went to see him and took it off before she went home.

"Hannah, if you're in trouble, you must let me help you. Tell me what it is."

"It's nothing." She hung her head.

"That's not true. All the time it gets worse. Now, tell me, you must. We're together in everything. I'm like your husband now, you said so. I'm here to look after you, man, tell me. It's money, isn't it? That's the problem?"

She couldn't answer. She couldn't say: "It's food, that's the problem." She couldn't tell him that that very morning she'd taken the last teaspoon of coffee from the tin, scraped out the dregs, then filled the tin with boiling water to swill out the last flavor and given it to her mother, knowing there would be no more. And how could she say that every day she went and asked the man who worked at the Post Office in Konigstad: "Is there a letter there for us? A registered letter? From my mother's husband?" But there was no letter. They did not know if he was sick, or dead, or had found another woman who needed the money. His work was very hard and his lungs were bad; they worried for him.

Finally Hannah said to Dawie, "I must go to Port Elizabeth to look for him." She did not tell him they had borrowed the money from her mother's sister, who had borrowed it in turn from a cousin. "I have to go tomorrow," she said.

He noticed how erect she stood, how little her lip trembled, how stern she had become except at those times when she lay and laughed up at him in the rosy light by the dam.

"Hannah, I've had enough now of your stubbornness. You must let me give you some money. Please God, man, are you trying to make me suffer or something? I can't see you like this. You have to take some money, or at least take some food to your family before you go. It would be evil not to, you know it." It sickened him, it broke his heart now to see how much they had at the farm:

how food was thrown out because it had been in the fridge more than one day; how the vegetables rotted in the garden or were given to the pigs.

"Pride can be a very bad thing too," he said. He felt that he and Zelda had made this pride of hers worse by making her see how poor she was, and because they had shown her no way to get for herself what they had by right.

It frightened him that she had begun to turn against their shared past; she would not let him talk of it. It was the dearest part of his life and it hurt him that she could take no comfort in it. She said it was not real, and anyway, it was lost, they could not have it back so why worry with it? She wanted only Now, because that at least could not be stolen. But she did not seem really to believe this. She would look at him with a patient, knowing look and he knew she thought he would abandon her.

"Never, I'm telling you, on my word, I won't leave you. True as God. You are my blood."

"Touch me, Dawie, just touch me. Let's forget about it." She gave him all of herself, but hid her life as if it were shameful to them both.

"You don't do me justice," he said miserably, "you make as if to punish me by not letting me help you. You'll take nothing from me and so you separate us. It's your own form of apartheid."

Her eyes grew wide with the effort of absorbing her tears.

She forced herself. "I will take some sugar and mealie meal for the children, and maybe some coffee for my mother, and a few aspirins," she said quietly.

He wanted to fill the back of the truck with food and unload it at midnight outside her door. But she insisted, "Only bring a few bags or else I can't say where it's come from."

When she said things like this, he knew that in allowing the secrecy of their life together he had entered a bondage: if he couldn't love her openly, how then could he keep his honor to her and his own self-respect? If he betrayed her daily by not being with her, how could he promise her anything and be believed?

He learned to cover himself with the reality of his dependence on his parents, his youth, his lack of money. All this would be solved when he was a lawyer, when he had money and freedom; then he would come back for her. But he couldn't tell her this, it would not be fair. He had to do it first.

"If you go tomorrow," he said unhappily, "then, when you come back, I will have gone to college." He kissed her hands rather desperately. "I won't see you for months and months."

He didn't see how they could manage the separation, either of them. But she was wearing that strange, enclosed look and it frightened him.

"Don't hide from me, Hannah."

She took him in her arms and rocked him. Life was giving her stronger emotional muscles than him, but the strength she was acquiring was only that of endurance. She thought bitterly that he would go off and learn the strength of power: the power of words, of the law, of the courtrooms.

"It will be all right there, you'll see," she said, thinking he worried for himself.

"I don't care about that," he said angrily. "How can it matter, when you are here."

"Nevertheless you must go," she said, "and you'll do great things, Dawie, be a great man and maybe even change the world a little bit." Though she said it lightly, it was not said in mockery; she believed it.

"I wonder how I'll know, without you to tell me."

She was thinking that there would be girls, pretty blonde girls, with blue eyes and pink mouths—the Cape was full of them. He had a big lust, he would sleep with these girls, he would do to them the exquisite things he and she had learned together. She would be left with the hunger again, a hunger deeper even than that for learning. For a moment she clung to him and almost wept.

He stroked her hair, "I won't forget you, Hannatjie, and I won't go with other girls. I never have and I could not, it would make me sick. It would break everything between us, you know that, don't you? It would be the same for you also. We must be loyal. No one else, I promise you. Now, you also must promise me."

She promised.

"Remember this, Hannah, remember everything. I'll come back, true as God. Just wait a little."

When she walked away, it was he and not she that wept, but by then she had already become quite good at pretending.

Five

I'VE GIVEN MY BODY TO ONLY ONE MAN; MY HEART WAS CON-
nected to it and I couldn't separate the two. The vow he asked me
to make before we parted and went in different directions was
unbreakable. I have lived my life by it. The very first time he
went into me, I told him: "No man has ever touched my body
before you." It remained that way.

The boy my mother wanted me to marry—the Xhosa boy with
the big nose—she pushed me toward him saying he would be a
good husband to me. I knew it. I knew he could probably take me
some other place and build me a house where we might be allowed to stay. Maybe give me some children and some happiness.
But I couldn't do it. Not because I waited for something that
couldn't happen, but simply because I could not do it. My body
could not. The gate on my heart had closed and my feelings stiffened. Also I was afraid what I might do to a husband whom I
couldn't love.

You get used to living on very little. Often at night I cannot
sleep and my body plagues me. It seems to remember what my
mind has forgotten. When I can't sleep for remembering, I walk
out into the moonlight. I walk over to the big netted run where
the roosting chickens perch and I watch them for hours. Sometimes they wake up and clatter their wings. They look strange
with their heads tucked away, sitting asleep.

Those nights send me backward. I seem to think of hunger, of being so scared of not being able to get any money, days when I did not think of my family's hunger anymore but only mine. When you are that hungry you think of nothing but food, nothing but food. You seem to see it everywhere in the town; in shop windows, people eating in restaurants, food being taken out of vans, children sucking sweets—food everywhere, but not for you. Stealing is not easy, but if you must, you do.

I did not find my mother's husband that time I went looking for him. I took a job working in a polish factory in the day and cleaned out a hairdresser's shop at night. I worked so many hours that when I was not working I just slept, and if you sleep you don't have to think of eating. It was a funny thing, but I even dreamed about food.

I would remember the squealing of the pigs when they were being slaughtered, the roasting of meat over open fires, everyone together, talking and laughing, waiting for the meat. Even things that had sickened me as a child returned with a certain pleasure because they were to do with food. Ja, it was very peculiar: the skin being ripped off a sheep's flesh, that sound like ripping paper or cloth, those kidneys in their pink bowls of lard and the good fat my mother made.

Then slowly, as things got better, I could think less of food and more of my home and the people I had left. I was sending them money regularly, so I knew they were all right. I had a little room in a woman's house, the rent was steep, but at least she did not throw me out like at the other place. There you could come back and find all your things thrown out because someone else had taken your place.

But I never liked the town life, I felt alien there. The people were strange, the ones my color the strangest, the saddest of all. I didn't want to be like them; they had no place in the world; no one wanted them. Because their skin was that bit whiter, they got little advantages sometimes, but mostly it seemed to be worse for the coloreds. But if they were strong, they really were strong, and some were great characters, with their drinking and their strange way of speaking.

I made friends with a colored girl who was very pale, with red hair and gray eyes. Her father was Portuguese and her mother a mixture of many things. She nearly was allowed into a white school, but then they found out and sent her away. Her brother, he also tried to sneak into a white school, and was accepted, then after a year they found out and threw him out. He hanged himself in the schoolroom there, the day he was supposed to leave.

I learned many things and I found out that there was a way to survive anywhere. That is why I have no real terror anymore. Very bad things are happening all over the country, it will catch up with me, I have fear, but no terror. My heart also learned to live on very little. I did not think of Dawie because it would have finished me. I just worked, worked, worked. And I suppose I have never stopped.

Once Dawie said: "We won't always have to stay here, we don't have to stay here now. We could go away, make ourselves a country somewhere else." But I couldn't go, I couldn't do that. You have to stay, but if you do stay, then you must not break your own laws.

Six

"RUTH!" ZELDA'S VOICE RANG OUT ANGRILY ACROSS THE room, "what the hell do you think you're doing?"

There was such force and authority in the voice that a small table shook. But Ruth, who also trembled, did so with pleasure, because she could hear panic in her aunt's voice. She turned toward her insolently, pushing the drawer closed with the small of her back. "What?" she asked, jerking up her chin.

Zelda pointed to a pile of papers. "Those are mine."

"Ja, that's right." Was it a sneer?

But, still, Ruth was afraid. She'd been caught in her aunt's bedroom, a place in which she'd never spent any time beyond putting her head around the door to ask for something, and always after knocking. Zelda encouraged no visiting. Her room revealed very little about her—being merely functional. The walls were bare and white, the furniture heavy. She cleaned the room herself and she locked the door when she went away for a night.

So they glared at one another, the girl with her back to the bureau, the afternoon light from the window harsh and radiant on her hair.

"Well?" Zelda said quietly, but not without menace. "What were you looking for? Money?"

Ruth's cheeks mottled with anger; she snapped, "What do I want money for?"

"To get away from here perhaps?" It was said almost with understanding.

Zelda walked over to the window and pulled the blind down so that the glare was cut a little. Then she moved to the center of the room, where she could look directly at Ruth, and waited, her arms folded.

Ruth, like a rabbit trapped and petrified by the lights of a car, quivered.

How odd, Zelda felt, to be afraid of another person. Her curiosity was quite detached; she had never been afraid, herself.

"That's what you'd like, isn't it?" Ruth said angrily. "Isn't it?"

"What would I like?"

Zelda's stillness, of a different kind from Hannah's, having at its center no serenity, unnerved the girl even more. But she would not give in.

"For me to go away, leave here, that's what you want." She started to shout "What have I ever done to you? Except been born—which wasn't my idea. Why must you always hate me?"

"I don't hate you." Wearily it was said. Zelda's shoulders moved forward as her broad hands clenched. "I don't hate you, Ruthie."

Ruth tried to remember when she had last heard her aunt use the diminutive, and could not. The soft tone made her suspicious.

Zelda picked up the suspicion immediately and it hardened her again. "I just don't like people messing around with my things. I don't go poking about in your room."

Zelda saw that the cupboard against the other wall had its door open; there was something furtive about the way she looked at the small line of oak drawers set into the hanging section.

"Don't flap, I haven't found anything." Ruth lolled to one side, her weight supported by the bureau. She gave the impression of holding it as one holds captured territory in a war.

"I have nothing to hide," Zelda said coolly. "You must just learn to respect other people's privacy, that's all."

"Oh, I think you do have something to hide," the girl said with an underhanded look.

"Really?" The heavy eyebrows went up in mockery.

"Really."

"And that's what you were looking for?"

Ruth drew herself up so that her carriage was proud. Something about the line of her jaw reminded Zelda of her brother when he wasn't going to be persuaded by her.

The whine always present in Ruth's voice had vanished. "Tant Zelda," she said, "there are things that happened that I want to know about. You don't have to worry about the gun, you know, those stories people talk about, or whatever it was that you did— I just must know about *me.* You have to tell me. I've looked and I can't find anything that helps me, so you have to tell me what happened."

"I don't have to tell you anything." Zelda said.

"I have the right to know about me."

"Oh, rights!" Zelda tossed the word up and caught it lightly like a ball.

"Ja."

"Well . . . not so much about me. What I mean is, I want to know about my father and mother— No"—she spread her hands with a jerk—"not that they're dead. I know that story, and I . . . I don't believe it. Well, I don't believe that *he's* dead anyway."

Zelda's eyes widened, their gray color went black; and when she spoke her voice seemed remote. "Well, then, what?"

Ruth darted to the door and turned the key in an absurd and dramatic gesture, then stood with her back to it. "You must tell me everything—*alles.*" She said the Afrikaans word roughly. "I want to know the whole story and until I do you're not going out of this room."

"Then I'd better sit," Zelda said with a laugh. She could feel the fatigue in her back from driving the landrover over bad roads all that morning. More cattle had been stolen. The guerrillas had come down again from the hills and driven off her stock, killing the herdboys. One of these nights she was going to be up waiting for the bastards. As she walked to her bed and sat down, Ruth felt confused, unsure of what would happen now.

Zelda was pulling off her boots. "I suppose there are things you should know, but you could have asked instead of carrying on like this."

"I have asked, millions of times."

"Not as if you really wanted to know." She looked up briefly. "It's not the easiest thing—locking you up."

Zelda laughed. With her lips pushed out stubbornly, her head high, Ruth reminded Zelda of herself: that time she had locked Dawie up in the storeroom overnight with the bats, because he wouldn't tell her something she'd wanted to know. She warmed to her niece a bit, and even wondered what exactly it was about the girl that made her so hard to take.

"Okay, then" she said, now that her feet were free of the heavy leather boots. "If you want to know, I'll tell you. It's about time. We'd better start with your mother. You can get away from the door, I'm not going to make a dash for it. Sit down, why don't you?"

Seven

IT WAS HARD FOR ZELDA TO TALK TO RUTH. THERE HAD never been any intimacy, except that of mutual hostility, between them. And now she must tell Ruth the things she should have been told years ago. She wasn't the right person to do it, she knew, and yet perversely she wanted to be the one to do it. When she spoke, her voice was brisk, her manner direct but uninvolved.

"I had a sister who died," she said, adding, "Well, no, not a sister, a half-sister. Annetjie. Your mother."

Ruth nodded. This much she knew.

"The reason we've never spoken much about her is that, well, Hannah and I felt there wasn't much point. Also, I didn't know her very well, not so I could describe her the way you'd want."

"I just wanted to know something, anything—you know, so I could see what she was like a bit . . ."

Zelda felt uncomfortable: the girl—young woman—sitting there on the floor of the bedroom, pliant, pleasant almost in her manner, was looking at her in a way that made her uneasy, guilty even. Better to get it over and done with as fast as she could.

"Annetjie was the result of my mother's first marriage—no use asking me about that because I know nothing about it, she never mentioned it. We just knew that Annetjie had been born long before us and that her father was not ours. No one"—she looked at Ruth caustically—"felt the need to explain anything to us in those days. They didn't consider it our business."

"This," Ruth said stiffly, "is a bit different, this *is* my business."

"Ja, well, maybe it is." She gave a small shrug. "Anyway, Annetjie lived with our grandmother in town, not on the farm. She'd once gone there on a visit and decided not to come back to live. But still, she did come and visit us on the farm." She smiled with wry amusement. "And we rather worshiped her. I suppose, thinking about her now, she was young and beautiful and quite unlike anyone else we knew. Also, she loved playing with us. She liked to dress us the same and carry us one on each hip. She always called us the babies, even when we weren't anymore. She was a bit wild. People spoke about her in a particular way."

"What way?" Ruth's face was intense.

"Well, you know." There was a touch of impatience in Zelda. "She was a definite person—nothing feeble about her—she was zany and funny, quirky even." Zelda smiled with something like affection. "She was sort of extreme, you know," she said quietly, and as she spoke she leaned back against the wall running along her bed, and in so doing, her body became softer.

"She had a special language of her own—words that she'd invented: nicknames, endearments, that sort of thing. And we began to use them too. She used to play a game with us. How strange, I'd forgotten all about that. She used to say: 'I'm going into a wood or pasture and there's a house in there, full of beautiful things—a piano, a cage of canaries singing, gold chairs. Now tell me what's happening in there, tell me what you can see. Let's go in . . .' "

Zelda stopped and looked down. Ruth was quite startled: it was as if, for the first time, she could imagine her aunt—long ago of course—as being beautiful, yes, quite definitely, she could see it. Beauty.

Zelda returned, went on slowly, "It was wonderful, she took us to all the places she'd been to, and all the places she dreamed of going to. Often, she'd be sitting quietly, plaiting my hair, and she'd whisper in her low voice, 'Let's go somewhere, I want to go somewhere wonderful. Where shall we go? Come on, Dawie, take us.' Dawie was very good at this game. She made our world magical—but then of course she was up and gone again and we wouldn't see her for a long time. Poor Ma—she loved her the best. When she'd gone, Ma wasn't the same person."

Zelda brooded. "With Annetjie gone, she was always off visiting, shopping, distracting herself one way or the other. And I used to try and get back at her. She didn't like me much, I don't think. Dawie was okay: everyone loved Dawie, no one could resist him. I suppose he was a good person, if there are such people: upright, just—but not stuffy, just . . . Well, anyway." Her voice had grown brittle and she was impatient again.

So was Ruth, "So what then?"

"Well, anyway, what happened then was that your mother came to the farm for a long holiday when she was about sixteen. I'll never forget it: the fuss, the excitement. Those two, my mother and Tant Ethel, they turned the house upside down. Oh, that house was much finer than this one; it was old and very elegant, full of shadows and coolness, long rooms with polished wood floors and high ceilings. But they turned it upside down, for Annetjie, painting her room in a lilac color—all the other rooms were white—putting up frilled curtains. You'd think she was coming to live.

"Of course Ma hoped for it. She wasn't above bribery: she filled that room with presents from town, with little scent bottles and ornaments and flowers and she even bought a little speckled puppy—he was a sweet little thing—for Annetjie. We were insane, my boetie and I, with excitement and jealousy.

"And then she came. I'll never forget how she looked getting off that train. As if she'd just stepped out of one of those fancy boxes packed with tissue and ribbon. When we brought her home, she seemed to float up the steps in a creamy silk dress with a big, wide hat that same color on her auburn head. Pa wasn't there. I remember that. He was peculiar with her, polite, stiff. She didn't care; it was as if she knew that she could make anyone adore her if she chose. She just hadn't got round to Pa yet— that's what she made you feel.

"When she was in the house my mother just stood looking at her and couldn't speak for happiness. We squealed like pigs. She had on lipstick and Ma didn't even reprimand her. Annetjie was aware of her beauty, all right, she was like a queen visiting her subjects, and I wonder now what she thought of us, whether she cared for us at all."

Zelda was silent for a while, not seeing that the child was almost suffocating with excitement and relief that she was at last blessed with such a mother. It was hard for Ruth to move, even to breathe. She wanted to creep closer to the voice that uttered these comforting things.

She leaned forward beseechingly. "And then? *Then* what, Tant?"

For a moment it was as if Zelda would not continue, as if she had righted, or remembered, herself, and felt foolish.

"Well then, she stayed with us," she said flatly.

"Ja, but what *happened*?"

"It didn't go well." Her hand rubbed her chin, she looked tired.

"Ag, please, don't stop now," the child breathed.

"In fact . . ." Zelda looked dazed. "In fact . . ." Her voice was very low. " . . . It broke Ma's heart, if one likes to talk in such dramatic terms."

But thinking of that time the phrase seemed to Zelda neither dramatic nor untrue, merely a fact. Watching her, Ruth felt as if Zelda had been transported into one of Annetjie's imaginary worlds and could not find the door to get out.

"What *happened*?" the girl insisted.

Zelda pulled herself away from the wall, so that there was now nothing to support her back. This was the way she usually sat. "She fell in love," she said dismissively, "or she thought she did. With a man from round here, a rough Afrikaner. He was blond, big—good-looking, I suppose. And clever as a snake. So clever that he ignored her—Annetjie. He ignored her, who all her life long had never been ignored, always been doted on. He paid no attention to her when all the local boys were hanging around. So, of course, she began to fall for him.

"It was pathetic. It was even laughable. But she had to have him. She couldn't rest for scheming to trap that stupid man. And yes, he knew just what he was about: he played her like a violin and she didn't even see his fingers move. Funny, isn't it, what love does?" she sneered. "Ridiculous." And she didn't even notice the look of rapt dismay on the young girl's face as she sat there and seemed to feel the pain her mother had once felt.

"Well, she married her Pieter, you see. She made Ma arrange it and make it just as beautiful as she'd always imagined—silk, lace, lilies. We were dressed up in the same. But there was something very wrong with the day and our ouma wouldn't come. Annetjie kept saying, 'Oh, she'll turn up, you'll see, she'll come, she wouldn't not.' Even to the last minute she was saying this. And then, when it was clear that the old woman wasn't coming, she went proud and careless about it.

"I remember I cried when they drove off, but other people seemed to know something was wrong. Then, when they came back together, they went to live on the farm that Ma had given Annetjie when she first came home. It was the best farm, the one over the long mountains. You see, we were all to be given a farm when we were eighteen—only she wasn't eighteen yet. It was Ma's way of trying to make her stay. And clever too, because although Annetjie hated the country, she loved the old gabled house on that farm, and she loved being given things—big things. The land there was the best, the most fertile: it was watered by a good river and it was full of peach and apricot trees."

Resentment pitted Zelda's voice. "Ma refurnished the whole house—new chairs, thick curtains, expensive rugs. All to get her to stay. A manager had been running it for Pa and really"—her face stiffened with anger—"it was an exceptional farm, small but perfect, running like clockwork.

"Anyway, after their honeymoon the two of them went to live there and at first it was all fine, because she came over often to visit. Pieter got rid of the manager and began to run it himself. He bought Annetjie lots of presents and a little blue sports car so she could visit us. She got pregnant almost immediately. It was as if he then had everything he wanted: the best land for miles around and a wife who'd make a fool of herself for him."

Zelda sniffed. "Well, to cut it short, he squandered that farm away. He just couldn't keep money at all, he squandered it away in debts and more debts. First he sold off part of the lands, the little lands on the south side, and then the big lands. Pa must have been appalled. Then the stock went too, then the other things—furniture, the lot. It all went very fast. I don't remember it much, not the details, but we used to listen to our folks talking and rowing about it at night. Ma was beside herself with unhappiness. Pa was silent and furious. There was nothing they could do about it. I know they tried to buy Bloukops back, but they couldn't—God knows why. I would have found a way, but the thing was in Ma's hands. The land had been in her family forever; in a few months it was all gone."

Ruth sat very still, as if these things were happening even now, to her, and she was helpless to change them. Zelda, watching her face as it flickered eloquently with distress and perplexity, went on, more quietly now.

"And it was in that expensive little foreign sports car that he'd bought for Annetjie, it was in this very car that they were killed, on the road leading back to town. You were in the back and were saved. That's all. Now you know it all."

Eight

RUTH, SLUMPED ON THE FLOOR, BACK AGAINST THE DOOR, hands over her face, was sobbing with a strange and sensual abandon that Zelda, in acute discomfort, must now break.

"If you ask to know, you must take it," she said.

It was not the truth that devastated. It was the crushed hope. All her life Ruth had been sustained only by the fantasy of her mother's beauty and goodness, her father's courage and pride—and now, for the first time, they were manifest to her as people, real people, and really dead. The illusion, which she returned to each day with the same wonder as a first love letter, was over. Her father was dead; her mother was too. Her father had been the one to kill them. He was no good. She didn't begrudge him this; it made him more familiar to her. But he had made her mother suffer. And now they were both dead.

Her aunt watched her in silence, until she could endure it no longer; then she moved back on the bed so that she could not see the girl. The sounds of Ruth's sobbing rose and fell, rose and fell. The house settled into a late-afternoon torpor. A fly had found its way in through the netting at the window, and flung itself at the pane like the thud of hard rain. Zelda rose from her bed in quick irritation and killed it with her hand, flat.

Ruth looked up as if she wanted Zelda to say something.

"I can't tell you any more," Zelda said shortly. "What more must I tell you?"

She knew, of course, exactly what the poor thing wanted to know: that she had at least been loved. But even the word made her impatient. Anyway, how could she, Zelda, know about that? Her conscience suggested that she should be kind. Kindness was something that Ruth needed at this moment. She relented a little. After all, once you'd allowed yourself to be drawn into the mess of other people's emotions, you had to find the best way out again.

"I was only a kid, you see. I don't really remember much about it. Afterward, my mother wouldn't talk about Annetjie. It was a long time before my brother and I could play Annetjie's games again. For a while, whenever I said to Dawie, 'Let's go somewhere, come with me,' he got angry that I was trying to be *her* and he'd say, 'There's a coffin, I see a coffin with Annetjie inside it and beside her is the wheel of a car and through the spokes her hand is . . .' "

Seeing Ruth's distress, she said angrily, "See, I told you I shouldn't say any more."

"No, no, it's okay, really, just tell me anything you remember."

This pleading was so repugnant to Zelda that she snapped, "There's nothing else."

"Ag, please, man, there must be something. Even about Dawie, anything."

"No." Zelda flung her legs off the bed and stood up.

The sobbing began again, soft and rhythmical, until Zelda, her face twisted and ugly, roared, "Get out, go, get out of here."

Ruth ran. She charged through the house, through the front door and out into the heat, running blindly down to the dam.

Nine

ZELDA SAT ON THE BED, SHAKEN AND FURIOUS WITH THE girl: she was like a mosquito that buzzed around you, wouldn't let you be, and finally stung you. And crying like that, so loudly, huddled there like an animal, making that bloody awful din. As if she would never stop. How could anyone beg another in that way—it was revolting.

She sat with her hands planted flat on her knees, her hank of hair bound tight, making her features bony and stark. She had moved away from Ruth now, into different territory, but it was just as dangerous. There was something about the day, something about Ruth, that took her back, and, for all her will, she couldn't dismiss it as efficiently as she had the stupid girl. And on this airless, desolate afternoon when all she could do was remember, all she could feel was hate. Hatred was more palatable to her—it didn't stick in the thoat. She could swallow it eventually and feel nourished.

Charlie. . . .

Zelda at seventeen, radiant with her challenge of a new conquest: a man who looked at her and was not drawn.

She had taunted and intrigued him, encouraged and resisted him. And then, he had given way—but as if he didn't give a damn, as if it was only a game to him and his real concerns and love lay outside her desperate grasp. He played with her and learned how to break her on her own desire. He taught her submission, but not the submission of love—never that, just a surrender. Her will and the breaking of it, that he had enjoyed, only that.

The heat was like a scarf across her mouth; her lungs seemed to close in and push her heart together. "God!" she snarled, wiping the sweat from her palms on the bedspread. Then she leapt up and paced the room, back and forth. She had no strength to resist the intrusions of the past, to fling off the memory as he came back to taunt her.

"Come here, Zelda" (that soft whisper of his). "Do what I say. Kneel. Now crawl slowly to me. That's right. It's what you wanted, isn't it? I can reduce you to nothing. To dirt and plain hunger and greed. You thought you were above me, didn't you? Above all of us? Well, you're not, you're just like anyone else. You can be broken, you can bleed. And you can beg. I've made you into a whore, so I could make you into anything. I can play with your body or forget it. Now, do it nicely, do what I say. Don't you see, Zelda, it's the ones like *you* who love to lie in the dirt— that's where you push everyone else, so you're just waiting for someone to do it to you.

"You're lucky you found me, lucky I came to this godawful farm in the middle of nowhere, lucky I haven't packed up and left you. That scares you, doesn't it? I can see it in your face. Well, lie down, do as I say, lie down." And then in his sweetest whisper, a whisper that could just as easily have been hers when she was manipulating her own victims: "Do you know how I learned to do this, Zelda? By fucking sheep. That's right. Just the same, no difference, Zelda. Do you want me to stop, then? Is that why you're looking at me with such hatred? Well, then, maybe I will?"

Standing in the middle of the room, her body rigid, her heart had the hard, quick beat of a small animal's. It seemed to fill her whole body, the entire room. She went quickly to the window and opened it to try to breathe. There was no wind. There was nothing out there. The dust rising on the road far away seemed to settle on her tongue; the glare blinded her.

But she could not let it be. She remembered, too, the sheer pleasure of torment. And then she brought out her most exquisite recollection: that night—black, moonless—and she quite frantic with the undoing of all her powers, trying one last time to restore them, to get him to submit. But it was again she who submitted. There in the dust—kneeling, sobbing, begging him not to do it.

The next morning his two big brown suitcases stood in the hall, his name and address written on them already: SYDNEY, AUSTRALIA, the label said. The other side of the world. He, huge and careless with his hat tipped back, exposing that white slice of forehead that the sun never touched. His broad hands running down the sides of his thighs before lifting the cases. His mouth smiling, his body stooping, anxious to be done with it, beginning to forget already.

The shout. His turning, the laughter moving into a frown, then into fear. Then his voice: "You bitch, you fucking mad bitch, pack it in!" Her hands raised, ready. Her smile of triumph. Oh, how sweet, doing it back to him. Holding the moment, freezing it for ever. Then that beautiful blast. Silence. The second blast. Silence. As if forever.

Ten

"ZELDA!" HANNAH CALLED FROM OUTSIDE THE CLOSED DOOR.

"What?"

"Supper's ready. Are you coming? It's past eight."

"In a bit."

Hannah hesitated. But knowing the voice so well, and hearing it now with its broken edge, she opened the door and asked, "Are you all right?"

"Why shouldn't I be?"

Zelda's face, turning, had a heavy, depressed look; there was shame in it too. Her shoulders were slumped. She sat on the bed with her legs hanging down. Her face was flushed. When her leg twitched, her hand came down and gripped it angrily.

"Ruth was crying," Hannah said. "I thought you might have had a row with her."

"Since when do I have rows?" It was a matter of pride to Zelda that she never shouted, not even at the men who worked for her. She got off the bed quickly. "I just told her," she said, "to stop messing with my things. She was looking in my cupboard."

"What for?"

"Oh, some cock-and-bull story about wanting to know about her parents—the whole truth, that kind of thing."

"Oh," Hannah breathed out. Then she added quickly, "What did you tell her?"

Zelda turned sharply. "I told her what she wanted to know, didn't I? It was about time."

Hannah was startled. "What did you tell her? She moved into the room and closed the door behind her, looking closely at Zelda.

"Oh, you know, I told her about the accident."

"But she knows already."

"The detail, I told her the detail. Facts. About her parents, what they were like. She wanted to know what they were *like*."

"So what did you tell her?"

"Mainly I told about Annetjie." Zelda gave a grim smile, impossible to translate.

"Annetjie?" The black brows on Hannah's face seemed to lengthen.

"Yes, a nice touch, don't you think. And why not tell?" Zelda's voice filled with sarcasm. "I told her what a pretty, spoiled, but lovable person my sister was. Zelda opened a drawer in her bureau and yanked out an old black sweater.

"I see." Hannah was looking down at her hands and in particular at a dark bruise on one finger.

"Do you?" Zelda put the sweater on over her shirt. Then she asked with mock courtesy, "You don't mind, do you?"

"Me? No, why should I mind? She had to know." She hesitated, pulling at her fingers, "Did she—did she seem satisfied by what you told her?"

Zelda tugged at the sleeves with impatience; she was tired of it all. "How should I know?" She glared at Hannah. "What must I do? What would you have done? I don't really know anything, do I? I told her a good story. Kept to the basics. The rest I think I read somewhere."

"Can you tell me what you told her?"

"Why? For what? I'm tired."

"I'd like to know."

"Look, I can't remember, I was making most of it up, so it's gone, I can't remember."

"You don't remember a lot that you should, Zelda."

It was all Zelda needed. "Oh yes, and what should I remember, then? What's the bloody good of remembering anything, hey?

What good has it done you, tell me that? Don't think I don't know how you lie there at night and go over it all, again and again. It's crazy. It's pointless. Let's just forget it all—everything, the whole bang shoot."

Looking at her, mostly in anger, Hannah felt she had never seen the wound so raw in Zelda. It was always there under the skin, but now it had made a startling eruption. Her face was quite wild, her emotions smeared all over it, and she could control none of them.

Hannah tried to protect her. "When I remember," she said softly, "I try to think of the things that made me happy. I think of you happy, Zelda, ja, even with that desperate kind of happiness that Charlie gave you. It was better than this bitterness—"

"Don't talk like that," Zelda hissed, "don't you bloody well talk about that, you hear?" Almost reeling with rage, she snapped, "You ruddy well remember what you like, Hannah, you were always like that—but I have nothing to remember and nothing to forget. Okay?"

Hannah felt the old pity return, then alarm, and then, yes, a kind of excitement and relief. It seemed that at last Zelda might be cracking. Like a dam, she thought. Once that first crack comes, the deluge must follow.

She remembered how, long ago, she and Dawie had held Zelda down, physically prevented her from trying to escape from what she'd done. It was not something Hannah would attempt alone. That imperious streak was still there—that girl who dived naked between black rocks, who made slaves of those who loved her— that Zelda who had sucked a man dry and made him hate her— oh, she was still there.

"Come, Zelda" she said, as if she spoke to a child, "come now and eat. You're very tired."

Obediently, Zelda followed her.

Eleven

Dear Dawie,

I am writing to you only because I must. I would not other-wise interrupt your life. We have trouble here, of different kinds, and I feel I can't deal with Zelda as well as I used to. Also there is Ruth, and though I have never bothered you with her problems, something has to be done about her future. I am not your family, but Zelda and Ruth are and I don't think I can go on to make decisions without a word from you. I have been very strict with myself, and I am convinced that this is not an excuse. I need your help, that's all.

I will start with Zelda. We are having a lot of trouble with the Bureau and I know that bothers her—they are trying to force us to put all the men in the labor camp and, at the same time, the old village here is to be broken up. You will know how all this works and what the legal position is. Is there any way we can fight them? If so, can you tell me what we should do? We have been holding this up for months now by various maneuvers, but I want to be certain there is nothing else we could try before we decide to sit it out.

As for Zelda on a more personal level—she seems to me, now, to be reaching a crisis. I don't know why, but her bitter-ness is up and there are very few of those times of peace and quiet which kept me going with her before. She has become pretty hostile to everyone, and I find her wearying.

No, I know these are not your problems; she is only your

sister. But Zelda is my lot and I know I must get on with it. Our relationship is wearing thin and I want to make it better, if I can. For this I ask your advice. It is as if she still blames me for things: for the absence of you—for the hole in her life. And of course there is always the constant ugliness of Charlie in her mind. She won't discuss that at all. She won't discuss anything.

And what can I tell you about Ruth? You know nothing about her and I suppose it's too late to start. The point is, she can't stay here very much longer, and she has to be found some way of making her own living and being independent. Work will give her the dignity she needs so badly. I am afraid for her out there in the world, because she has lived the kind of life we did, shut off from outside influences. The only difference is that we had one another and she's had no one. I think perhaps it may be better if she were to leave the country altogether, go to England perhaps. She likes little children, and could perhaps train to be a teacher there. I fear for her; her life has been strange, will always be strange. She does not fit and perhaps never will. England might be her only chance.

Can you please tell me what you feel about this?

There are so many things to say to you, to tell you, that I can't do justice to any of it. But I do have to try because I just keep feeling that things, all sorts of things, are drawing to a close here and that we cannot keep them away any longer. Sometimes I feel it so strongly that it's like a physical pressure in my head.

It's as if we hide here, from everything, all of us, and now life is prizing us out.

Please understand that I am not asking you to come here— Zelda would go crazy if she even knew this letter was being written. I know how your life is. Though we see people seldom, your cousins sometimes drop in and your nephew Andries was here not so long ago. They of course hate what you are doing and call you a traitor. Zelda says nothing for a bit, and then shuts them up. So I know how things are with you, and I would not make anything difficult. I am only asking that you write to me.

I am also sending you copies of all the papers and orders we have had from the Bureau and our response to them, so you can see precisely how the thing stands at the moment. You will see how urgent it has become.

I know this is a dreadful letter, and it may just confuse you. The trouble is, I have written it so many times that now I must just send it off and hope you can make out what I am trying to say. It is such a very long time ago, sometimes it's as if it were someone else's life and not mine, were it not for the results that live on to haunt us. But I suppose I would change nothing.

Hannah

PART THREE

The timeless, surly patience of the serf
That moves the nearest to the naked earth
And ploughs down palaces, and thrones, and towers.
ROY CAMPBELL

One

DAWIE LOOKED UP FROM HIS DESK AND THROUGH THE WINDOW overlooking the port. He could never do this without feeling a sense of loss that the ocean liners of his childhood—those elegant boats with names like *Windsor* or *Caernarvon Castle*—no longer sailed into port with their streamers flying in the wind. The first time he'd seen a Union Castle boat—meeting his mother after a trip to Europe—his small boy's wonder had known no bounds; his curiosity was awakened by the engine room, the holds, the vastness of it all. Zelda and he racing up and down, from first to second class, mad with excitement, forgetting why they were there, until their mother's expression pulled them into line. The most wonderful part was telling Hannah about it, seeing that small face, those dark eyes, sparkle with excitement.

A young man popped his head around the office door. "Are you still wanting to go to the trial, Mr. de Valera?" Dawie didn't answer straightaway, so the young man added, "Only it's getting late."

"Ja, I know, thanks. Of course I'm going."

"There's a big demonstration building up outside the court-room. Police are everywhere."

"Okay, just get the car ready and leave enough time for delays. When d'you think?"

"Twenty minutes?"

"Okay, fine." Dawie looked more directly at his assistant. "And Kenneth?"

"Ja, sir?"

"I want you to come with me." He smiled. "You're not going to be much good to me unless you get the smell of these things. And de Klerk is a great judge, a really fine man. You shouldn't miss him."

The blond-haired boy looked excited. "Oh, I'm coming sir. You couldn't stop me."

"Good. Twenty minutes, then."

Dawie shut his door and took the letter from Hannah from his pocket; again he read it. It had been a shock to see that handwriting again. And the tone of the letter exactly as he remembered Hannah, too: clear, to the point, proud in that there was no mention of herself in it. No rebuke. Just like that day when he had stood before her and spoken, miles and miles of speech, of justification—and she, silent, sad, watching a man drain away in front of her.

On this occasion, as on the previous one, he would have preferred a rebuke. The letter had been so impersonal, as if they had never had a life together. Of course it had to be so. It was her way. There was no hidden message for him there. She asked about Zelda and about Ruth. He had been thinking a lot about Zelda in the past weeks, almost as if that twin connection had begun again. The letter confirmed his instinct that she, like him, was nearing a crisis point in her life. When they were children and this happened, each would draw off from the other whatever was needed; their personalities would forge, making each stronger. But all he could feel in Zelda now was a desperate weakness, the weakness he had experienced when he had left Hannah.

It was horrific to remember that business with Charlie. He'd never understood why she'd chucked herself at a base Australian like that. Charlie was one of those men that other men instantly recognize as corrupt bastards, but to whom women are drawn almost because *of* the corruption. An old sense of responsibility about the affair returned to him. After all, Charlie would not have been on the farm at all if he, Dawie, hadn't gone off to study law. Charlie came to help on the farm. He knew all about sheep and was just increasing his knowledge in another part of the world. He gave the impression he knew all about women too, and in particular, one Pauline: a freckle-faced girl who smiled out of a photo kept in his wallet. When his year on the de Valera farm was up, he was going back to Australia to marry Pauline.

It was this loyalty to Pauline that had challenged Zelda, but it had taken her months to work him round. Dawie remembered how there had been a certain satisfaction in seeing her fail: in seeing Charlie stick loyally to the girl in the photo. It was hard, always had been, to identify with Zelda in trouble. When she began to fall, you watched her the way you would watch a great tree topple.

But then she had begun to conquer him: there was a difference in him and a difference in the way they behaved together. The sharp banter continued between them, but it had altered. Zelda had wrenched the power from him. She had made him want something very badly from her. It was disturbing to watch them together, as slowly the way he treated her became disdainful. Dawie frowned, trying to remember exactly what it was.

She forced him to do things and then he made her pay for it. I remember she made him write a letter to Pauline. I'd heard them arguing about it the night before, and he had refused to do it. She was relentless, but clever about it—she never whined or wheedled. It was clean, direct manipulation, not woman's stuff: no tears, no pleading, just force and logic. He wrote the letter, all right. I saw it. Only I don't think it ever got posted, but she thought it did.

I was amazed by his ability to play her. Perhaps he could only do it because he had something on her, some power, probably sexual, that he had learned to wield. She seemed to be intrigued and horrified at the same time by what was happening to her. I feel sorry for you, Zelda, thinking about it now, because it must have been hell. You were like animals fighting for dominance: pacing, taunting each other with little jabs until the right moment, when one would go for the other's throat and finish it.

When you thought that letter had gone off, breaking the engagement, you coolly began to plan the wedding. You worked round Ma. At first she refused to have anything to do with it.

You didn't give a damn that the whole thing would remind her of the past, of another wedding—you just forced her. She went ahead, stonily, and we were forced to listen to you going on about how the wedding would be, like a small child determined to get her own way. Charlie would lie back in his chair and smile in a particularly nasty way he had—cruel and amused. You went off and chose the material.

It lasted a month, the tensest month of our lives—the endless preparations, the rows—you, Zelda, like someone beating back time. And all the while something physical about you was changing. Hard to say how, just an aspect of another, darker side of you, something loose, slutty, a bit sick.

At times I used to feel that you were acting out some kind of revenge on Hannah and me. You insisted on telling us stories about what you and Charlie did together, until it was too disgusting to listen to. I almost hit you a few times. You began to taunt us about our own future. There was a peculiar need to hurt and destroy us then, as if you could not bear the quiet of our relationship— as if you were, as always, making comparisons, and what you couldn't have yourself you wanted to destroy. I gave you hell, but Hannah withdrew from you. And then, inevitably, I suppose, the thing that you'd always dreaded happened—

There was a knock at the door and, when Dawie called out, the tea lady came in with her trolley. "Will you have your tea now, Mr. de Valera?"

"I will, please, Martha. Thanks, just put it there."

She closed the door and whispered, "How will it go today, mister?"

He cleared a space for his teacup. "Hard to say, Martha. Not good."

"My brother and his wife, many people, they've taken time off work to wait outside. Last night the police came and took away fifty people. But the rest are still going." She put in a second lump of sugar and stirred it vigorously. Beneath her faded pink uniform the sturdy armor of her underwear stood out in ridges. "I think," he said quietly, "there will be plenty trouble today."

"I'm afraid so. People were killed last night in the raid." She raised her head. "One white policeman. Of our people shot dead there were sixty, though they say five. And many, many with bad wounds."

"Ja, Martha, but that one white policeman last night makes the whole case more difficult."

She nodded her head up and down gravely. "Hm, mm, they'll go to prison, mister?"

"Ja, they'll go. A long time."

"And the people they thrown in jail from last night?"

"Unless they can find clear evidence of sabotage, they won't be in too long. Do you have family in now?"

"My brother's child." She sniffed, but her eyes were clear. "The ones who did the bombs, Mr. de Valera, what will become of them?"

"That will be determined today, Martha. It's not my case, you know, Mr. Greenberg is handling it. And no one could be better."

She nodded her head hard. "I know it, mister, I know it. He is a good man. We are praying for him every night." She began to push her trolley to the door. "You going down there?"

He nodded.

"Well, you take care now, you watch out, hey? There's plenty trouble coming."

"See you tomorrow, Martha. I'll find out about your nephew. Write down his name for me, okay? I'll check it out later."

"I'm thanking you, mister." She turned and made the old-fashioned bob to him, then walked quickly away, shutting the door behind her.

Dawie took up his cup and sat a long time drinking his tea, then let it go cold. It was that feeling of being quite helpless; it frustrated and angered him. His partner, Abe Greenberg, never lost hope, never lost his sense of humor, never seemed to feel he was licked—he always went in like a man certain he would win. Dawie couldn't do it that way. He went in prepared, determined and furious; but if he lost, the defeat—and it was nearly always defeat in these cases, or paltry hold-ups before defeat—felt like a personal failure.

It was, he knew, quite stupid to take it so personally. It was an old failing. He'd felt something similar with his sister: nothing to do but watch events unfold. The court hearing today would be the same—for all the courage of the judge, his insistence on the law, and all the brilliance of Abe. You beat your hands against the wall until they bled, but beat you must, or become the wall. And yet, tomorrow Abe would march in here and begin all over again, working for another appeal, maintaining some extraordinary belief that the law was still working. And, yes, he had to admit it: Miraculously, justice did still go on—some basic decency in human nature kept surfacing in the most unexpected places.

He had loved so ardently the idea of justice, believed with all his heart that it could change their world; that the law would be a blockage against tryanny. He had made Hannah believe it too. He had left her to go and build the foundations of this dream—and then became intoxicated by his own cleverness, by the speed with which he had climbed those dizzy heights where honor, truth, and virtue could be represented by his person in a courtroom. He'd been true to himself—had come out bravely as a man prepared to show his political bias, and work for it.

But something had gone wrong inside him. Something had made him say to her: Don't wait for me, get on with your life. I must get on with mine. Personally, he couldn't take the heat. He'd let his professional life take over and had hidden behind it. He'd left her.

In the same way, he felt now that he'd abandoned Zelda at a crucial time. He had watched her destroy herself. Of course, she was responsible for what had happened to her, but did that make her more guilty? She too was a victim. She had put her fate in the hands of one man, as Hannah had placed herself so trustingly in the arms of his great dream. Only, he now felt, Zelda had had more guts than he. She'd run her course to the end. And it destroyed her, sharply and cleanly. Not like him, with his protracted, daily farce—the outer hero masking the hollow inner man.

Zelda just did it. Charlie announced, one dinner time, that he was leaving, in the morning. It was a week before the wedding. He gave no explanation. And Zelda had spent the afternoon on a table with pins in her mouth as the dressmaker put the finishing touches to her wedding gown. No one said a word.

The effect on Zelda was electrifying. She went white all over, I remember even her arms went pale, and then she let out a scream. It was quite shocking, like a single shot from a gun in a silent night. After that, she just sat there, her eyes wide open, her body stiff. I remember how he just continued to eat. I got up and smashed him out of his chair. Zelda didn't look up. He left the room—which surprised me. I thought he'd beat me to a pulp.

We all went to bed. Later, much later, she began to scream at him. Finally they left the house and went out into the night....

There was a light tap at the door and the young man walked into Dawie's office, saw him with his head down, and said quietly, with some concern, "The car's waiting, Mr. de Valera." Then, a little awkward, "Hey, are you okay, sir?"

"Ja, sure, are we all set?"

Dawie got up and gathered together a pile of papers on his desk, stuffing the letter back into his pocket. He picked up his briefcase.

His assistant, who admired him, hesitated, then said, all in a rush, "Er, sir, can I ask your advice about something?"

"Of course. What is it?" He looked directly at the young man for the first time, his voice concerned but his manner somehow a bit detached.

"Well, it's just that I'm having hassle at home, sir, about working in this office. I mean, my parents, well, they think, after spending all that money on law college, they think that working here will ruin my chances. I got into real trouble last night about this Greenberg case." He look embarrassed. "Well, they're just not the most liberal people in the world, you know, keep calling you lot a bunch of pinkos! Sorry, sir."

Dawie's voice was strangely severe, the boy thought. "Is that your way of saying you want to leave?"

"Oh no, sir, no, I don't. I want to stay."

"You knew what you were getting into from the start, Kenneth."

"Yes, I did, sir, ja, of course. It's just that I'm wondering how to counter their criticisms."

"You can't, Kenneth. They're right. Come on, let's go down to the garage."

As they got into the lift, and it was empty, Kenneth said, "Look, sir, I think what you and Mr. Greenberg are doing is

wonderful, I'm proud to be here, really I am—I believe in it."
His face had a flushed sincerity that made Dawie want to laugh
out loud, or cry.

"If you've got the stomach for it, stay, man. If not, get out,
now—not in six months, when it will be a bit late. If you stay,
you've got to get in further, you know that?"

"I know, sir."

"In that case, I suggest you move out of home." He stepped
out of the lift.

"Well, yes, I was thinking of that," Kenneth said, a bit
uncertain.

Dawie laughed. "I think maybe you're thinking of that raise
we promised you, hey? And that with it you could afford to move
out"—he looked Kenneth sharply in the eye—"and then devote
yourself wholly to the honorable course—without any aggro?
Is that what this little chat's been all about?"

"Well, it would help, sir—the money I mean." He blushed.

"Clever little bugger. You'll make a good lawyer all right.
Now, drive this car and get a move on. We're going to be late
as it is."

"And I'll get the raise, sir?"

"If you get us to court on time, you will."

Two

DAWIE, SITTING IN THE PACKED COURTROOM, HIS MIND WAN-
dering from it to a remote farmhouse and back again, from
Zelda to Hannah and back again, suddenly found himself quick-
ened by the proceedings of the trial. It was Abe. Abe, who with
his small, unimpressive stature, his round, bespectacled face—a
man who might seem unable to catch the attention of a bored
commuter on an empty train. He had them, the whole courtroom,
stuck fast in the power of his eloquence.

The Africans up in the crowded galleries, sitting pressed
closely together or standing along the walls, all watched him
with rapt attention. Some rocked their bodies slightly as he spoke,
others leaned forward gripping the rails, and always, when he
stopped, heads would nod gravely or a soft chant would rise and
then merge with the tense atmosphere.

He was asking the jury to judge these men (only men, he
insisted, not the violent terrorists that the prosecution would have
them be) only as they would judge themselves. Could they, he
asked, being brave men and women, submit to a regime that gave
them no right and no future in their own country? Would they,
if their country was overrun tomorrow by the Russians, not fight
back with every means available? Could any of them honestly
say they would give in helplessly to tyranny? And, if the situation
were reversed, and their own color miraculously altered—only
this one thing—would they not rebel too? They must ask them-

selves where they would stand, with a silent, broken people too intimidated to fight back—or with the ones who were prepared to risk imprisonment, torture, even death for the sake of freedom. Could they really not imagine, in this short moment of time, how it must feel to be black in South Africa?

He was like a marathon runner, Dawie thought. His life—the loss of his entire family in wartime Germany—had trained him for these exhausting and solitary fights against the odds. "The greatest danger," Abe said quietly, "is when one man thinks another so different from himself that he ceases to treat him like a human being." Then he roared, "Think about it, *think* a little, imagine a little. Do it *now*."

Always he began quietly and steadily, taking his pace from the audience in the room, aware of their fluctuations of mood. As he gathered momentum, it was as if everyone in the room joined him. They were no longer watchers, they were participators in the race. When he had them all like this, locked into his fight, then he would urge himself forward with all his strength for the last lap.

"Do none of you out there understand passion?" he asked now in a quiet intimate voice. "Have none of you felt, reading famous trials in your papers, that a crime of passion was one you could most readily understand?" Now he had them. "Those men in the dock acted from just such passion, just such despair. They had reached the end of their endurance. Think of it: years and years of protest, of being shot down, clubbed to death. Could you go on believing in the eventual decency and goodness of others? Of you people out there? Would *you* carry on? Or would you do what they have done? Yes, I'm talking to you people out there—you, man, you and you."

When he had stopped speaking, there was a hush. But when he turned and began to walk back to his seat, everyone stood up and a roar began.

It was remarkable, Dawie thought, the way his speeches seemed to touch them all with the same brush—a tar brush—so that, for a moment, each forgot the one thing that separated and regulated their lives: their color. In that safe and enclosed place, he seemed to make them one shade, one people.

It was the phrase "a crime of passion" that kept reverberating in Dawie's brain. "The crime," as Abe had said, "that each man or woman committed when they betrayed all that was decent and fine in themselves out of cowardice, greed and fear. A crime that could only reproduce itself and destroy the man as surely as it destroyed the society he lived in. A crime that meant the death of the heart."

Listening, Dawie had begun to sweat. He felt faint; the room and Abe's voice blurred. He felt the most acute mental pain he had felt for a great many years, the kind he'd not dared to feel again after leaving the farm all those years ago. He could hear Hannah's quiet voice: "It's you I am sorry for, it's you who will never again be the man we both loved, it's you who have died today."

He left the courtroom for a few minutes. When he came back, is had all changed. How quick, how easy it had been. Another man striding up and down the courtroom, spouting a few in-flammatory clichés, was able to divide the room neatly in two again. He had gathered the jury back into the laager. It was all so predictable. But not quite. Something else was happening. High in the galleries an atmosphere of calm dignity prevailed. It was as if the words had no meaning for them, as if they didn't even hear what was being said. They seemed just to wait. Not for the verdict; they knew how that would go. No, they just waited.

The men in the dock shared this same patience. The low drone of the summing-up penetrated no farther than the ears, and the ears did not hear because they listened to other things. A white man stood and made a fist. A child woke and began to wail. The women began to gird themselves. Outside, the police in their armored vehicles waited with the crowds. It all seemed very still.

Inside, the judge passed sentence. He looked around the court-room, he spoke with contained anger, he announced five sentences of death, ten of twenty-five years' imprisonment, and one ac-quittal. There was a deep hush—no gasp, no movement, no breath. Then a lone voice began to sing a hymn. Other voices joined in and slowly the harmony deepened, the voices swelled, reaching higher and louder, obliterating the calls to order, the thud of the hammer, the pandemonium in the benches below.

And in the midst of it all, a woman stood. She rose up on to her chair and shouted out a name. One of the men being led away stopped and turned to look at her. Her arms outstretched as if to enfold him, she called out in a proud ringing voice, "Twenty-five years! My husband, it is *nothing*, it is nothing!"

Three

DAWIE WALKED OUT OF THE SIMONSTOWN TRIAL, PUSHED HIS
way through a furious crowd, and walked very fast toward his car.
Behind him he could hear a loud hailer ordering people off the
streets, the sounds of shouting and abuse as clashes broke out
between the crowd and the police; finally, shots being fired,
screaming, people fleeing in all directions, the smell of burning.

As he too began to run, a woman rushed toward him, holding her
crushed bleeding face. He turned instantly to help her, but she
reared away from him in terror and ran off in the opposite direction. He tried to follow her, but he lost her.

He drove home. He went straight to his study and closed the
door. He sat there a very long time, deep in thought. Then he
took up a pen and began a letter to Hannah. He wrote it many
times, discarding each attempt and beginning again. In the end,
the letter was short and to the point; he put it in an envelope to
post.

He sat and waited as it grew dark. The woman who had called
out in the courtroom sat with him, she seemed to hold him tightly
in her grip, there was no escape from her. As there was no escape
now from what he must do. This very night when his wife came
home, it would be done.

Four

———————

"HECK, YOU'RE LOOKING SO DAMN PRETTY THESE DAYS, Ruthie," he said admiringly, looking at her pink dress and her breasts pushed hard against the soft material.

She had a solid, sweet body, long-waisted and tall, with the grain of her skin running smooth and flawless. It pleased him to look at her, to touch her and smell the clean scent of her flesh. There was nothing cheap about her now; she had changed and he took a little credit for it. Those stupid stiletto heels were gone, her feet were as brown and bare as her legs. She wore no makeup, but the skin was very pale—her legs might brown, but never her face. Her hair was pulled up in a high ponytail and it bushed out at the back; little strands of gold sneaked out around her face. They didn't cover that mark, but she didn't seem to care so much. Ja, he thought, she really looks beautiful. Something more womanly, quieter, about her. There was none of that flaunting that made him worry that he would forget himself with her.

The change had happened quickly. Just a little while back, when that thick Dutchman cousin of hers had come to stay, she was still bad. She was looking for trouble then and the skellum Andries seemed to know it, sniffing around her like a dog wanting to get up on its hind legs. But now she was different. Hell, now he could even take her home to his mother, his ouma even—that elegant old lady would approve, would pull her red blanket close to her and nod.

"What will I do without you, Willie? You're the only one that says such nice things to me." She took his hand and squeezed it.

He kissed her quickly, a little awkwardly, on the side of her face. She looked at him quietly and held still, then moved her face forward and kissed him on the mouth, hesitantly and shyly, but full of curiosity too.

He looked a little startled, then he said tenderly, "Wait, now, we haven't yet made a plan for you, Ruthie. This here has just been my plan. I come first today, but now it's your turn." He laughed so widely at her that the shadows beneath the trees seemed lit up by the whiteness of his teeth. "You don't think I was going to leave you here with no plan, did you, hey?"

She moved closer to him for the reassurance it gave her. "No," she said modestly. "You go first, you still haven't told me just what you're going to do." As she said this, as if fascinated, she did what she'd always wanted to do and reached to touch his hair. It was grizzled, strangely impenetrable, but soft and quite unlike wool.

"So—what you do that for?" he said gruffly, as if reprimanding a child.

"Niks," she said, shrugging her shoulders.

He laughed a little. "Once I wanted hair like yours. I thought if I put oil in it, it would go like a white person's. Once"—he smiled more broadly—"I thought that to be smart I had to be like you people. Funny, hey?"

"You're the smartest one I know, Willie."

"That's just because I can make the stars dance for you," he whispered enticingly, "because I sing to you in the bush like a honeybird, and play my mouth organ till your feet wipe all the dust away. Isn't it, Ruthie? That's why you think I'm smart, because I make you happy?"

"Oh ja, all of that," she said impatiently. "But now get on with it. I want to get to me, you know."

"Ag, well." He settled himself down. "It's simple, man, here's the plan. Machine Mike, well, he's got it all sorted out for himself in P.E. He's got a lekker little business going, really good."

"How come?" she interrupted. "How can he do that?" She was always quick to point out the limits of possibility for Willie.

"Ag, you know nothing! There are plenty businesses going along in spite of the law. Machine Mike, see, he has set up a garage in the grounds of a smart girls' school—one of those places that turn a blind eye. It's far enough away from the main buildings for them to say they didn't know about it. It's an old unused sports hall, something like that, but big, and he's fixed it up good. He lives in the school grounds, at the back, with his woman. She works there in the school kitchen, feeds him, washes his clothes, the lot. He's got a good deal, all right. It was his woman who suggested he make a garage there and he's had it nearly six months now and no trouble. Well, he says he can tuck me in there nicely, give me a job at the garage—he needs another mechanic and I'm pretty good."

"Ja, but Willie . . ." She frowned. "Who's going to bring their cars to be fixed by you in a place that doesn't exist?"

"Ag, don't be so clever. Already he's got customers." He waved his arm extravagantly. "Many, many. He goes out, collects the car and then drives it back when it's fixed. No questions asked. He's good, man. They don't care how the work's done, and he can do it a bit cheaper too. So then, the word gets round and off you go. That's what Machine Mike says: word of mouth. Any paperwork the girl can get done for him. Where there's a will there's a way, hey?" He nudged her in the ribs again.

"Anyway, I'm happy as Larry about it. He'll pay me forty rand a week to start, and as long as I watch myself and don't break the curfew or anything stupid, they won't catch Willie-boy, man, not a chance. He'll dance out of sight like a spring hare."

She looked at him, slightly in envy, more in admiration. "You're lucky, you know, you people. There's always some excitement, some fight for you. You have laws to break, risks to take. It makes life exciting. For us, everything's on a plate."

"Well, Ruthie, my sweet potato, if that's so, then take it off the plate and eat it, man! What you waiting for?"

"Ag, Willie, I don't know what I want." Her ennuis returned, and with them, the flat tone, the slackness in her body.

"You want the same as me, man," he said firmly. "There's no difference: you want a job, money, clothes, a chance to live your life good. That's all anyone wants. Am I right?"

"But Willie, you at least can do something, you can fix cars and things. What can I do?"

"You just need to be trained, that's all. That's why we're sitting here like goggos in the shade; we're going to work out what it is you want to do, then you can tell them that you're off to do it. That's all, true as God, easy as that. No one will stop you."

An apprehensive look crept across her face. "Willie, you see, there may be a problem with all this," she said quietly.

"What you talking about?" He looked at her sharply, his instincts jangling like bells.

"Ag, niks." She turned away.

"Don't give me that niks. What's the problem? You just tell me now or I'll klap you one, no word of a lie!"

"I said it's nothing. Really." She looked at him sheepishly. "I just don't know what's going to happen to me, that's all." She fumbled about in her mind for something to convince him, and came out with, "Well, it's a difficult time for them at the farm now, with the men from the department coming all the time to make trouble. I think I should stay. Tant Zelda says she's going to fight the order, so maybe there'll be a bit of trouble and excitement for us, all the same." Her face was bright, and it convinced him.

"Well, that's a bleddy miracle," he said happily. "Somebody who's going to say no to them for a change, someone white who'll put up a fight. Jeez, just one person needs to have the balls to do that and it could really start something, hey?"

"Ja," she said vaguely.

But then Willie began to worry about his family, about leaving them. "How can I leave my ma, what'll she do without me if things get bad here?"

"Ag, Willie, don't get upset. You know Tant Zelda, she'll show them off. Don't you worry. I promise you, we'll look after your ma and the kids. No one's going to kick them off the land, I promise you. You must just stick to your plan—go off and make good money for them."

But then Ruth's hands flew up to her face: she thought of the trouble coming, she thought of her own private trouble. Without Willie there was no one to share it with, no one to help her.

"Oh, but Willie," she wailed, her hand rubbing her birthmark angrily, "what'll I do without you here? Who will keep me alive? What will I do when you've gone, Willie? What will I *do*?"

She flung herself into his arms and sobbed. He felt her breasts against him, her heart against his, the wetness of her face in his neck. Her face came up slowly to his and hung there imploringly. How could he not comfort her with the only words, the only ways he knew?

Five

EARLY IN THE MORNING, THE KITCHEN QUIET AS A SUNDAY, the black stove making a soft roar and the *putt-putt* of hot porridge bubbled in an open saucepan. Ruth, hair fizzing about her sleepy face, sat at the long table watching Hannah as she took out a bowl and, with a spoon, ladled out thick dollops of porridge. Ruth spooned on golden syrup and small dribbles of milk.

"This'll go straight to my hips," she said.

Once she had been so thin, Hannah thought, watching her eat. Now she could almost be called buxom. Her breasts and hips were no longer childlike. Her face too was changing, the flesh becoming taut across her bones, lengthening and refining her features.

"What time is it?" Ruth asked, eating the porridge slowly, taking it from the outside edges in long circular strokes.

"It's nearly four." Hannah turned her head to the window to see a slender moon set in a dark and glittering heaven.

Ruth said quietly, "Hannah, what would you say if I told you something bad?"

"What sort of something bad?"

"Just—something bad."

"Well, I'd want to know it, whatever it was." She spoke gently and went about her business—filling the saucepan with water and setting it on the sink, drying her hands, putting the lid on the syrup tin. Then she made the tea. Ruth lost her nerve.

"Why? Do you have something to tell me, then?"

It was the same voice, the girl thought, that sheltering sound that she could never imagine turning cold or careless or cruel. But still she hesitated, because it was such a bad thing and to Hannah it would be a sin; Hannah would have no knowledge of such things. And sometimes she felt that if she didn't claim it, it would not happen.

"Is it to do with Willie?" Hannah asked, making her voice casual.

"Willie?" Ruth looked up. "No, not Willie. Well, no. . . ." Her spoon was curling into the deep edges of the bowl with the efficiency of a cat's tongue. "But I do miss him," Ruth said quietly. "He's only been gone a couple of weeks but I miss him already."

"Ja, it is hard." Then Hannah stopped, considered, and made herself say the rest. "But you also were thinking of going away, weren't you?" She hated to say it, to bring the absence nearer, but when would another time as close as this happen? How long had it been since Ruth had come to her room at dawn and woken her to say: "I can't sleep, can I stay with you a bit?"

Ruth pushed the empty bowl away from her and drew her arms up high around her breasts. "I don't really want to go, not really, not now. Well, I do a bit, man, but I don't also. *She* wants me to go, isn't it? It's she who wants me out." There was even something resigned about it.

Hannah took up her cup, warming her hands around the bowl. "No one will make you do anything you don't want."

"I did want to. Only, well, after talking to her and making her tell me about my people, well, I think she's lied to me again." She was busy pushing her finger along the grain of the wooden table.

"What about?"

Hannah placed the cup centrally in its saucer. "What did she tell you?"

"Ag, you know. She must have told you."

"No, she didn't, she didn't tell me anything about what she said to you that day."

"Well, I think she lied when she said he was a Dutchman."

"You think he's English?"

"He's not Afrikaans, he's English. I know it." She leaned forward with an intense and frustrated movement. "She said he fooled my ma. Well, a Dutchman's too stupid to do that! And she said he schemed to take her land and farm away from her."

"There was a farm once, over the mountains, that's gone now," Hannah said.

"Ja, well, there might have been; it might even have been true, bits of it. In fact, I think what she told about my ma was probably true enough—you could tell Zelda was jealous of her sister, so that rang true." She was scratching the back of her head slowly as she thought. "But not about my father. That bit I don't believe. She was lying through her teeth about that. I know her."

"Hm. So what do you think, then?"

"I think"—the girl scowled—"that she thought she was fooling me. The question that I can't answer is why. Oh ja, I think my mother is dead, all right, some way or the other, but not my pa, he's not. I believe rather what Andries said."

Hannah was uncomfortable with the conversation now. She said quickly, "Andries is not a reliable human being, he's not even very nice. He's just as likely to lie."

"Ag, I know that, of course he is. But he's got no *reason* to lie to me about that—and Zelda has."

"Has she? Why?"

"I don't know." Ruth's face was stubborn and angry. "I just know she has her reasons, I just know."

Hannah wanted to leave the conversation, but she couldn't. "Tell me, then, Ruthie, what makes you so sure your pa is alive?"

"I've always felt he was. I've always known it."

"And your mother? You've never felt that about her—that she's alive I mean?"

"No." She thought a little. "But maybe it's because I don't mind so much about her. I always had you, when I was small. When I needed that sort of thing there was you, so it wasn't the same. But there was no man ever, no person to protect me."

"Except Willie," Hannah said.

"Ja, except Willie." Ruth was despondent. She didn't want to talk now, and not about Willie, who'd left her.

"You do know, Ruthie, don't you," Hannah said gently, putting her hand on Ruth's, "that there's nothing I can tell you about all this, don't you?"

"Ja, I know." She was surly, dissatisfied with it all. So much so that she didn't notice the pain in Hannah's face, or the way her head dropped and her eyes stared steadily at the tiles of the floor.

But Ruth had changed her mind. "No, now look," she said quickly. "I'll tell you, even though I swore I wouldn't. It was Andries who told me, it was he who told me everything. But he made me say I'd not tell anyone."

Hannah went pale. "What did he tell you? He knows nothing, that boy, nothing." She sounded nervous, Ruth thought, very much so.

"Ja, he knows things, he can dig up dirt anywhere, that one."

"So what did he say, then?" Hannah was calm again, remembering things that made her feel safe, things that neither Ruth nor Andries could ever dream up.

"He said that Tant Zelda had been in love with a man when she was young." It seemed so extraordinary to Ruth that she found it hard to believe. "But this man wasn't in love with her. He was in love with someone else. And so—these are family secrets, and no one talks about it—she was in love with a person she shouldn't have been. Ag, Hannah, don't look like that, man. With Zelda anything is possible. Anyway, she got so mad with this man, one day when he wouldn't do as he asked her, she shot him, right through the head."

Ruth was flushed and excited, and got up quickly and walked over to the stove, where she laid her hands quickly, once, twice, on the hot plate, and then spun around to say, in the same high voice, "Don't you see. Hannah, that *must* be the truth, man, it must be, because those were always the stories I was hearing at school: 'Your auntie shot a man' . . . 'find out who he was.' All that stuff. But you see, what Andries says is that the man disappeared, so they weren't ever sure whether he was dead or not. Zelda might have buried him, or he might have got away. What Andries says is that he was shot, ja, that's true, in the head or throat, but after that he ran off—he definitely did not die and neither did he marry the girl he wanted to—someone saw him long after, and that's how they know he wasn't dead."

"You know, Ruth," Hannah said with a touch of amusement, "your aunt is a hell of a shot. If she was going to shoot a man, then she'd kill him dead, with one bullet, don't you think?"

"Ah, but what you're not thinking straight about is that she *loved* this man. That makes it quite different."

"I see."

"Ja, and the other point you've missed is that this one didn't marry the girl he wanted to. So . . . Do you know who *she* was?" Ruth was drumming her fingers against the table as if to egg on Hannah to ask.

Hannah complied. "Who was she, then?"

"Why—my ma, of course!"

Hannah laughed, the girl was so carried away.

"No, think about it," Ruth insisted. "My mother was the elder sister, the pretty one. Oh ja, it's simple, the man was in love with my ma and Zelda couldn't stand it." She sat down and went on quickly, "You see, with Zelda I was trying to catch her out, to find out if she'd tell me the truth. I knew plenty already but she didn't know that, so I asked her to tell me everything. She told me a pack of lies. Then, at the end of it, I pretended to be very upset. I cried buckets, and tried to see if she'd tell me more, but then she clammed up. I was hoping that maybe she'd drop a clue, give me his name, or something to help me find him maybe."

Hannah waved her hands quickly from side to side to stop the rush of words.

"Now, hang on a minute, wait a minute now. If you're saying that Annetjie was your mother and this man was in love with her, are you saying that this man was your father? And are you also saying that your mother didn't *marry* this man. Is that what you're saying?"

"Ja—exactly." Ruth was up again and she went back to the stove and leaned carelessly against it, almost sitting on it, facing Hannah. Very quietly she said, "I'm illegitimate, you see, that's the other thing. My mother had me after he'd gone, cleared off by shotgun Annie back there"—she jerked her head dismissively in the direction of Zelda's bedroom. "*That's* what people knew about me, that's what made them horrible to me. But really, man, that's not the important bit, I don't mind that now. The important bit is that he's still alive."

Hannah had had enough. "Ruthie, come now, this is all a lot of conjecture and a lot of it doesn't make sense. You must let it be. You mustn't listen again to Andries. He's a nasty piece of work. He was like that since he was a little boy. I remember once, when he came here for a visit, he threw one of the kittens into the water tank to see if it could swim. His mother spoils him because he's good-looking and cunning. I for one would not trust a word he said. Maybe he was teasing you—or being cruel. Seeing if you too could swim or not?"

Ruth shifted uneasily. "Ja," she whispered, "I know all this. That's why I tried to force Zelda, to see if any of it tied together. Now I'm all mixed up like before."

"Ruthie, come sit. Look, I don't know what to tell you. All I can tell you is that there was a man once who Zelda loved. That is true. It went sour and she did shoot him and that destroyed her life."

Ruth sat. "Why didn't you tell me that before?" she demanded accusingly.

"It wasn't my business, it wasn't mine to tell. I only tell you this now because you're unhappy and Andries has filled your head with stories."

"Hannah," Ruth said grimly, "there's more you can tell, there's other things you know. Tell me, tell me *now*." She wanted to shake her.

Hannah swallowed hard and walked back to the kettle on the stove—the water was spitting on the hot surface as it came to the boil. "No," she said, "you must let me alone, Ruthie. I can't tell you anything." She turned back to face her. "Was this the bad thing you wanted to tell me?"

"No, not really."

"So what was it, then?"

"It was about Andries." Now she didn't care, didn't care about a damn thing. "Andries is a pig," she said quietly. "For him to tell me those things, he made me do things."

"What things?" Sharply, Hannah looked up.

"Just things."

"*What* things?"

"You know, you know what things he made me do."

Six

ZELDA SAT ON THE STOEP DRINKING HER MORNING COFFEE. It was only nine-thirty but the heat seemed to rear up and move in closer. Black beetles crowded onto the stone floor, crawling over each other's backs—to no purpose, it would seem, since there was plenty of room and no clear destination. She kicked them and they scattered, then began their relentless scramble again.

Zelda was waiting for Mr. Mantagisa to get back from the lands to go into town with her. As she waited, her face became morose; her jaw set. Things had gone badly for her in town the day before and she didn't particularly want to go again. Manty would help, but not much. There was a show on; it was the annual event for buying and selling stock; she couldn't afford not to go. There had been a bad scene yesterday.

In the hotel bar, where most of the business went on, she had found herself the target of a certain hostility. In the past the farmers had treated her with cautious respect, and she always sat and drank with them. Yesterday there'd been a definite coolness. Talk was about how tough things were getting, about inflation, high prices, poverty, white unemployment. But the emphasis now fell on how dangerous the blacks were, how their violence was beginning to be directed more at whites and less at each other; how the riots were spreading beyond the cities now. She had noticed little jibes directed at her, the old "kaffirboetie" slur. Once a joke, it now had real resentment in it. If she persisted in doing things her own way with her boys, then she would pay for it.

As her coffee cooled and the day heated up, she began to wonder if van Reenen had been stirring things up in town.

Manty now drove up outside and came striding up the steps onto the stoep. He sat down beside her, relieved to be in the shade. He flipped his old hat onto his knee, revealing a neat, closely shaven head from which dark and humorous eyes shone. His history made him more than fifty, but he didn't look it—his skin was firm and shiny, his small body quick and athletic, and his belly round but tight as a drum. At the back of his neck, deep lines were etched and his hands were scarred—old knife scars that were so well acquainted with his skin as to seem an original part of it.

"Ai, what a day. I'm certain the work stopped the minute I drove off." He was amused, bringing out his words in little puffs.

"You sure you still want to come with me, Manty?" Zelda was looking for an excuse.

He wouldn't let her. He took the coffee she offered and said, "I'm telling you, there's a lot of things I'd rather do than go with you into that dorp today, but that's what we'll do. You're not going alone—so you can forget about it. Boykie tells me there's plenty bad rumors going on about us down there—people looking for trouble."

"Don't I know it. The worst is that it's going to affect us financially—I don't give a damn about the rest. You know how, normally, they're after our stock like hyenas? Well, yesterday it was different. There was interest all right, but then they shied off, particularly if other farmers were about. I got the feeling that if I could get them alone, I'd have made plenty of good deals, but as it was, they gave me this rot about the prices being too high, the sheep not prime, not fat enough—that sort of thing, when we've been stuffing them with all that high-protein fodder."

"They're in perfect condition, every one I checked myself." Manty was indignant, "Ag, no, that can't be it. So what's the problem, then?"

"I think we're being made to pay for not allowing van Reenen and his lot to clear the labor off our land," Zelda said thoughtfully. "Word's got out that we're not toeing the line. Everyone else has obeyed the order."

"Eh he." He sucked in his breath. "Is there then any point in going in today?"

"You're bloody right there is," she said angrily. "Today's the day the people from out of town come in—we could do better with them."

"Ja, that's true. We did well last year, particularly with Strydom. Let's try for it, or else we must wait for the next show. But by then the prices will be higher and also we'll have the transport expense."

Zelda sighed. "And we'd have to keep up this expensive feed. I'd rather get shot of what I can now. I've never had any trouble selling," she added. "People fight over our animals. This whole thing stinks."

"Ag, well"—he smiled at her encouragingly—"we won't let them get to us, hey? It's been a good year, we at least have plenty of land for grazing and don't have to feed as much as others. The drought has hit a lot of people very bad."

Zelda leaned back. "I heard talk of animals being poisoned— hundreds of head of them found dead. Is it the men in the mountains? They all said it was."

"Ag, I've heard those stories. But those people"—he sounded disdainful—"they wouldn't mess with poisoning. If you're hungry up in the hills, you'd kill the sheep to eat them, not poison them."

"I don't know. You only need a few to eat, so why not poison the rest?"

"That's true, man, but it's not their way. Before, if they wanted to make trouble, they would cut off a hoof from each animal, something like that—I don't go with this poisoning story."

"Hm." She was thoughtful.

He felt they should make a move, and stood up with determination. "Let's go, then, Zelda, hey? Don't look so serious, man, that lot, ag, they're just a lot of chicken shit. Let's not worry."

She laughed loudly. "Talk like that, Manty, and one of these days they'll send a lynching party after you."

"What about you, man, don't think they'll spare you," he teased. He hit his hat hard against his thigh. "Let's get going."

As they walked to the van she said quietly, "Manty, you've

worked for me a long time now. You know that this is just the beginning of trouble for us. That things are going to get worse. I don't expect you to stay with me. A lot of our boys would like to be up in the mountains with the terrorists."

"Not our boys," he said brightly. "They're happy. And don't you worry, we'll manage."

"And, Manty"—she turned her face away from the glare—"do you think it's possible that van Reenen is behind any of this? It wasn't nearly so bad in town a week or so ago. He has a reputation for making things difficult for people in all sorts of ways."

"Ja"—he was serious now—"it's possible. This is a bad situation for him. If it was our people now, refusing to follow the law, then he'd just bring in the guns. But if you people, white people, begin to make trouble—what can he do, hey? His hands are tied. Ja, that's his trouble. He doesn't know what to do, how to bring it right. So maybe he hopes you'll get trouble from other white people and they'll fix you for him. There's no danger that anyone will side with you. Round here they're all the same. They're making plenty-plenty money, they like the things that the Bureau is doing. 'Cleaning up' makes life better for them. They can keep us at arm's length and feel a bit safer too."

"Well," Zelda said, reassured a little by him, "we'll just have to wait and see. You driving?"

He nodded. She got into the passenger seat and opened the door wide to let the hot air out. "Jeez, hell would be cooler. Somehow I never feel right if I'm not behind the wheel," she complained.

"Time you had a little rest," he said with determination and started the engine.

"Time you people saw," he added lightly, "that now it's our turn to be behind the wheel."

Seven

RUTH TOLD HERSELF THAT IT WASN'T REALLY VERY DIFFERENT
from the times she had done it before. In those days she had simply
packed a small brown suitcase with her favorite things—a doll,
sweets, and oranges—and run off into the bush. But this was much
worse. She'd spent a long time thinking about it in the attic above
the house, where the suitcases were kept. She'd spent even longer
deciding that she wouldn't tell Hannah.

She had found an old suitcase that she thought she'd take with
her. Inside it were some faded initials and a name: D. H. DE
VALERA? The first initial was barely readable but looked like a
D. Zelda's brother, she thought, not someone she knew much
about—an uncle who, like the rest of them, had fulfilled no duties
toward her.

Just a name, some old person somewhere I'm connected with
who doesn't want to know me. But perhaps that isn't my fault,
and is more because he and Zelda aren't speaking anymore, haven't
spoken for years and years. The last time they did, so Hannah said,
they were in the same room together and Zelda would only speak
to him through Hannah. Just like Zelda to be such a mad bitch,
and who knows what about. Perhaps she'd just wanted the whole
farm and everything to herself, because it must have been about
the time Oupa died and the old lady went to live in Cape Town.
Those were also people who'd gone and died before she'd had

time to meet them, and so now she had no memories of them either.

So few memories at all, nothing to look at and remind her where she'd come from, who her family was, who she was. Just the name: Ruth Miranda de Valera; pretty, but so very empty.

She sat in her room and tried to convince herself that now Willie was gone, it wasn't the same anyway. But still it was hard to leave, and as the minutes passed it grew harder. The room was the only place she'd ever felt safe.

She didn't see how little there was in the room, because she had nothing to compare it with. To her, she was leaving behind a wealth of precious things, the most precious being all the dreams she had hatched here, lying on her bed. Well, today it began. But all she could do was to look with sadness at her handful of souvenirs: some confirmation cards, a few china ornaments, some letters Hannah had written her when she was at the boarding school, one from Andries, six from Willie (with kisses at the bottom), and one containing a pressed flower that he'd sent after the rains had covered the veld with wild flowers one year when she was away. The letter had ended with a plea: "Don't forget to come back now, don't forget all about your sweet William with all those fancy people." The only part of letters that counted was the end bit; that was where people said the nice things, if they were going to. Except for Hannah; she always *began* with the nice things. She would miss Hannah.

Ag, shit.

All these treasures she packed carefully, then added her clothes and shoes, a large amount of makeup, and finally, a photograph. A photograph of a young woman wearing what looked like a first dance dress. It was long and full and low across the shoulders; there was a rose at her waist. She was beautiful and she was smiling a little. Ruth had found the photograph among Zelda's things. Of course it was her mother.

She had stared hard at the features and tried to find her own. After a while they seemed to appear, and by then the face in the photograph was so familiar that she didn't need to look at it very often; she knew it by heart. Her mother: Annetjie de Valera. It had comforted Ruth to see softness, even frailty, in the large, widely set eyes, something full of hope and longing in her expression as she gazed down the years at her daughter, and smiled. Such a possession: she would kill to keep it. If only, if only Zelda had given it to her years ago, how it would have helped her endure it all.

She looked out of the window at the garden, the garden where Willie had once whistled and watered, wearing that disgusting woolly hat like a kaffir. There was the mulberry tree with the purple earth below; the peach trees that she loved best in the short springtime, their roots jutting out of the sand where once she had played and talked to Willie.

It was morning; Zelda on the lands, Hannah gone into the dorp to shop. She could hear the women singing, moving about with their brooms and pans, complaining about old Ilsa, who sat in her kitchen like a despot unable to relinquish power. She allowed no gossip, no giggling, and no loose talk in her kitchen. And if there was any cheekiness, she gave no second chance. It was the only way she could stay on and still feel useful.

Ruth knew that she would miss the old woman, would miss the ritual of her household, even miss being chased out of the kitchen by that scowling face. It was hard to leave. She considered putting it off for a bit, but knew she couldn't; time was running out. But she slowed down, taking things out of the suitcase and repacking, smoothing and tucking everything in. She could hear the doves' wings flapping in the acacia trees and below them the soft slap and flap of washing being done in an old tin tub. The smell of wood smoke and strong, coarse soap; a woman kneeling with her baby strapped onto her back; the black pot of pap that was bubbling for the maids' lunch. The dogs asleep under the pink canopy of bougainvillea that trailed in the white dust. She felt close to tears. Home.

She slammed the lid of the suitcase to, she picked it up and tested the weight. Then she took up her handbag and emptied it, then put everything back in and waited for the sound of the truck that should soon be here to take her away.

Eight

"WHAT DO YOU MEAN, SHE'S GONE?" ZELDA ASKED WEARILY, resting her arms on the kitchen table. It was too much—after a stinking hot day, driving miles to check that the sheep she hadn't been able to sell had been moved to new lands—to come home and find a domestic drama.

It was late. Just the two of them at the kitchen table, the dirty things stacked in the sink for the maids to wash in the morning. Hannah had kept the news of Ruth's departure from Zelda until now, because moving the sheep had upset her.

She brooded and wouldn't talk about it. Then: "She left no note for me I suppose?" Zelda said.

"No." Hannah was sharp. "I think she felt you wouldn't care."

"I don't, really. It's just another thing to have to worry about. I am her aunt, after all." She added accusingly, "We should've done something sooner. Where's she gone?"

"I don't know."

"You don't know!"

"No," Hannah said angrily, "I don't! Her note didn't say where she was going, only not to worry."

" 'Not to worry,' " Zelda sneered. "Let's hope she has the brains not to go to Joburg."

That morning they had heard on the news that two hundred young men wearing strange uniforms had been slaughtered in ten minutes while on a protest march. The army had taken over the township. They said they had shot without provocation because of the uniforms; the uniforms bothered them.

"Of course she won't go there," Hannah said tensely. Why did Zelda always contrive to make things more difficult—she was incapable of conciliation.

"Well, we can't tell the police, that's for sure," Zelda said. "Van Reenen would just love it."

"It's not necessary. She seems to know what she's doing."

"How can she know what she's doing? She knows nothing. She's barely been off this farm, apart from abortive visits to schools—and she couldn't even manage those."

"She says she's gone to look for her father," Hannah said.

"Oh, terrific! That's just what we need. And where does she think she's going to find him?"

Hannah looked closely at Zelda. "I think she's gone to find Willie," she said, hoping it was true.

"How the hell can Willie help her find her father?" Zelda got up and went for the coffeepot on the back of the stove. "Willie's going to be in trouble himself before he knows it, he's too clever by half. And I can't really believe that she'd be so naive as to go to Willie."

"Yes, she would," Hannah said defensively. "She hasn't got many alternatives."

"Well, you seem bloody calm about it, or are you following one of your 'instincts' again? Do they tell you we should ring up the police station and get them to start looking for her?"

Hannah snapped, "I'm sick of you, Zelda, I'm sick of your bloody selfishness all the time. Now talk about this reasonably or I refuse to discuss it."

Zelda was flabbergasted. She took Hannah's reactions so totally for granted that this display of anger shut her up. What was happening to Hannah? She'd never spoken that way before.

"What about money?" she asked, after a pause.

"Her Post Office book has gone. Those payments have been going in since she was tiny. There's stacks in there."

Zelda noticed that Hannah's hands were shaking.

"I just hope," Hannah said tightly, "that she's nowhere near the rioting. There's so much—everywhere, so much now. Those killings this morning, there've never been so many. It's as if it's got out of hand finally."

"She'll steer clear of that," Zelda said briskly. "She's never had a political thought in her life."

"Have we?"

"Of course we have. Our lives are a political statement."

"I don't think so. They're just the way we want to live."

"What do you want, then? To be out there going on funeral marches waiting to be shot down? Is that what you want? Something more public?"

"No, that's not what I want," she said bleakly, thinking that they couldn't even get it right in private, didn't even have the guts to try it on a small scale.

"It's too late for all this," Zelda said, affected by Hannah's quiet. "Let's go to bed."

"In a minute I will. *You* go."

Sitting on in the kitchen, Hannah felt she had never been so alone. Now that Ruth had gone, there was no one to give her life an excuse—a pretense that she stayed on in her hiding place for any reason but cowardice.

Nine

DAWIE SAT WAITING FOR HIS WIFE TO COME. HE WOULD HAVE expected, now that the time had come, that he'd feel apprehensive. He didn't, he felt instead a kind of pity, for them both, for the wastage of their lives. When she came, she stood at the open door of the study in a way she had: unsure, her eyes nervous. As if she knew. Looking at her, it was as if he saw her clearly for the first time in years, with an intimacy that had been one of the first casualties of their marriage.

"What are you doing?" she asked.

"Writing a letter." He turned the pad over. She wanted to ask him who he was writing to, but didn't.

"Are you busy?" he asked, feeling his nerves tighten. "Can we talk?"

"What about?"

She was unsettled this morning, he could see it in the way she fiddled with her hands. It was eight in the morning and she'd just come home. But this wasn't unusual.

"About our marriage," he said, watching how her body stiffened.

"What marriage?"

She looked tired. And he found it so hard to say, after all these years of collusion, compromise, deadness—it was still so hard to say it.

"Well, since there is no marriage, perhaps we should be more honest about the whole thing?"

"How you love that word," she sneered.

" 'Honest?' "

"Ja," she snapped. " 'Honest.' You love it. We've been honest about everything, haven't we? Never had secrets, lies. We're honest all the ruddy time, aren't we?"

"Don't blame me because you couldn't resist telling me you had a lover!" he said angrily, and then pulled himself up; there would be no finger-pointing.

He wondered what the years had done to her inside, in all the places that were inaccessible to him. But strangely, as he prepared to leave her, he felt that he did know her well, in the particular way people who have wounded one another do. He did not know her as her lover knew her. He knew her as someone he had broken on his own disappointment. Now, quite suddenly—almost as if he was already looking back on it—it seemed extraordinary to him that this was the woman he had climbed into bed with most nights for nearly eight years, woken with, reared a child with, in all the close habitudes of marriage.

"Isn't it time?" he asked, "that we stopped the pretense and separated? There's nothing here for either of us."

Her first reaction was anger, that he had said it before she could. But when that passed, she felt defeated. She'd always waited, half in dread, half in suspense, for him to come out with it: to break their bargain—that was the best way to think of it—in the way they'd both broken the vows between them. Though, at the beginning, she remembered now with some surprise, there had been some desire to be good to one another, to share a life and make it close. But then she'd lost the child: he seemed to take that as a personal punishment. Things had altered after that, so much so that she began to feel she had trapped him by getting pregnant, and trapped him again by losing the baby. He'd not have married her otherwise, she knew, though he would never imply it.

She looked at him with suspicion. "You've been quite happy to let things go on up to now, so why the change?"

He turned his face a little, to see the garden through the window. "There just comes a time, things happen, and you see your life for what it is."

She was hurt by the certainty in his voice—the way it excluded her. She retreated to a safer place to ask, "Is it because of Abe?"

Abe had been arrested a few days after the trial; under the Emergency regulations Dawie could do nothing to help him.

"Partly," he said. "I don't know how long it'll take to get him out. The system's seizing up."

When he didn't continue, she persisted, "Are you really going to give up the practice?" She couldn't understand this decision of his, coming immediately after the Simonstown trial, even before Abe's arrest. She hadn't gone to the trial, never did, but it was the same night: they were watching the news on the television and he got up and said, "I'm getting out of the practice, probably for good. There are better things to do." Just like that, and he wouldn't discuss it further. And Dawie not a man for snap decisions. It was all he cared about, his work. But having said it, it seemed to change him—he was like a different man.

She thought, sadly, that she liked him much more now, he seemed more the man he'd been when they'd first met. Their life together, their marriage, it had diminished them both, even altered their characters. Now he seemed restored, but she didn't know why.

Watching her, he could see that she was puzzled, but he couldn't tell her about the woman at the trial. It was too late for that.

"Well," she said tersely, "I can't say I understand any of it. As for Abe—well, Jews are just suicidal, aren't they?" His face closed with a smile that was full of disdain. She regretted what she had said, but couldn't take it back.

"Could you, or would you, want to live with John?" he asked.

She went white with anger. "I don't think that's any of your business. And don't think because you want to off-load me, you have to reorganize my future."

"I just wondered what you would do, that's all."

"Well, you've certainly made up your mind about what *you* want to do, haven't you? This is hardly a discussion, is it—more a fait accompli?" Her voice narrowed. "Have you met someone else, is that it?"

"No." The obviousness of it made him laugh.

"Well, why then?" Now her face also seemed to narrow, as if this way she could nose into his thoughts. "You were quite happy to live with me like this before. You said you understood about John, that it was okay."

"I had to understand about John, didn't I?" Suddenly he was furious with himself for the stupidity of it all.

"*Why* did you have to?"

"Because of the way our life was."

Slowly she seemed to be relaxing, to be getting acclimatized to it. "Well, I'm not so sure," she said, moving into the room, going to sit on the couch. "I'm not at all sure that it's what I want, you see. We agreed, three years ago, if you remember, to stay together, because of Marina mostly, and I'm not so sure that you can just go and change your mind and presume I'll go along with it."

"What good would trying to prevent it do?" His hands were folded in front of him, but she could see that he looked at the letter to one side of him.

"Well, perhaps you should tell me your plans."

"When I've closed up the practice from my side of it, I'm going away."

"Nice of you to tell me."

"It's a recent decision."

"Oh ja?" she had a sudden urge to smoke, though she'd given it up many years before.

"I'm going back to the farm," he said.

"But you haven't been there for years. You never even send a Christmas card to your sister. What do you mean you're going back to the farm?"

"I mean the old farm, the one we were brought up on, not the one Zelda has. I'm going back to my father's place." The idea of it was like a haven to him as he waited for this confrontation to end, knowing that more blood must run before it would.

"Why?" She was suddenly furious. "Why now?"

"Because," he said patiently, not wanting to hurt her now, seeing her alarm that his plans were further along than she realized, "Because now is the right time. Perhaps I should have done it years ago instead of messing up our lives and playing at being a good man out in the world. But I didn't. And then"—he was almost conversational, as if explaining something important to a friend—"one day you just know it, it seems simple, you think you can start again, in some way, try again anyway."

"Don't tell me," she almost wheedled, feeling the cool steel of a knife at her disposal at last, "don't tell me that this has something to do with that little colored girl who was your childhood sweetheart? The one who ran around barefoot with your heart between her teeth?"

He looked appalled. And she hated him for being the kind of person who would never deal such a low blow himself. Because he was a clean fighter, she always felt the need to make up for the deficiency.

He wouldn't answer, but felt a hot rush of blood. He'd told her, in a rare moment of trust, at the beginning, about Hannah. He'd wanted her to understand, and she had. It was the first time she'd turned it back on him. But in spite of that, he congratulated himself now for having never trusted her with anything else that she could use against him.

"You never did get over that, did you?" she whispered with some pain. "If you knew, if you had any idea of the jealousy . . . Well, what does it matter now?"

He saw that she was crying. The truth of it affected him as nothing else had. "It does matter," he said. "It wasn't fair to you." He knew now that he'd never loved her—even though he'd tried— for all the good things she was. And yet he'd lived with her and pretended to the outside world that a workable marriage existed between them.

"And Marina?" she asked him. "I suppose you've made plans for our daughter too. At least you always loved *her*."

He felt sick. He asked gently, "What did you want me to do about her?"

Sara began to cry, but the tears did not affect him. Her tears had too often been manipulations. He knew that she was crying for herself, not her child. She was afraid of being alone out there. She needed his charity.

Quietly, he said, "Sara, please don't worry about things like that. You'll be well provided for and so will Marina."

But, beside herself with anger and hurt, made ugly by her power-lessness and dependence, she lashed out at him with the best weapon at hand. "Don't worry," she said, "and don't pretend either. You're not her father and you know it "

It was as if he saw the small, sweet girl untangling her plump arms from around his neck, running down to the end of the garden, where she disappeared among the tall flowers and was lost to him for ever. "Ja," he said quietly, "I always knew it. But I loved her as if she was my own."

"How bloody noble," she snapped, "how bloody noble you are." And she ran from the room, having delivered the final insult.

Ten

HANNAH WOKE FROM A DREAM TO HEAR VOICES IN THE YARD and hammering on the door. It was four in the morning and still very dark. She leapt out of bed, and ran down the corridor, praying that nothing happened to Ruth.

Boykie stood there, wild-eyed, shrieking at her in Afrikaans and pointing backward, trying at the same time to pull her outside. She didn't need to go any farther, though, to see, and her skin, even at this distance, could feel the heat: the barns were on fire, all six of them, engulfed in flames, the smoke so thick that it looked like blankets caught in the wind. Smoke was also whooshing out of the high silos where the fodder was kept—the stench was nauseating. There was no point in calling for help, she kept explaining to him, it was too late, they were too far away. Men were out there with buckets and hoses, but they couldn't get close enough, and, compared to the billowing flames, they seemed like little ants rushing around the edges of a bush fire.

In a little while Hannah was aware that she was not alone. Behind her in the darkness, Zelda stood watching. In silence she looked at the veld, which all around was quite radiant with the light, the acacia trees black and stark behind sheets of red. She was mesmerized, her face quite awesome in its concentration and stillness. When Hannah ran up to her and took her arm, she turned and looked at her almost inquiringly. She was above it all, beyond it.

Seeing her so passive, so unlike herself, Hannah began to panic, making frantic suggestions as to what they should do.

Zelda's voice was quiet and firm, almost gentle. "You know there's nothing to be done. If you must do something, then tell them to stop. It won't do any good, and people will get hurt. We must wait till it burns out."

Hannah went over to Boykie and sent him back. People were coming from the village, carrying buckets and cans, rushing back and forth from the taps.

You never knew how she felt, Hannah thought, walking to the other end of the stoep, where she too now stood and watched. In a short time, however, it was as if the fire had become a different fire. Oh, that fire—how it had destroyed everything. Not even a tiny green shoot could escape its conflagration. Thinking of it, Hannah's pain was so intense that the fires merged. . . . All those years ago, when they had stood outside and watched the farmhouse illuminated, like a castle with tall candles at every window. The thatch was a flame rising higher and higher, until the whole glittering facade seemed to explode and then slowly, slowly, sank and died. And Zelda howling like an animal, running back and forth in front of it as if she must at all costs get inside, rescue something precious from those flames.

Zelda's voice now came to her soothingly. "There's no wind. It can't spread to the house." She stood and watched, with no trace of emotion. The men were still out there, with the women, valiantly trying to put out the fire. She repeated, "Go and tell them to stop, tell them to let it be."

Hannah looked at her in wonder, with a kind of love she'd felt long before, when watching Zelda as a child, when she'd seemed one of those rare remarkable creatures beyond judgment or definition.

"It's so quick," Hannah breathed. "It's all going up so quickly." But the tears she felt pressed against the back of her throat were tears for the fire before. She felt her body move a little closer to Zelda's as they stood side by side and waited for this fire to die. Neither said what each was remembering.

Then Zelda urged again, "Tell them, please tell them to stop."

When Hannah had sent them all home and come back to Zelda,

she felt she couldn't tell her about the jerry cans she had seen stuffed behind some bushes. She did not tell her any of the rumors and speculation she had heard either.

Zelda was sitting in the rocking chair, moving back and forth with her hands held loosely in her lap. Her face, for the first time in many years, had lost all its severity. She sat as a woman sits when she has lived the thing through, seen the ending—but there was no joy in this look, only acceptance. She did not speak when Hannah sat down beside her on the brown chair; she did not turn her head to one side; she looked steadily ahead of her. But, after a long silence, she suddenly spoke.

"I started the fire," she said, and, looking quickly at Hannah's shocked face, she added, just as calmly, "No, not this one. The one before."

She leaned forward and, looking directly at Hannah, she whispered all in one breath, "I burned the old farm, I burned Bonnington, I burned the whole thing down. I did it. Then she breathed out the way someone does when they have held their breath a long, long time.

Eleven

THE NEXT DAY, VAN REENEN CAME UP THE SHORT FLIGHT OF steps in two easy leaps, then stopped and looked about him in an arrogant and familiar way.

Zelda had been sitting, watching him in silence. Now she said rudely, "You're not wearing your uniform, van Reenen. I can't believe this is a social call." She noticed also that the colored policeman, a strange, silent man, about whom peculiar stories with regard to his relationship with his boss were told, was absent too.

"Condolences, Miss de Valera," he said in English, but with a glutinous accent. "I was sorry to hear about your bad luck with the fire, all that damage. Shame." He found himself a seat. "We're having a lot of backfire from all the trouble up near the Cape, isn't it? Maybe that Joburg mess too? Seem to be little bits and pieces of sabotage all over the place, hey?"

"You're not suggesting mine was sabotage, are you?" she snapped. "And you're not suggesting one thousand dead is little, are you?"

"Ag, ja, of course, man," he said lazily, "there are terrorists all over the place. That's what I keep telling you. But you won't listen to me, you think it's all mischief in my mind, hey?"

His smile, with its mixture of sneer and leer, was repellent to her. She glared at him furiously.

Only now did he turn his attention to Hannah, in a deliberate and cool way, as if to suggest that she had not been worthy of his gaze until that moment. She was sitting on the hammock in the far corner of the stoep, reading. It was as if she did not want to be noticed; they both knew the rules of the game, and how to play it. He continued to stare. She felt on edge.

"Tell me," he said seductively to Zelda, "the name of your friend here. I don't think we've met." His voice swayed with innuendo and menace. "Bit rude, isn't it, not to introduce us?"

It was Hannah who replied, in a steady voice: "Hannah," she said shortly, and then felt that rush of despair to see that she had answered him according to the code, not giving her surname—like a servant. She forced herself to speak again. "Hannah du Bois," she said, as she always did, giving her father's name, not the Xhosa name of her mother.

"Are you from round here?" he asked pointedly, in Afrikaans now.

"No, she isn't," Zelda interrupted, so that he turned slowly to look at her. "She's from Graaff-Reinet, she's just visiting."

Hannah experienced both relief and dismay—dismay that it wouldn't all come out and be over with, the strain, the hiding without papers. She had always felt, like murderers do, she thought gravely, that there'd be some kind of peace if she was found out.

"Is that so?" He smiled politely. "I wonder, perhaps I could just see your papers? I wouldn't normally be uncivil, but"—he smiled again—"in these troubled times I have to watch out for everyone. You do have the new papers, don't you?"

"Oh, come on," Zelda said coolly, quickly, putting her hand up as if to detain Hannah, who in fact had not moved, "this isn't something for a quiet evening when you're off duty, now is it? A bit rude, don't you think?" She smiled with an expression borrowed from his own face.

To their surprise, he let it go, with the assurance of a man who could come back to it any time. Zelda began deliberately to make conversation and Hannah couldn't understand why she was prolonging his stay, unless it was to convey that she was as relaxed as he was.

"So there have been other fires, then?" she was asking.

"No, not that I'm aware."

"Well, what then? What other 'little bits and pieces of sabotage' were you referring to earlier? What else have you been investigating?"

He lost his cool a little. "Locally, you mean?"

"Of course." She smiled falsely. "It's just that I haven't heard of any. It's been quiet down your way too, hasn't it, Hannah?"

His face flushed as Hannah was included in their conversation, and he turned his chair a little so that he almost had his back to the hammock. "No, we've had no trouble," Hannah said.

"Well, you out-of-the-way people don't get to hear everything," he said.

"Oh, I disagree," Zelda said. "There are no secrets around here. That's the trouble with a small community, isn't it?"

"There are always unresolved matters," he said, turning his attention full on Zelda so that Hannah felt that they too had a code of their own. "Ja," he smiled, "there are always those things that get pushed under the carpet, isn't it? Skeletons in the cupboard." Then he became suggestive. "I'm telling you, if I was to let on the stories and peculiar happenings that go on in a farming district, you wouldn't believe it. True as God, it's a mucky business all right."

"I've even heard stories of murders," Zelda said smoothly. "Guns that went off by mistake, so to speak—people who vanished. How else does a quiet place ease its boredom?" She was leaning back in her rocking chair.

Van Reenen stared at her in amazement, his cockiness gone, even a touch of admiration in his face. "Well," he said, as if he was about to leave, "I just came round here to help, see if I could do something for you." He even managed to sound a bit put-out.

"It's kind of you," she said, "but we don't need any help."

"Oh ja? There's a bleddy great mess out there," he said, pointing to the charred buildings. "And the stink's terrible, man."

"Yes, well, fire's not something you can hide well," she said pointedly, "there's always evidence."

He looked startled. "Did you find anything?"

She ignored his question and said, "We'll clear the ground tomorrow and then rebuild."

"Insurance is a wonderful thing."

"It certainly is," she countered. "Especially when you don't know where the sabotage is coming from."

He rose quickly, adjusted his crotch and said, "Of course to reinsure will set you back a lot."

She smiled. "In farming there are so many things to take into account." She was as unruffled as a lily on a pond. "You expect it, you see. Animals you can't sell suddenly, things like that. These things happen in the life of a farmer, so you have to be prepared."

She too rose, to see him off. He was trying hard to think what the feminine form of farmer might be, so he could correct her, but couldn't. He left with a curt goodbye in Afrikaans.

"How rude"—Zelda was smiling broadly at Hannah—"not to say goodbye to you."

Hannah said roughly, "Don't look so smug, Zelda. I don't like him coming here. He didn't believe you about me. Someone's told him. He'll be back, and next time he won't let us get away with it."

"Who could have told him anything?" Zelda said. "There's nothing to tell. There's no crime in you sitting on the stoep talking to me, is there?"

"You know what I mean."

Zelda wouldn't be drawn. "I'm not worried about him, the little creep. I think he'll watch his step with me from now on."

"Why?"

"Oh, he understood my crack about sabotage—where it comes from. He started our fire, or rather, got someone to do it for him. Sabotage is okay if you're the right color—his lot have had years of practice. It seems to me too many things are beginning to go wrong for us for it to be a coincidence."

Twelve

WALKING OUT OF THE HEAT INTO THE POST OFFICE, ZELDA knew immediately that something was wrong. On the surface of it, everything was as usual. The Post Office was filled with farmers' wives, small shopkeepers, people who worked on the railway, and, at a separate counter to one side, a long queue of blacks. It was the atmosphere that was wrong: it was thick, rank, pressing in around her—directed at her. The small group of people clustered around the other counters turned and looked at her, looked and turned away. Immediately she knew what it was. It was the killings. A white farmer and his entire family had been slaughtered the day before, on their front stoep, in broad daylight. Now everyone was terrified. The sabotage and killings of the cities was moving in closer.

Their hatred was as tangible as the heat and the smell of sweat in the small room. They'd always resented her; now they hated her. She felt that their faces had grown fangs and whiskers. Mrs. de Wet, peering through her pink-rimmed spectacles, a devout member of the kerk, seemed to be drooling a little at the mouth, and the doctor's wife—said to be an angel—looked as though she would go for her throat. Clerks from the bank, always a servile bunch, glared unpleasantly. She felt almost afraid of them and more separate than she had ever felt.

Contemptuously, she strode over to the first empty counter. As she walked past, one woman spoke to another, loud enough to be heard.

"It's not often that you see *her* here, is it?" Then she couldn't contain herself and spat out, "Kaffirboetie." Then she shrieked, "They'll cut *your* throat as quick, I'm telling you. Don't think you'll be spared."

The other woman said, "Ag, she probably hasn't even heard what happened, and wouldn't care. You know her, she's always too busy buying up land us people have to sell—just like her old man."

A man's voice from beneath a turned-down hat: "They're all just the same, that lot. Peculiar. Live in a world of their own. One of these days the brother will be arrested too."

And another, with satisfaction: "No, man, it'll be *her* first, I'm telling you, one of these days they'll come and get her."

Zelda, putting her hands on the counter and looking straight at the sharp-faced assistant behind it, demanded her mail. The young girl hesitated before she said, "I'll see now." Her manner was offhand enough to make her affiliation clear. She went to the rows of post boxes, turning her back. Behind her, Zelda could hear a chorus of whispers; she didn't look around. It was like being a child again, in a game: if you turned, they would freeze; if you looked the other way, they moved in. She began to sweat.

The girl pushed the pile of letters toward her rudely. Zelda took them up slowly and stuffed them in her shirt collar. The girl turned away quickly. Zelda braced herself to walk through the crowd again. They moved back to let her pass—surly, watching, waiting, but silent now.

Zelda saw a face she used to know: Jeanette. Yes that was her name; she'd once been in love with Dawie. Now, dried out and thinned by the sun, two children hanging onto her, her beauty was gone. Catching Zelda's eye, she turned away in embarrassment, then looked at the other people with a glance that tried to convey that she was from out of town and did not know their problem with Zelda.

Zelda felt she had made it; could reach the door safely when a man moved out from the crowd and barred her way. She stood quite still. He didn't budge. He was tall and thick set, with big bare legs planted like timbers on the ground. Instead of trying to make him move—which clearly he would not—Zelda stepped to one side of him. He followed her with a surprisingly graceful movement for so large a man. She was no longer aware of the faces behind her, but took in the fact that all activity had ceased, that everyone was watching.

She knew him of course: Swanepoel's son, Stephan. She'd known him all her life. Their farm had once been the closest to her father's, when they were both children, before he'd bought a farm of his own. She'd often gone there for coffee and koeksusters when her father had made the trip.

"What's your problem, Stephan?" she asked, her head to one side, looking him full in the face.

"Ag, no, it's not *my* problem now, is it, Zee?"

"My only problem is your body blocking my way to my van. Move, Stephan," she ordered, remembering him as a small boy, very inventive and clever, making machines out of his father's fruit boxes, and how Dawie had once spent a whole week at their place.

He became aggressive because she still frightened him. He was remembering her as well: the way she had of dripping poison into his head with the mean things she said.

"When you going to come right, man?" he asked. She just looked at him, but he faltered and his voice became coaxing: "We only want for you what's best. Then there's no trouble—then we can go on like we always have."

"Whatever you're referring to isn't any of your business," she said, still not moving.

"Oh, but it is, Zee, it is. It's everyone's business what you do. It makes trouble. You get away with breaking the clearance order and then our boys start to make trouble, they also want to stay with their families. They make strikes, they start to kill and take over the farms—"

"Well, then," she said, her composure returned, "perhaps you'll have to learn to treat them better and pay them more. Ever considered that?"

She said it quietly enough, but he felt menaced and moved back, just the merest fraction. It gave her the advantage. She moved forward boldly and hissed at him, "If you don't move your ugly carcass, Stephan, I'll blow a hole right through it. Perhaps you've heard how good I am with a gun?"

She pushed past him and he let her pass, but not without calling out, "It's a shame, it's disgusting, how you boast about that terrible business."

She did not look back but walked solidly to her van. She climbed in it and roared off, leaving him, leaving them all, as they crowded around the door, to eat the dust of her departure.

Thirteen

IT WAS DUSK AND THE SUN HAD SET. THE WIND ROSE AND BLEW dust across the road; birds flew up into the trees and Africans trudging the road drew their blankets closer, pulling their heads into their shoulders as if, once the sun was gone, they became cold. But the heat was still intense and the only relief was the absence of glare.

Zelda drove a little farther and then stopped at the crossroads, by the left fork that led to the farm. She looked down at the two letters on the empty passenger seat, both in the same hand, one opened, the other sealed. She picked up the sealed one; it was heavier than her letter and this made her unhappy. All afternoon she had avoided going home. Now there was no alternative: it would be dark very soon. The roads were dangerous; at night, desperate people broke the curfew and made their way from one distant dorp to another, looking for work and food, or simply hiding—from the police, from strange people who might attack them, or from the army.

She, however, felt no sense of menace and sat quietly waiting for the darkness to close in. She could see where her lands began and how far they stretched—to the horizon. Their size was a great comfort to her. It was also why those people hated her. She didn't care, for look, there it all was: land—permanent, indestructible, her own. She felt native here, rooted to the place, knowing the exact shape and feel of it, every outline of trees, the rocky paths that led to the koppies, the koppies themselves with their nests of vultures. Her people, her animals—these were the only things that mattered. But it couldn't quite comfort her enough. Not today, not after Dawie's letter.

He can't come back, I can't have it, I won't. If he comes, everything will change, as it did last time. He'll take Hannah. They'll slot together like bones do. When he tried to take her before, I had to do something final. It worked. But now I can't rely on how she'll be, anymore.

He thinks he was so straight in the letter: telling me his plans, asking was it all right if he bought the old farm back. As if I give a damn. As if it'd make any difference if I did. He'll just do precisely as he wants, as he always has. But he won't take her away. I have to have someone. I'm not like other people. I can't join. And I'm not peaceful like the blacks, just waiting for the days to pass and life to take its course. I want. And I don't want. That's all. I want Hannah. I have to have someone.

Hannah said I wasn't human. I don't mind, I'm not. She was trying to make me tell her about the fire, about burning everything we loved. Well, I created it so I had the right to burn it. I had to. There was no other way. No, I'm not human anymore. Each year I become more like this drought, year after year the same. In the end I'll be buried deep in the earth and it'll all go on without me. What does it matter?

I have had my moment of ecstasy. They all misunderstood. It was not him and it wasn't the shot, nor the next one, finding its mark, perfect, right through the heart. (The first one was just to frighten him, taking a little skin off his neck.) No, it wasn't him. My moment was long, long ago: waiting in the kitchen for my brother to come home. Hearing his footsteps, how he dragged his feet in the sand, up the path that led to the door. Then he stopped and I knew that he was looking up at the sky. The door opened and he stood there, walking into a circle of light, smiling, thinking of other things, but letting me into them, into that secret world behind his eyes, the private place that we two knew. He walked silently and sat down beside me, putting a blue flower into my tumbler of water. We watched as it began to stand up straight, pushing out its petals. Then the moment was gone. No one else had it, so it will mean nothing to them. But it was my moment. Mine only.

Abruptly, her mind came back to the van, the darkness, Hannah waiting up at the house. So completely was she able to discard her memories that it was as if she'd forgotten them entirely. As she drove down the road, then across the gravel driveway, she was excited. The letters made her excited. For when last had anything touched her so keenly? She looked at Hannah's letter and was filled with the power of being able to make it vanish. She had nothing to be afraid of, there was nothing she couldn't handle. Let him come, let them all do what they would, she would prevail.

She jumped out of the van and let down her hand to the dogs, who leapt and barked at her return. At a word they retreated, sat, were still. They were her dogs, broken in, trained by her, for her. If she left a dog in one place with the order to stay, she could be gone for years and would come back to find it still there. Dead, but unmoved. She was certain of it.

In the kitchen the wind made a low moan that seemed to Hannah quite human. She didn't hear Zelda come in because she had turned on the radio and was listening to a concert. She had flour on her hands and the table in front of her was covered with it. There were strong smells: of cooked meat cooling by the stove, of yeast rising, of a cake baked and of something else, something Zelda couldn't identify.

"What are you doing?"

Hannah looked up, startled. When her face relaxed again, it was beautiful. Yes, it was shocking to think it, but her face was beautiful. She was perfectly content doing what she was doing.

And then she said, "I wanted—" And stopped.

"You wanted?" Zelda held it up for inspection. "What?"

Hannah laughed softly. "Just to make something," she said, "something new, something out of the recipe book, your mother's."

"Oh." Zelda abandoned it.

Zelda sat at the table and waited, keeping the letters in her pocket, touching them secretly sometimes; she wanted to choose her moment. Finally she said, "There was a letter today. For you."

She watched Hannah's face. She held the moment longer, unraveling it slowly, like the thread in a hem. Hannah said nothing;

she took the dough from beneath the cloth and began slowly to knead it. She would not ask for her letter.

Zelda pushed it across the table. Hannah glanced at it quickly and then away. She went on with her kneading, shaking on more flour, stretching the slack dough into its own folds.

"I had a letter too," Zelda said.

"Oh?" The brown eyes held Zelda's for a moment, then dropped.

After a while Zelda said, "Aren't you going to read it?"

"No."

"He's coming back," Zelda announced flatly.

"Yes," Hannah said, "I knew he must."

Fourteen

AN HOUR BEFORE DAWN, THE CITY SLEEPS ON IN SILENCE. Most of it was evacuated after the bombing, and the people who sleep here are strangers, passing through. Once these streets would have been busy with people making their way to the factories, but the factories are burned-out shells, the houses gutted and looted, and skeleton roofs look out at the sky. An army tank lies on one side. A few dogs scrounge among the debris, their tails down, their ribs showing through the skin. Some black birds shift and shake their wings in the charred treetops. Someone scuttles, a small figure, through a doorway, then vanishes. In four hours the next patrol will pass.

It happened early one Sunday morning before anyone was awake. This was the first city to go, the next was in the Eastern Cape. The next in the Transvaal. Whole cities wiped out in a series of carefully organized attacks with sophisticated weapons. So sudden and so devastating that the white population was too stunned to even retaliate. For the moment, chaos: not quite a state of war, but without doubt a revolution.

A young woman sits with her back to a wall and her knees drawn up, sobbing very quietly. Ruth. The room, with slowly dulling stars for a roof, is filled with people, but she can't see them, can only hear their breath, hear their movements and smell their odors. Occasionally, she stops sobbing and listens as someone rises to walk a few feet and urinate. Then the soft gasp of tears begins again.

A baby whimpers and is stilled. The night air is dense with the lingering traces of wood fires, of liquor and meat fat. Before the next patrol, all these people, and the traces of their passing, will be gone as if they'd never existed. It's a dead zone. But for now, they hoard these last few hours of sleep: children lying across their mother's knees, men propped against the walls in the drooped positions of sleep—twitching, snoring, wakened suddenly by dreams.

Ruth pushes her hands into the floor in an attempt to straighten her back. Her pregnancy makes it impossible to get comfortable for long. She grows quiet but doesn't sleep. She moves again, and then again as, imperceptibly, the sky begins to lighten. The faces are still in darkness and in any case she doesn't want to look at them. In a far corner she hears a small movement and then a low moan: they're having sex again. Her lip curls in disgust. In the filth and the crush, two people are doing this to one another. She knows the result of that—and hates it as she hates her swollen body and the creature growing inside it. In the corner, their breath comes to her, quick, shallow, and then the woman cries one long painless cry. Ruth wants to scream out, "Stop it, stop it!" but is afraid.

More light filters into the sky; the stars lose their hard luster. People are waking, stirring, and the splash of urine is regular and loud. She can make out faces, hurried movements as people pull their pitiful possessions together to get ready to clear out. She sits quite still and watches them, retreating into the wall, deciding in this instant that she won't go with them, that she'll stay behind by herself.

Because what does it matter if I stay here? They won't shoot me like they shoot them. Anyway, I wouldn't care if they did. I won't go, I can't get up and walk again. I'm going to wait for Willie. Perhaps he'll come back, or perhaps he's dead already. But I can't go on, true as God. I'm finished. I'm tired of living as they do, doing what they do—I have to copy them because I don't know what's going on. They laugh at me, they say things about me in their own languages. I don't know these languages. They're not Xhosas, they're from all over, just what's left over after they've rounded up people, and sent them to the camp. "They just have to get rid of people," that's what Willie said, after the bombings and burnings. The police shoot them down and the rest get put away. In that camp. No one seems to know where it is. Only blacks go there; there's another place for whites who make trouble. Sometimes, I've seen white people hiding too. They look dazed, and dirty like me. I don't know what they're doing. Just hiding like the rest of us. I've nowhere else to go now, so I have to just wait here for Willie, like he said, because everything else is gone.

Now they are ready to go. The women strap their babies to their backs and lift bundles to their heads. They are frightened, hurrying, pushing at each other, stamping out the last traces of fires and covering them with sand. They talk abruptly to one another, but say nothing to Ruth. A small boy drinks water from a tap that stands in the street, his mother comes and pulls at him: "Come now, quick, quick." Three men stand in a group, smoking, making a plan. Their heads are alert, tilted to one side, listening for the patrol.

All activity accelerates as the sun rises. Now there's something frantic about the way they shake and fold their blankets and begin to leave the shelter; they're irritable with the children, fight over scraps of food, fill cans of water hurriedly. A siren can be heard far off. They begin to run—out of this exposed part and into the surrounding bush, where they will split up and hide until it's dark and time to travel again.

Ruth moves into a corner and watches them go. A big Swazi woman talks to her kindly in English, asking her if she wants to go with them, but Ruth shakes her head.

"I'm waiting for Willie."

"Oh yes, I see. Well, God be with you. You take care now, okay?"

"Where are you going?" she asked dully.

"To the Free State. I have a sister there. We'll be all right if we can get there." She laughs. "She has a place. We'll get there. Quick," she hushes the children, and pulls the baby tighter to her back by yanking the ends of the blanket together. And waves goodbye. Figures vanish behind buildings. Soon the place is deserted. It becomes quiet, Ruth sits on.

She's alone and afraid, but not of the patrol. It will sweep by and take no notice of these broken walls that she can crouch below. They'll search the more intact buildings farther along where a few ignorant people may be hiding. It was her second night, so she knew it all.

Someone has left a shard of mirror behind. She picks it up and looks into it. Her face becomes elongated because the mirror is so thin. She finds her face quite hateful: I'm ugly, so ugly, my face is as thin as a lizard's. I'm dirty and I can smell myself. My mouth's dry but I can't risk running to the tap. My legs have cramps. Why doesn't he come? He should've come last night. Perhaps he's run off? Or been killed? I could have loved Willie, but only when he's happy and laughing, not now that he's brought me to this terrible place.

It was all right at the beginning. When I found him at the garage, I could hide there for a bit, but then there was some trouble nearby and the police came, searching everything. The school was shut up, the nuns went away. We ran away to Machine Mike's cousin up in Klerkfontein, but then the riots began and everything went up that one night when the big bomb exploded. After that, we had to keep running. Once they caught Willie and stuck him on one of those trucks, but he managed to run away the first night and got back to me. Now I don't love him, because he keeps trying to make me go *home*: he's tired of me; I slow him down; they'd shoot him for being with me. And I don't love him because he's not here. He's left me like everyone else. I didn't think he'd do that, true as God. I always thought Willie would stick by me. Now I don't know. Now I just love my father. I can see him sometimes so clearly, you know, walking down a corridor, smoking, walking toward a heavy door with his name on it. I can see him so clearly, I'd recognize him the minute I saw him.

Oh, that bitch Zelda, that bitch, bitch, bitch. For sending me all that way for nothing, for bloody nothing. When I got there no one had ever heard his name. She'd made it all up. She told me to go to that place, but no one knew him there.

They thought I was mad. But I kept on looking, through the whole town, in telephone books, everywhere. But no trace of him. She lied to get rid of me, to get me away from Hannah, to make me suffer all over again.

Ruth began to sob like a child, loudly and painfully, then tried to smother the sound and almost choked.

Slowly, as the sun began to gather force, she wilted and her anger evaporated. The patrol was far along now, in the distance. She'd heard shots, but that was not unusual. Now that the patrol had gone, there was nothing to look forward to. Her head began to reel. She slumped down as she had done when the patrol roared by, but this time it was involuntary: she just slipped down, her body falling to one side, her knees coming up and curling around. The flies buzzed around a pool of urine in one corner. She watched them, then tried to cover her face with a rag. The sun beat down on her.

Fifteen

"WELL," ZELDA SAID WITH DETERMINATION, ROLLING UP her sleeves, "We can't get slack around here. We've a helluva lot of work to do—and your mind's not on it, Hannah." She slapped her hands down on the table, disturbing Hannah's cup of tea, which trembled then spilled into the saucer. "What are we going to do?" Zelda said, sitting.

Slowly pouring the tea back into the cup, Hannah said carefully, "Zelda, I know how you feel, but you've got to go easy. It's not our lives that you're playing with."

"I'm not playing with anyone's life," she said evenly, "you saw for yourself. The men all stood there yesterday and refused to go—it was nothing to do with me."

"But it was you who inspired it. They wouldn't have had the nerve to disobey with the place crawling with police."

"Crap. It was their decision."

Hannah touched Zelda's arm quickly. "I know that, I know they were refusing to go because they didn't want to. But it took their courage to refuse and it's going to take a lot more before it's finished with. Don't push them. They all lost their labor papers, remember."

"Who's pushing?" Zelda snapped. "And so what if they've lost their papers? They don't need papers to work for me."

"Zelda, has it ever occurred to you that this farm could be destroyed any day? That you could be arrested tomorrow? That the men could be forcibly removed. Probably will be?"

"I don't spend my time thinking about things that aren't going to happen."

"The paper this morning said that more than five thousand people were missing, presumed to have been taken to that place."

Zelda sniffed. "I'm not sure that I believe in that place."

"Well, believe in it or not, people are disappearing in vast numbers—and they're not in prison."

"So? The whole country's in a mess. Everyone's all over the place, hiding, blowing things up, sneaking into Botswana. How can anyone tell what's going on—or where anyone is?"

"Zelda, the point is this: we have to think about what's going to happen to us. After all those murders, things are getting bad around here too. There are rumors that the army's coming."

"They've got too much to worry about to mess with little problems like farmers being murdered."

"Ten farmers murdered and all their families? Fifty white lives?"

"Well—so what do you want me to do?" Zelda asked angrily.

"Just go easy. Don't stir things up anymore. There's too much pressure on everyone."

"I'm not stirring up anyone."

"You know what I mean. It's just that you don't have to go through what they do."

"And you do, I suppose?"

"Not yet, but I will."

Zelda came back, "I do have to go through it. Don't forget what's happening to this farm, and don't forget that my van was overturned in Konigstad yesterday and no one was looking to see whether I was in it or not."

I wonder if she's actually enjoying it, Hannah thought with dismay. A personal revolt: they'll follow her to the ends of the earth—and she wants to see how far she can make them go.

Zelda stood up. "I'm off, I want to be here tomorrow when they come back—and I've got a lot to do. Keep them working on the barns today. We must finish."

"Zelda," Hannah called after her, "don't be late, or I'll worry about you."

"As if anything could happen to me."

Sixteen

"RUTH, RUTHIE, WAKE UP, MAN."

She woke slowly, but didn't pull herself up. Instead, she curled her legs closer to her body and said, "I was dreaming I was home. At the farm, with Hannah rubbing my head." She began to cry in her ecstatic way, "I want to go home, I miss my dolls, I shouldn't have given them away, you shouldn't have brought me here, everything stinks." She retched, then went on with a shrill, quick voice, "Oh, I wanted a red silk dress, a room with white curtains and carpets. Oh, Willie, oh, Willie," she wailed.

He gathered her up into his arms. "It's okay, it's okay. Just wait a bit, hey. Soon you'll have the red dress and all the jewels, like I told you."

His face was still handsome, but it was haggard now and he looked older. His jaw was broken. His clothes looked clean, the creases were still in his trousers, but his shoes were ruined, one toe pushing through the leather. His face, as he cradled her in his arms like a child, was exhausted. Feeling her big body against his, he felt quite desperate with responsibility.

"Where were you? Where've you been?" she sobbed.

"I came," he said slowly. "You should have stayed with the others like I told you. If I'd have been shot, who would look after you, hey?" He shook her gently. "Don't be such a domkop. Use your brains next time."

"I hate them, I hate them all."

"Ja, ja, I know it." Then he said nothing for a bit. He was planning, or trying to, but nothing would stay still in his head. He was lost and miserable: a man without a plan was nothing. And anyway, what would he do with her if she refused his plan? Where would they go? They were so conspicuous alone like this.

"Are there patrols here in the day?" he asked.

"Only the one at dawn, then nothing till dark. Then all night long." She moved her position and looked at him. "Where've you been, Willie?"

"Looking for transport," he said shortly, then changed his tone, more by an act of will than anything else, and said with his old enthusiasm, "I've got us a car. Someone left it abandoned by the side of the road. White people, running away. It was bust, but I managed to get it going. The petrol had been scaled, so I had to go back and get some. Anyway, I've brought the jalopy here for us."

"Where?" she peered above the wall at the rubble and destruction that had once been the north side of the city.

"Parked out of sight behind some buildings. Ruthie"—he took her face in his hands—"now, listen to me and listen carefully, my girl. I'm going to take you home. No, listen, *listen*, man," She was shaking her head wildly. "Look, you *must*. You have no choice."

"You said I could stay with you."

"Ruth, now listen, man." He held her shoulders firmly. "If they catch you with me, what's going to happen anyway? They'll bury me in that place in the desert and where will you go? Ja, now you're cottoning on: they'll send you home, man, or to hospital. But first they'll be horrible to you. You know what those pigs are like. I can't take the risk."

"You just want to get rid of me." Her head was down.

"Of course I don't. You're my little koeksuster, you know it. I just have to decide these things, what's best for you. I must look after you," he said desperately, feeling the old sense of duty and pity.

But now, everything was so complicated; it wasn't like at the farm, when he could make a plan for her and tell her, "This is what you must do, and this you mustn't." It was too late for that.

Now he just had to do his best. His best was taking her home. After that, well, he didn't know yet, and he hadn't had time to think of himself yet either, but he'd have to keep away from the city. Port Elizabeth was no good anymore. Those days of city life were over. Now there was just a fight to survive. But he couldn't even begin to think about the future until he'd got her back home, safe at the farm.

Hannah at least would understand; she knew how it was with Ruthie. Jeez, how he longed for the sight of Hannah, walking toward him to take Ruth into the house. Ag, the thought was even more beautiful than the thought of an iced beer.

"Willie," Ruth was saying more quietly, "I can't go back, I can't face them. I've failed at everything. I can't run back with my tail between my legs. Zelda will just kill me when she sees I've come back. I promised, man."

"Look here," he said furiously. "That woman should really be ashamed of herself. Your family, after all, and doing something like that to you. She did a terrible thing, sending you away like that. Lying to you, deceiving you with false hopes. Ag, man"—he threw up his hands—"I've never known such a cruel thing. So, you don't worry now about your tant. That place is your home, you've a right there, isn't it? Hannah won't let her be unkind to you. She'll be so mad when she hears about this, there'll really be hell to pay."

At the thought of Hannah, Ruth's face relaxed. But then she whispered sadly, "What will she say to me after I went off like that, after all I've done?" She looked down. "Just look at me."

"She'll forgive you," Willie said simply. "It wasn't your fault, nothing is your fault. Things happen to you, that's all. Only you and Zelda know that she threw you out. You could split on her, so she'll watch herself a bit. And Hannah will be just *happy* to have you home, honestly, man." He was getting excited, feeling she was responding at last. "She'll take care of you like she always has."

"Without you, I'll be frightened again," she said, rubbing her hand up and down on a piece of earth between the broken lino.

"Who says I'll be going anywhere?" he joked. But she just looked at him and then down again. "So—come on, now. Come with me and let's take a look at this motor, hey?" He pulled her up.

In the car he said, "Here, I have food for you. You must eat." He rummaged on the back seat for it. "Oranges and a pawpaw and some bread. It's stale, but okay. We must go now, we have to find somewhere along the way to hide out till it's night. We must go now—now," he said urgently. "It'll take days to get there." He wondered bleakly if they'd make it at all, the odds were stacked against them.

"I'll go, only if you'll stay when we get home," she said desperately, clinging to him. "If you won't go away again. It was so bad without you, so unhappy after you'd gone."

He considered just for a second, then said, "Ja, I'll stay. We'll go home together, we'll stay together now. It's what we must do."

And although he'd said it originally just to make her go with him, now that the words were said, it was right and he would do it. It was his duty to look after her as long as she needed him. It was his duty also to be with his mother now. Soon the bad troubles would be around her too. Not just the cities, but the farming places also would see the guns and the bombs. It had to be so, he wanted it to be so, it was time. Because of all these things, his own life must wait. Duty after all was love; and love, loyalty. He would stay with her.

"We'll get by, Willie," she said softly, taking his hand and reaching across to kiss his face. "We'll get home, I'm telling you. We'll survive."

Because now that he was here and now that he was succeeding, she loved him again. But he was saying bitterly, "If I must walk this earth for as long as fifty years, then I must do more than just survive. I want to live, I want my chance, and God's truth I'm going to get it. This much I know. This is what it's all for. Ja," he whispered softly, "this is what it's all for—what my oompie and my pa died for: to be Afrikaners, to live right in our own place. Ja." He nodded his head softly and slowly. "Ja, that's the way it is."

"Come," she said tenderly, putting her hand on his arm. "Come, let's go home now, Willie, let's go."

Seventeen

HANNAH SAT IN HER ROOM SEWING. THE ELECTRIC MACHINE
whirred under her hands and the cloth sped past the needle, making a heap upon the floor. Sometimes she stopped, looked up and
frowned. The house was empty. She listened. Then lifted the
cloth out, bit the thread, and pulled the seam straight. She stopped
again to listen. It was as if the house was full of strange noises
today; she kept wanting to go and see if anyone had broken in.

She went on resolutely with her sewing. She was making a
dress for Ruth, something she hadn't done for years. She liked to
believe that doing this for Ruth might make her return. Because it
was as if, when Ruth had gone, she'd taken life with her. Hannah
had come to feel that her own life had no tide anymore. It would
just drag and slow, having no capacity for change. And then the
letter from Dawie had come and he'd said that he was coming
home. He'd said that it was time to beat back the past, to embrace
the future.

For days she had been excited, thinking of these words. But
now she only felt panic. Perhaps he would look at her and then
away? Perhaps he would feel: That is not it at all—not what I
wanted or expected, not the woman I once loved. She touched her
face. How had it changed? She was not so old, nor he; they'd not
even lived half their life—so why this dread, this fear of time
passed?

Then her foot ceased on the pedal and she began to think in a way she had never done before. Yes, she thought, he has found his courage again, he has borrowed it from some black woman in a courtroom. Now he feels he can redeem himself and he asks for my courage. Just the touch of a sneer moved her lips. But perhaps, she thought, perhaps she didn't want him now, didn't need him? The thought was so audacious that it shocked her. Then it invigorated her. The suffering was all past now, and she had endured it without him.

Everything was changing: the whole country was in uproar, and whatever happened it would never be the same again. The simple fact that it would soon be theirs, to share or withold—that was her power now. It had come at last into her hands. She was no longer the one to wait or endure. Life was open. Soon, any path could be taken, no door would close on her face. His great dream had come to pass, but it was not his to give her, like money or a gold chain. It had not come about by his dedication to the law—even he knew that. She smiled sweetly with the triumph of something deeply hoped for and long awaited. It was coming to pass, in her own lifetime: she would be free. And then she would take him, and then maybe she would not.

The ruching of the cloth formed into soft pleats; she spread the front of the dress on the floor and seemed to see Ruth's arms lift to flop it over her head, and then turn and pirouette. One day, she would go out in a long dress and dance in a fine room full of music and laughter. She would know love, would marry and bear children, be proud and take her place in the world.

As the clock struck eleven, there was a loud, impatient knock on the door. Insantly it was followed by another, more loud. Hannah started, but did not move to open it. She picked up the cloth from the floor and drew it into her lap; slowly her hands relaxed. Then she heard the stoep door slam, feet on the gravel, the sound of a car starting up. They were going. For now. But they would return.

Eighteen

RUTH LET HER HEAD FALL FORWARD ONTO THE DASHBOARD.

"Are you okay?" Willie asked, touching the side of her face where the birthmark was, making her flinch.

"Ja." Her voice dragged itself over to him. It was so hot and she couldn't bear to look out of the windscreen a minute longer. She hated driving in the daytime. You saw horrible things beside the road: dead bodies lying where they fell, left to rot; once a small child. But Willie insisted they just keep driving, day and night.

They were tense all the time now. Willie barely spoke. The day before, the car had broken down and they'd had to push it off the road and behind some trees. He had worked all day, trying to fix it, saying not one word. His silence had upset her.

"You don't have to do this for me, Willie," she had said in a childish voice.

"For who else should I do it?"

"But you're cross with me."

"I'm cross with the engine."

Now his clothes were no longer clean, sweat and grease were smeared on his shirt. She had never smelt him before, only that nice clean pine smell when he was going out on the razzle. Now he was a bit offensive to her.

"You'll never fix it," she said.

His face came up from under the bonnet wearily. "That is not the way a woman must be to a man who's working. You don't say, 'You're not good, you'll fail.' You say nice things. Try a bit, hey? Make an effort, my friend."

She looked around her, rubbing her foot in the dirt. She hated the bush. It was full of birds that startled you, scorpions, flies, and when she'd tried to wander off for a walk, he'd snapped, "Don't go in there. There's bad things in there. Stay here."

She cleaned her nails with a long white thorn and, later, she slept.

When she woke up and saw him still working, his head under the bonnet, she felt sorry. She came up to him and put her hands on his arm to make him look up. "I'm sorry, Willie. I don't deserve you," she said. And she gave him a bit of hard bread and the last of the water.

He ate without appetite. "We must go into the next town, we can't stay on this back road anymore. We must go in because this repair it will not last for long. We must find a garage."

She looked at him and said nothing. Then, as if the thought of danger revived her from her apathy, she said, "We need food and things to drink."

"Ja, but we'll have to be careful. I have no papers, so if they ask me to show, I'm finished. You must go to the store and I must go to a garage—separate. This is my plan" he said.

"How far are we from home?" she asked, as she had a hundred times.

"Not far, not too far. A few hundred miles. But I can't fix this car so that it lasts." He was angry with himself for not looking after her better.

She was thinking about how tired she felt, and how she wanted, for the first time in her life, to lie in a deep bath, wash all the filth away, sleep in a bed again. But she was quiet because all his worry had moved to his limbs and they no longer had that vibrancy, that dance in the blood that she loved to see. Now he just concentrated on one thing: getting there, getting away from the open road and places where people could stop them and ask questions.

Often in the night as they lay huddled together away from the road, they could hear the army vehicles thundering by in convoys. Once she'd got up and watched them: tanks like you saw on the newsreels about Namibia. Hundreds of them, one after the other, as if they'd never end. This was the danger of the night. It was when the army moved, so that people would not know how serious the problem was, how much it was spreading.

The tanks going by was terrifying, like being thrown into a foreign country at war. Was it war? No one could answer that question. There were so many false rumors circulating, and the government was trying to hush everything up by hiding things, not just from the outside world because the economy had collapsed now, but from the white people who were fleeing wherever they could.

"Why does it have to happen now, Willie?" she said, lifting her head from the dampness her sweat had made. "Why, just when we were trying to get out in the world?"

He laughed in the old way and began to tease her, "Ag, man, they were just waiting for us two to get out to start them off." Then he added, "We are nothing in this, Ruthie, just a spit in the sand. This is just the beginning and it will take a long time. Yes, my friend, a long time will pass before they stop the shooting."

"What will happen?"

"Bad things, very bad things." He looked out into the bush a bit.

"And, in the end, will your lot kill all the white people, or will we kill all of you?"

"There will be plenty killing," he said morosely.

"Do you think it's everywhere, Willie? The whole country?" She turned so that her back was pressed against the car door and she could watch him.

"Now, I don't know. In Joburg they got things under control again."

"How? How did they do it?"

"The same. They killed as much as they could and the rest they put away. But," he added more confidently, "P.E. and Durban was full, full of trouble and the faster they shot, the more there was coming. But listen, we don't want to be thinking of this now. Our plan must be to go inwards and we must try for a very small dorp and hope for the best with a garage."

Time seemed to thicken. She didn't want to ask him now: "How long? How far?" She sat in silence and after a while he said, "As for me, I'm not happy with this trouble. It's right, man, I know it's right, but I'm not happy with it. Too much suffering—what's the good of it? I'm a peace-loving boy."

His concentration returned to the car. She could feel his body tense as the engine of the car stuttered, as a banging sound erupted from under the bonnet. He stopped the car, got out and adjusted something without saying a word.

After some miles, the road began to improve and he knew that one of these miles a dorp would appear at the end of the horizon. "Soon we will find something," he said, cheering up.

She thought of Coca-Cola in one of those bottles with icicles running down the side; her craving for it made her more thirsty. She drew idly in the dust on the glass clock on the dashboard and then just sat, gazing out of the insect-smeared window at the white sheen of the road.

Then they saw what they needed: a few ugly, low houses leading into a single street, which had a general store, a chemist, a Barclay's Bank, and a shop selling farm machinery.

"Shit," he said, "I can't see a garage."

"Keep going, we'll drive right through and then turn back," she said, alert now, peering to the left and right of her.

A few men in dark hats walked up the street; a large Mercedes came to a halt outside the farm shop and a few women got out of their cars and entered the store. Their own car was noticed as it drove by.

"Let's try up there, down that little street," she said, pointing to where the road made a single right turn up ahead.

He did so and at the far end was a petrol station with a scruffy café beside it.

"You get out here," he said, his voice brusque and nervous. "There's no one about. Walk back to the store. And be quick, now. I'll go up to the garage."

She rummaged in a red purse and thrust a lot of money at him, which he quickly divided and put into various pockets. "Say you're a long time?" she asked fretfully.

"No ways. If they have what I need, then I'll just buy it and go. I must get petrol too. So when you see me outside, you come quick and jump in. Okay?"

"Say you can't get what you want?"

"Say we die tonight!" he said impatiently. "Just go now, quick. And listen, man, if anyone asks you anything, you just hold your mouth, hey?"

"Ja, all right. Now stop being so bossy. I'm not two years old."

She was fine, she was okay; in the bush he knew things, he was the boss, but the dorp was her territory. Here she could do the talking and have people listen to her. So she walked up the street, her head high, until she remembered her ugly fat body, her dirty smelly clothes, and began to panic—pushing her hair in place, looking in dismay at her marked dress. "Jeez, they'll think I'm a kaffir." She wanted to run and hide and would have done so, had she not been so thirsty and had she not begun to feel a certain responsibility toward Willie.

He drove the car slowly up to the garage. There was a white man inside a booth and then there was a sprawl of junky cars and what looked like some kind of workroom. Willie drove the car around back and parked it out of sight of the man in the booth.

Two men were sitting on the ground outside the workroom eating sandwiches. He approached them, conscious that he was a stranger. He smiled, greeted them in Afrikaans, and let them return the greeting before he made any request. Then he stated his business and they listened. The older of the two shook his head but went into a long discussion of the problem. The other got up and went to the car and took a look. The two of them peered in; Willie was explaining, but the mechanic was slow. Willie was sweating. Finally, he thought of a solution, and led Willie through the workroom into the back, where the spare parts were kept.

Eventually, after much looking about, he found what he wanted, turned to Willie and asked, "Can you do something with this? It's for a Ford but maybe you can mess around a bit. It's all we have. It's hard to get parts these days."

"I'll take it," Willie said, conscious that time had passed, that Ruth was waiting, that the white man was strolling over, smoking a cigarette.

Seeing him, the mechanic said, "Here, give me the money. I'll take it to him."

"I need petrol also," Willie was whispering, as if there was a problem, and the mechanic said, "I'll drive round and fill it for you." He too seemed nervous, didn't want his boss any closer; but he'd arrived.

"I'm just going to fill up the car now, baas," the mechanic said. "I have found the boy here what he wanted."

"Check the price on the list. I'll come over and ring it up," the owner said, not bothering to look at Willie.

The old mechanic got to his feet and wiped his hands on his overalls, moving back to work. Willie went with him, breathing more normally.

But then the white man called out, "Where you from, boy?"

They both stiffened; it was as if a link had forged itself between them. Willie said quickly, "I'm taking my baas to Upington, but then we had this trouble with the big end, so now I'll take this and go fetch him."

"You going to fix the car yourself?"

"I'm a mechanic, baas," Willie said quietly. "I will fix it for him."

Willie and the mechanic walked on in silence and waited for the man to enter the booth before they approached the pumps.

When the tank was full, the mechanic said, "Is there nothing else you need?"

"No, I can manage now. Thank you." He gave the man the money, and waited for the owner to unlock the till and ring up the money. Then he turned to go.

The man in the booth called out after him, "Hey, boy?"

Willie turned slowly. "Baas?"

"Aren't you wanting your change? And here's the receipt. Your baas will want to see it, isn't it?"

Willie walked back slowly and took the slip of paper and the coins, both of which he was handed very slowly. He turned back to see that the mechanic had flipped a wet cloth over the windscreen to clean it. Willie got into the car and drove it slowly away.

"Something cheeky about that boy," the man in the booth said to the mechanic.

"He's not from round here," the other replied, walking away.

Ruth, having bought two carrier bags full of groceries, stood at the door nervously, waiting for him. He was being ages. People came in and out, staring at her, unfriendly, the way people were in small places.

The fat lady behind the checkout stared at her and then said, "Why not sit down a bit, hey? You'll feel better." She pushed a stool towards her.

Ruth was quite desperate to sit down, but she said, "No, no, I'm fine," and moved closer to the door.

The woman shook her head. "You should sit in your condition."

Ruth ignored her and pulled out a can of Coke. It was very cold, covered in condensation. She was going to open it, but stopped. Not until she was with Willie. Not until they could both drink. She'd been horrible to him and she was ashamed. The can was blissfully cold against her skin but she put it back with the others to keep it that way. She went outside onto the stoep, where a few Africans sat, waiting for the bus; they all had children and bundles. Ruth stared impatiently up the road, looking for him.

When he came, she ran down the steps and he opened the door from the inside. She got in with her carrier bags and he drove off quickly.

"I feel like I committed a murder or something." She laughed, hurriedly. "You should've seen the way they looked at me, and my dirty clothes. I was really embarrassed, I'm telling you."

"We must get away from here and back on a dirt road." He was nervous, looking behind him.

"Did you get what you needed?"

"No, but I can sort something out with what I got. We'll find somewhere to stop later."

"Is it being with me that makes you scared?" she asked, ripping the ring off the Coke can.

"Ja, of course, man," he snapped. "It's okay for you—who's going to give you a hard time?"

"But if you weren't with me, they'd have stopped you already."

"Maybe." He took the Coke she handed him and drank deeply.

They drove past a flat-roofed building with the police sign outside and breathed out again when they had passed it. He drank again. Then he said, "We're out of there, we'll be okay now. That place gave me the creeps. I had a bad feeling about it. But now we're safe." He hit her affectionately on the thigh. "You all right, my friend, not too tired?"

Just then, the road made a curve, and, a little ahead, no more than a couple of hundred yards away, was a barrier—a roadblock with a white policeman standing by it.

"God's truth, you never should've said that, Willie, you should have kept your mouth shut. Now I'm going to have to get us out of this. Don't say a bloody word, or we've had it. Now stop. Stop, now. He's got guns hanging off him like oranges."

Nineteen

DAWIE HAD PACKED THE CAR. HE HAD TAKEN ONLY HIS BOOKS, clothes, and a few paintings and records. While he put things in the boot, his daughter stood in the driveway and watched him.

"Marina," he called to her, "come over here." He put out his arms to her and she walked—and than ran—into them.

"Why do you have to go?"

She was a serious child and she had often seemed more like his than Sara's, probably because he'd spent more time with her. When she was tiny, she'd slept in his study in the afternoons and he'd had his clients come to the house rather than the office. It was such a joy to watch her sleeping and then wake her and see her head lift and turn as she smiled up at him. He had tried hard with the marriage then, because of her. It had been a peaceful enough time at home—looking out at the garden, walking with Marina at the back with the washing flying in the sunshine, the smells from the kitchen, the servants singing and talking all day. Sara wasn't around much, but she was grateful that he looked after the child. They didn't argue. Perhaps, even then, they'd gone beyond that, into quite separate compartments. He hadn't twigged about Marina then.

"Mommy says you're going away," she said, studying his face.

"Yes, that's true."

"And that you're not coming back."

"That's not true. I will come back and see you."

Was she actually looking at him with doubt in those blue eyes? He couldn't bear it, he felt his throat tighten. He reached into his pocket and took out a piece of paper and wrote some numbers on it. He was crouching down, and sat her on his knee so that they could look at the numbers together.

"You can read those, can't you?" She stared at the paper and nodded. "Well, listen then. You keep this piece of paper in your secret box, and whenever you want to talk to me, or if you want me to come and be with you, then you ring those numbers on the phone, the way I taught you, and I'll come, I promise. Is that all right?"

He'd always talked to her this way; her mother's baby talk infuriated him. When he looked at the piece of paper, clutched tightly in her hand, he saw that he'd given her Hannah's number. It was the only number he could give. It was an act of faith. He was glad to have done it.

Marina was happier, but she still looked at him questioningly, and finally she frowned and said, "Why are you going, Daddy?"

"I have some very important things to do."

"Then you'll come back?"

"Yes, I'll come back."

"And live with us like now?"

He hesitated, she was only five years old, after all, barely that. "No," he said.

"I didn't think so," she said, with the troubled expression she'd had from birth puckering her forehead.

When he lifted her down on the gravel, he could see Sara's shadow near a curtain window. Marina folded the paper carefully and put it in her pocket. He felt a sharp sense of loss. It was all he could do not to grab her and hug her against him. In her quiet, watchful way she had allowed herself to be reassured, but her smile told him she was not fooled.

She pushed a stone around with her naked foot as if deep in thought. But then, looking up at him, trapping his emotion on his face before he could release it, suddenly she began to wail, her round face gripped with sorrow. Helplessly he went over to her and picked her up, rocked her, talked to her quietly.

In an instant Sara was out of the front door, rushing across

the drive toward them. She tore the little girl away from his arms
and said savagely, "When you're leaving, at least have the decency
to do it quickly."

Marina went very quiet. She leaned away from her mother's
body, looking hard into her face. But when the child began to
struggle to get away from her, Sara's anger returned and she
began to scream, "Go on, get out, you're making it worse, you're
making everything worse."

He left, having no choice, not being able to touch Marina
again. It was a double blow, this messy, painful departure, with
its echoes of other desertions. He could see the little girl standing
stoically beside the woman, not crying now, just watching him
go. He wanted to weep, because he loved her like his own blood,
and because her courage was so reminiscent of Hannah's.

He got out of the city as fast as he could, and out onto the
open road. The broad road, usually so busy, was almost deserted.
People were abiding by the official advice to keep off the roads.
Here he could see the ravages of the drought; the bush around
him seemed to creak, it was so dry. His car was covered in dust
in seconds and there seemed to be more insects than he could
ever remember. He felt a sudden, deep longing for rain, as if
it might in some way purge the past, wash him clean the way he'd
always felt it could when he was a child.

As the miles sped by, slowly his despondency passed. He had
begun. Sara had not been vindictive; she had even admitted that
it was "fair" and that neither should be held responsible for the
failure. He wondered if it would last. He thought he would
probably receive a letter making financial demands—if that was
all, then he'd be happy. Marina— Oh, but that was harder, too
hard to think of right now when he was raw with it.

He stopped in a small dorp for a beer and sat at the bar with
the traveling salesmen, feeling that particular loneliness that
travelers have. Unlike them, he did not want to be pulled into
conversation. A woman with mangy black hair approached him,
almost apologetically, and in his pity he would have liked to just
give her the money, but felt he couldn't. She walked away and it
was her feet that he noticed; they were calloused and cracked and
seemed to sum up her existence. At the back of the bar the radio

was quietly murmuring the news. No one seemed to be paying any particular attention, though the voice droned on about sabotage, bombings, arrests, troops gathering in the east. It was as if a numbness affected everyone. They could only get on with their business by pretending nothing was wrong. It was an extension, after all, he thought, of the way people had always lived.

He left. The heat outside felt like a punch in the head after the coolness of the bar. The road shimmered and became hypnotic. It was hard to stay awake and he became aware of a great fatigue. He was feeling, in its conclusion, the effect of the strains of the past months. He worried about Abe; his letters were as witty as ever, but they both knew he'd be lost for a long time. The firm would go on, doing its best. Kenneth was coming along well, he had that powerful emotional appeal that Abe had and would become a fine lawyer. And yet it all seemed so far away: he found it hard to believe he had lived his life all the years that he had.

And Hannah—how would she be now? What had the years really done to her? What had he done? Perhaps she would have grown numb, simply not care anymore? He couldn't imagine her bitter—that was too self-indulgent for her. But it was possible that she just wouldn't care. The only thing he could fix on was his need to protect her; that, at least, was valid.

Up ahead of him, he approached a roadblock—yet another—and he stopped behind the car already there.

An officious policeman was giving a black man a hard time, shouting, abusing him. The young man looked very frightened. He was with a white girl who was arguing on his behalf with all the power at her disposal, but he could see that she was exhausted, at her wit's end, and heavily pregnant as well.

He got out of his car and walked over with authority. "What's the trouble here, officer?" he asked in Afrikaans, curtly, as if he had the right to interfere.

"It's this boy here, sir, no papers. They think they can just wander all over the country without papers, doing what they like. She says they come from round Konigstad, but how the bleddy hell am I supposed to believe that? Look at the pair of them. Perhaps I'm thinking there's something a bit funny going on. I want to take him to the police station."

"Quite right, that's just what you should do," Dawie said, "but in this case it's not necessary." He smiled quickly. "As it turns out, I'm heading that way myself, on business, and I happen to know this boy." He looked briefly at Willie's hands. "He's a mechanic at one of the big garages there, fixed my car a couple of times."

The policeman looked confused. "Ja," he said, thinking, "he did say that he was a mechanic and that he was taking this lady's car for fixing, but still, man, I can't take a chance now, not round here. This is not where I come from—"

"No, of course you can't take a chance," Dawie said smoothly, "but I can. Look, this boy's a good worker. I wouldn't like to see him in any trouble. Here, take my card and if you get any trouble, then you can call me and I'll sort it out. Okay?"

The legal card did it. The policeman backed off, shrugging his shoulders.

He became unpleasant again when he turned to Willie. "Now, you just get the hell out of here before I shoot you. And if I ever catch you again without your papers, I'll do for you. You understand, boy? Now bugger off."

Willie looked in amazement and relief at Dawie, and got quickly back into the car with Ruth.

"Who the hell was that?" she breathed.

"Never seen the man in my life," Willie laughed, "but he was a good one. God bless that man for saving my skin. These Dutchmen can be great fellows."

"Come on now, Willie," she said urgently, "please hurry. I'm worried, man, I feel sort of funny inside."

"What d'you mean?" His face whipped round to hers.

"Just go, go, please, now. I want to get home."

Twenty

HANNAH WOKE, CERTAIN THAT SHE'D HEARD TRUCKS IN THE yard, but that couldn't be right because the clock beside her bed said five o'clock and the lorries to take the men to the lands shouldn't be here for a couple of hours yet. It was dark, the birds were still quiet, she felt she must have dreamt it. But then she heard sounds again: wheels on gravel, an engine petering out. Voices. Many voices. By now, she was fully awake and she knew exactly what it was. She jumped out of bed, flung a jersey over her nightdress, and ran to Zelda's room.

Zelda was a heavy sleeper and she didn't wake when the door opened, nor did she have that mechanism that sprang into action when someone approached her in a darkened room. Hannah had to shake her a couple of times before she would wake up.

Zelda looked vacantly at her for a moment, then sat up very fast when she saw how agitated Hannah was. "What's up?"

"There are lorries in the yard."

"What lorries? What time is it?" She was fuddled and impatient.

"Five. And these aren't our lorries."

Zelda swore softly. "It's him, isn't it?" she breathed. "He's making one of his dawn raids, little bastard." She got quickly out of bed. "You keep out of this, I'm going to really sort him out this time. Stay inside."

"Okay. But, Zelda, you be very careful with him, I don't want you arrested."

"Me?" She laughed.

"Yes, you. And being a martyr isn't going to do any of us any good."

"I'm not the type for wings." She pushed back her thick braided hair and pulled her boots out from under the bed.

"Zelda, please. I'm asking you not to encourage any violence when it comes to it. Please, now."

"D'you think I'm that dumb? We haven't exactly got an armory out back, and we all know he's just looking for an excuse. Stick a bullet in me and the whole district would probably club together to buy him a medal."

"Well, you know what I mean. I know they've all decided to refuse, but— Oh, I don't know." She pushed back her hair in confusion.

Zelda looked at her with a determined and intoxicated glare. "Look, I promised I'd help them all I could. If I don't, they haven't a chance."

"Ja, I know, but you just have to watch your motives."

Zelda stopped in her dressing, looked startled, and said, "Well, this is no time for a philosophical discussion of my motives," and made for the door. Then she turned back. "What are you going to do? Say he decided to search the house?"

"I won't be here. I'm going to get my mother."

"Your *mother?*" Zelda was taken aback, as if she'd never considered the possibility of Hannah having a mother.

"Yes, from the village."

"So that's who you sneak off to see?"

"I don't sneak off, but yes, I go to see her."

"How will you get there?"

"I'll take the blue van." They were both talking rapidly now. "If they start clearing out today, they'll get the men, then go and clear the village. I can't have her taken somewhere where I can't find her."

"You'll bring her here, then?"

"Yes."

"Fine. I'll see you later then."

When Zelda opened the back door, she could see a whole fleet of open trucks with their headlights on. There was something very sinister about the way they stood there, flanked by four army vehicles. The yard was filled with police, armed and waiting. They wandered around as if they owned the place.

"Where's van Reenen?" she demanded of a youth lounging against a lorry.

The boy looked at her disdainfully and pointed toward the quarters behind the storerooms. By the time she got to the men's quarters, she could see them all standing outside. They stood quite still as the last of the laborers were rounded up. Those who lived with their families were separated from them and told to join the other men; the women and children huddled together.

Van Reenen stood with his colored assistant. The two of them were watching the proceedings without saying a word.

"What the hell d'you think you're doing on my land?" Zelda roared.

"We want the men out of here by sunup." He was cool, unperturbed by it all.

"You have no right to march onto my land in the middle of the night."

"You were thinking of having me arrested?" he sneered, giving an intimate little smile to his flunky. He turned back to her, put his hand out toward the policeman, who took a folded piece of paper from his breast pocket and handed it to van Reenen, who handed it to Zelda.

"The law, you see, is the law, and can't be avoided forever."

"I would prefer if you spoke English. I don't understand much of your dialect." She was frowning at the papers. Then she handed them back to him with no flutter of interest.

She looked over at her men, who had worked the land for so many years, and she felt their listlessness, their apathy and fear. Crouching at the door were the little children. She was shocked to see the same emotions reflected in their faces: resignation and defeat in those who had barely begun to live their lives. Their mothers stood with them, silent, but somehow not as passive as they appeared. She remembered how in her childhood these people had been vibrant and happy. How on church days they would dress up in their Sunday best: little girls in frilly nylon dresses and white socks, their hair in tight pigtails, small boys in white shirts and dark trousers, their hair oiled and parted on one side, their faces round and shiny. They would walk down to the church beyond the bluegum trees, and later, when she was having her breakfast, she would hear their voices rise up and make the morning wonderful.

"Van Reenen" she said steadily, no trace of emotion visible, "my people have decided to disobey your order and stay. They don't want to go to your camp."

"They can't remain on your property. It's against the law," he said patiently. "No blacks on white property."

"Precisely. We are prepared to break the law."

Looking at her face, he couldn't tell what prompted her. Was it a refusal to be ordered about, a personal desire to thwart a man she despised, a will to manipulate the lives of her workers, or maybe even something less selfish? "We?" he asked icily, "who's we?"

"The men, and me. We've agreed on it."

He smiled confidently and turned to say something to the officer beside him; there was something both intimate and contemptuous in the way he did it. Then he stood forward and ordered the men to get onto the lorries around front. Zelda could see Manty in the center talking quietly to the others.

"Hold on a minute," van Reenen said. "Have you all given up your papers? Not the passes. I mean the new papers. We have to have the new papers. Okay?"

There was a silence and then Manty told a few men to do as they were asked. On the outskirts of the crowd some of the men began to grumble and move away from the walls behind them, causing a stir and a tension in the air which the police responded to immediately by closing ranks. Slowly the last of the papers were gathered up. Then the men stood quite still. Van Reenen stepped forward and ordered them to get on the lorries—when they got to camp they would get their papers back. The police had moved back again. The silence was extraordinary in its quality of strength and resolve. Zelda stood watching them, her face impossible to decipher.

Then one of the women began to wail softly, and the sound had a curious, unsettling effect on all the men. Their attention was broken; their trance, which had united them, seemed to shift.

It was as if they no longer felt as one—individual reactions, desires, fears, and intentions began to decimate their solidarity. They were restless, becoming uncertain. Zelda went forward quickly and stood with them, talking to them lightly; it was as if she sensed a breaking up of resolve and must somehow physically stop it.

Van Reenen saw his chance. The way he seized it surprised Zelda, because it was subtle. She watched, dismayed and afraid, as he said, agreeable, fairly, as one man to the next: "Come on, boys, let's have no trouble, hey? Nobody wants that. Just come with us up to the camp quietly now and we'll fix you up good. No troubles. Things are good there—good food, beer. Later on, the buses will come and take you to work. We'll give you your papers back and everything will be just fine. We'll fix up your families in nice houses where you can visit. Okay? What more can I say? You must just come and see for yourselves. Then if you've got a problem, we'll sort it out."

Zelda could feel her will pitted against his. Her men looked over at her, then at him, then at neither of them. They were shuffling about. Their earlier stillness, which had seemed so im-placable, had now been replaced by an aggressive confusion. A child cried.

Van Reenen began to speak again, in the same reasonable tone. "I don't have to tell you what will happen if you refuse. After me comes the army. They're not going to mess around with you people. They'll force you or they'll shoot you. So you have a choice. Come quietly now, or go later and there'll be reprisals. Which is it now?"

The crowd moved forward a bit. The sun just begun to rise and they no longer felt cold. They no longer looked at Zelda, nor at the police, but only at one another. They understood one another, they were united again, but in their own way, quite separately from Zelda and her desires. She felt it, she felt them move away.

Van Reenen had lost his composure a little, he didn't know how it would go. No one was paying him any attention anymore. Then he saw one of the men move forward with determination, turn, and begin to walk in the direction of the lorries. A thin trickle of men began to follow him, then more and more. A solid group remained, Manty and Boykie at their center. Then the edges of this group broke up and followed the others slowly. The flow began to speed up, the little group still close to the storeroom walls diminishing until perhaps only a dozen remained.

Zelda's face was white, the skin stiff-looking. Van Reenen walked up to her and said, in English. "You think that I like to do this sort of thing, Miss de Valera? I'm a policeman, I'm degraded by having to implement political policies. It's not good for the police. But we have no choice."

"Ja, I do think you like it," she said.

"Well, you're wrong there. It's not my job, herding blacks about. It makes life difficult. There are too many laws, too many bleddy amendments to laws. A man can choose what he wants to enforce. That's why there's so much corruption."

"Spare me your conscience." She barely heard him because her attention followed her men as they walked away in silence.

"You see there"—he pointed at her angrily—"That's the whole problem with this country now. No one will listen to anyone else. The army's in charge of internal security. We're all fighting each other, getting nowhere."

"They are not my laws, van Reenen."

"That's what I'm telling you—they're not mine either, man. Half these ruddy laws were invented by the British, long before the Nats even took over."

"Let's not attempt a political discussion when people are being forced out of their homes, okay?" she snapped.

"Forced? I don't see anyone being forced? I know you'd like to think of me as a Nazi, but I care for these people too, you know. I'm only doing what's best."

"Ja, ja," she said wearily. "And they're only doing what they can't avoid any longer, so where does it get us?"

She strode off, back to the house. Manty walked quickly up and began to say to her, "I must go too, we must stay together. Since this is what they want, I must go."

He looked as helpless and frustrated as she felt. She nodded.

"Tomorrow we will come back," he said, touching her arm,

wanting to reassure her. "Tomorrow we will come and work just like before." He peered anxiously into her face. "You okay, Zelda?"

She nodded again, like someone in shock, not really aware of her surroundings. She could not even begin to think what she would do if they were not allowed to come back.

Twenty-One

A FEW WEEKS PASSED. ALTHOUGH THINGS SEEMED TO GO ON much the same, in reality everything was different. So Mr. Mantagisa thought as he drove the tractor down the side of the soya field toward her. It was nothing you could point to, it was something you just knew. Zelda sat under the acacia tree with her knees drawn up, her hand protecting her eyes from the glare, and she looked as she always had. But all the same the change had broken her, they all knew it, and there were some who took advantage of it. Life could change its shape, reorganize itself, but some people could not; she was one of them. He knew that she missed the men and their families. He, too, felt a great difference. There was an empty, lonely feeling to the place. No chickens scratched about in the dirt at the back, the women didn't sit under the trees with their pots, no children were running about or sneaking up to the back door to ask Ilsa for sweets. It was a sad thing and he felt for her, he felt for all of them; their old life had gone away for good.

He went to sit down beside her and she smiled up at him. Still he felt it, he could not shake the feeling: she had hardened to them. She felt their betrayal. Suspicion had entered her mind.

"How goes it?" she asked.

"Not so bad, we will finish it by the end of the week, but the blade on the machine is gone."

"Oh." Her hand went back to her eyes. "Can it be fixed?"

"No, we must get a new one."

They both knew they could not. The factory that made the parts had closed two months ago when the labor force had walked out.

What about that place in Konigstad. There's a good mechanic there. Couldn't he fix it?"

"That boy, he was shot the week before last in Port Elizabeth."

"How?" she asked with a shock. He'd only been about eighteen.

He shrugged. "He was with that crowd that took over the white hospital. The police got a few of them and beat them to death."

She shuddered. All the white hospitals were like fortresses now, shopping centers and white suburbs guarded and fortified against attack.

She looked at him; it swept over them both, the impossibility of things getting any better. They did not like to talk about it, and it seemed, as time passed, that there were more things that were difficult to talk about.

She did not like to ask him about the place where they now lived: the labor camp with its hostels. She had driven past it to see. It was a raw, ugly place, with no shebeens, just brick buildings in long lines. A place to sleep when the work was done, that's all. But the work was done just as efficiently as van Reenen had predicted: the men came in on buses and walked the last miles to the farm while the rest went on to the munitions factory. They worked just as hard, but it didn't feel like the same work, for the same end—an effort in which they all shared. They were now working for, rather than with, her. Their houses and plots of land, which had belonged to them and been worked to provide food, now lay open and unused, a reminder of better days. So much so that Zelda considered pulling them all down, but couldn't do it: it would seem like yet another capitulation.

Now, watching them work, Zelda saw that there was something automatic about it—the picks and spades hit the ground with the same strength, but without intensity or enjoyment, as if some muscle had gone slack. They took less interest in the animals, and when she spoke to her men they seemed to look away. They were disheartened and they blamed her for it.

"Manty," she said quietly, "we should be thinking of getting the sheep back for the show."

"If there is one," he said.

She felt frustrated, even angry. It was as if he was no longer interested. He never asked about the decisions and economics of the farm. Things were not going well. She wanted his help, as in the old days, but couldn't ask for it.

Now he turned to her and began to speak. He rubbed his hands together as he did when things had gone wrong and he felt to blame. "Zelda, there is a hard thing I must say."

"Then just say it, Manty."

It was not his way to come out directly with things, and he was a little insulted that she pushed him. She knew his ways, that he liked to present it slowly, spelling out the pros and cons. It was rude not to do so, as it was rude of her to be impatient with him.

"It's the men. They are making decisions and it's for me to tell you them."

She didn't want to hear it. She had a great longing for her old problems to return: that so-and-so had been fighting or that someone wanted more land or a better piece, that a wife had run off and there was trouble, that a child needed hospital treatment and could she arrange it. Now what he had to say would be none of these.

Painstakingly, he spelt it out for her and she listened, not hurrying him, not looking at him, just passive and resigned. "The men, one hundred and six of them, have decided that they will go at the end of the week."

She said nothing, so he felt obliged to explain. "It's not that they are unhappy with the extra wages, it is just that they know their families at the village will be sent away to the Ciskei very soon. There is no place for them here, no reason to stay."

"Where will they go? To the arms factory?"

"Oh no," he said with scorn, "no, it is not that. They would not do such a thing. No, they are going to join the men in the mountains."

Then she looked at him in the face, long and steadily. "They know what this means?"

"They know," he nodded slowly, sweat standing out in drops on his forehead.

"And you, Manty, will you go too?"

"I will."

"And what about your wife? Who will look after her?"

"She is coming with me. We have no children so the risk is not so bad. Also, if one is shot, we must both be together," he said simply. "It is better that way."

She got up slowly and brushed the dust off her legs.

"Many, many farms," he said, as if in justification, because he felt so bad leaving her like this, "many have had to close because the people have gone."

She gave an ironic laugh. "With no workers, there's nothing."

"That is so," he said, with no sense of triumph. "Slowly everything is breaking down and no one can stop it."

"A long, long time ago," she said softly, "my great-great-grandfather came to this part of South Africa because he said he could breathe here. It was so full of space that a man could do as he pleased and not be stopped. He built his farm, fenced it himself with his brothers, and slowly got more and more of the space that he wanted. He had got away from the British and was a free man at last."

"Ja," Manty said, standing beside her, watching as she did the men singing as they worked. "Ja, it always comes back to the same."

"I would prefer it," she said softly, "if they were to stop tonight, straightaway. I don't like things hanging over me. I will pay them, of course."

He nodded sadly and noticed that her eyes were very shiny. "I will get it done," he said.

Now, as she turned to walk away, he saw that her back jerked involuntarily and sobs shook her so that he felt as if that tall, strong body had grown small and weak. He watched her for a moment in awe, then he walked to her, pulled her against him with one movement, and kept her so until she had grown still.

Twenty-Two

HANNAH WAS IN THE KITCHEN SCRUBBING THE LONG WHITE shelves that lined the walls upon which the plates stood. Miriam had offered to help, but it was the time, after lunch, when the maids went to rest at home. It was oppressively hot. Two o'clock. The blinds were drawn against the glare, but she could almost see the hard shimmer on the thorn trees beyond the garden and the white reflection on the stones and caked earth. There had been not a single cloud for days.

Her sleeves were rolled up above her elbows, and below them her strong arms pulsed with the effort of scrubbing and wiping down the painted wood. The quiet was oppressive and the sudden quarterly chime of the clock unnaturally loud. Sometimes she would look up and think, and then smile, and if anyone had walked past the window they could be forgiven for thinking that she spoke to someone.

It felt to her like the child's days when she had spent hours building a house out of stones on a swept patch of yard outside the kraal. There was the same satisfaction and sense of expectancy: someone would come and inhabit the house she was making; soon she would fill it with her precious treasures. As a child, no one had come to sit in her house outside the kraal, and later it was not a game that she could play with Zelda and Dawie because Zelda refused to play it. It was odd to feel the same emotions today.

The sense of expectancy had been going on for days. Zelda was quiet and on edge; work on the farm went on as best it could, but things were becoming very simple: only what had to be done was done. Zelda brooded. They both watched the village, waiting for the trucks to come, but life over the blue koppies remained miraculously intact. And so the days passed, the feeling of anticipation becoming at times almost unbearable. Dawie was never mentioned, yet each was so obsessed by his possible arrival that it felt as if he, or his ghost, stalked the corridors and watched their every move.

Hannah stopped and wiped the drops of sweat off her forehead, then put the plates back carefully, one by one. When she looked around the kitchen, she felt she saw it through someone else's eyes. She was tired, and went to sit in the chair by the window and saw the dust lying thick on the window sill. She took her cloth and cleaned it, knowing that in a short while it would be back.

Resting there in the chair, she almost fell asleep, but kept jerking her head upright each time it fell. A wood pigeon called sleepily from the peach trees, but there was no reply. She could hear one of the dogs scratching about the back door. A small lizard shot up the wall and startled her. Then the silence rose up again and became one with the heat, and she dropped off to sleep.

She was wakened by loud barking out in the yard. The dogs didn't bark in that shrill way when Zelda came home. Then she heard footsteps running across the yard and, as she got out of her chair, the door swung open and Willie stood there, breathing so hard that he was unable to speak.

"Calm down, Willie. What is it?"

He gave up his attempt at an explanation and grabbed her hand instead, pulling her out toward the kitchen door and through it into the afternoon light.

Out in the yard the heat was suffocating. Hannah could feel it scald her arms and there was a high sound, like cicadas singing, in her head. Willie rushed her over to an old car that seemed to stand like a whipped and exhausted mule under the trees. When they neared the car, Hannah forgot the heat completely and ran very fast to the front seat, where Ruth lay slumped forward, absolutely still.

"Ruthie?" She shook the girl and then moved back in alarm as

Ruth looked up from a tangle of dirty, damp hair, her face dark from the sun, her lips cracked and her eyes bloodshot with fatigue and pain. She toppled to one side, into Hannah's lap almost, and began to cry loudly.

Putting her hands to her belly, she said quickly, "The contractions started, ages ago they started. I can't bear them anymore." And she clawed at the dress across her stomach as if to pull it off.

"Willie, help me" Hannah ordered, putting her arms under Ruth and lifting her. "Quick, put your arms round her here. Ja, that's right. Now lift."

She could see that he barely had the strength, but he did so, and between the two of them they managed to half carry, half drag Ruth across the yard from the trees to the back door.

The minute she was in the kitchen, Ruth doubled up and let out a loud scream. Hannah gripped Ruth's arms and had to resist crying out herself as the girl's fingers dug deep into her arm. Then Ruth relaxed, her body flopping forward so that she had to be supported again.

"Willie, how long has it been going on?"

"Since early last night," he said. "But then it stopped for a bit. But in the last hours, bad, very bad."

"We'll take her to my room. How often do they come?"

Willie looked dazed. "Every ten minutes, something like that. One is bad, then the next not so bad. I didn't stop, just drove, drove, drove like a madman."

He let go of Ruth and ran to the sink, where he was sick. When he straightened up, his body was shaking. Hannah waited. He turned, they looked at one another, and then slowly he walked back to Ruth and they led her out of the kitchen and down the corridor.

"Ag, Willie, I'm so sorry, so sorry. Look what I've done."

Her head lay against his shoulder and he hushed her. "Come on now, let's get to the bed before another comes. Soon it'll be over, my friend, very soon."

Hannah grasped her firmly and led her the last distance to the bed, where they let her sink down onto the cover. Hannah lifted her legs up onto the bed.

"Willie, I'm sorry to ask you when you're so tired, but can you go and get Miriam? They're not here anymore, you'll find her at the village. I'll explain later. Things have changed, that's all. Your ma is fine, though, don't worry. Just hurry. I don't know"— she whispered the last bit—"I don't quite know how to manage without her. Tell her to come right away. Take the blue van; the keys are on the kitchen table."

He ran.

Ruth turned on her side and began to moan, "It's starting again. Oh bloody hell, it's starting again."

"Of course it is," Hannah said briskly, "and now we must start to count the minutes in between, to see how long you've got. Soon it'll be over, so relax, breathe. Stop that, just relax. Okay?"

When it had passed, Hannah pushed back the girl's hair and said reassuringly, "You'll be all right, I promise, you haven't got much more to go. And you're home. It'll all be fine now, you'll see. Just try to be brave a bit longer."

Ruth looked around her with a dazed look, then she stared at Hannah and tears began to run down her cheeks. "I'm sorry," she whispered, "that I didn't tell you. I wanted to, so many times, I wanted to—"

Hannah stroked her hand. "I know. Forget about that. Just remember that it's nearly over. Miriam will be here soon. She's had so many babies she'll know just what to do, so don't worry now, hey?"

Another spasm came and Hannah reckoned them to be coming every seven minutes or so. Ruth was covered in sweat and there was blood on the coverlet, more than she felt there should have been. She wouldn't let her mind dwell on it, and concentrated on getting towels from the cupboard, wiping Ruth's face, giving her little sips of water, holding her hands and talking about as little as she could.

Willie returned with Miriam, who sat down beside the bed and began to laugh and talk softly to Ruth. "You come back to give us a big fright, eh? You kept that baby well hidden, nothing showing all those months. Well, I was like that as a young girl. After the first baby, then you swell up like a watermelon, quick-quick."

Her easy manner and calmness relaxed them all, apart from

Willie, who stood in the doorway, his face gray with exhaustion, his eyes like red beams watching Ruth.

"You don't stand there like that." Miriam said briskly. "Go into the kitchen and make the water hot, then come back again."

Ruth began to scream like someone demented. "I won't have it here, I won't. I want to go to hospital, I want a doctor and the right bed. I want the pain taken away, now, now." Her body contorted.

Miriam leaned close to her and said, "Scream, scream all you like, little missy. It's close now, it's coming. You scream plenty."

Hannah was shaking, trying very hard not to show how frightened she was. The best way was to keep busy. She pulled Ruth up in the bed and adjusted the pillows behind her. "Come on, let's sit you up a bit, and then you can lean forward and push with your body."

"No" Ruth wailed weakly, "I can't, I just can't. . . ."

"You want it over, don't you? Now try, for heaven's sake. Try."

"Now, close your eyes," Miriam said. "Close them and rest till the next pain is coming."

When the next contraction came, Ruth bit into Hannah's wrist, leaving blood.

"Now the head is coming. It's there!" Miriam said with excitement and pleasure. "So the next time you push like bloody crazy and the pain's finished, okay? Now wait, you feel it coming, hold, hold me tightly and push."

Ruth screamed one long, splitting shriek as a dark-haired head pushed through.

"Now!" the woman urged. "One more time to get the body out—slow . . . slow now, not so hard, or you will hurt later."

A little spilled body lay there, quiet in its pool of water and blood, hands and feet open, as if appealing to them—a mouth beginning to part and cry. The women breathed out, Miriam began to laugh and then stopped and then laughed again, a strange bewildered sound. Hannah began to cry. No one reached to take the child.

Twenty-Three

RUTH LAY IN BED IN A DARKENED ROOM; THE SUN WAS SET-
ting on the far side of the house; the fan whirred above her head.

Hannah came into the room and tiptoed across to the bed.
Ruth's eyes were firmly closed although she wasn't asleep. When
Hannah bent to put the small white bundle in the empty space
next to Ruth, the girl came violently to life.

"Take it away, it's not mine. Take it away!"

The infant lay very still against Hannah. She shielded it from
its mother's rejection and walked slowly over to the chair, where
she sat.

Ruth had turned her back and was quiet again. It was a relief
after the hysterics. Hannah knew she shouldn't have tried to make
her look at the child—she needed time, she needed a lot of time.
Now, if she would sleep, if she would only sleep.

But the next instant, Ruth sat bolt upright, with her eyes still
clenched, and hissed in a low, hateful voice: "Get it out of here,
take it away! It's not mine. I hate it. Get rid of it, just get it out of
here!"

Hannah, very pale, feeling the pain spread all through her body,
took the baby from the room and into the kitchen. She handed it
to Miriam, who looked at it sadly and stroked the little cheek.

Willie was sitting at the table, his head slumped onto the table,
asleep. He woke as if feverish, and looked around him. When he
saw Hannah, he said quietly, "The child is not mine. It was before

she came to me. She will not say who." Then it was as if he would weep.

Miriam walked over to the stove, hushing the baby, which had begun to cry. She sat down and held it close to her, solemn and protective.

Hannah said, "I know it isn't your child."

"Who then can be the father?" Miriam asked. "Who did this thing?"

"It doesn't matter," Hannah said wearily, "it doesn't matter."

"I don't understand this," Miriam said, looking down at the little face.

Hannah could hear Ruth calling frantically for her, but she didn't want to go.

"Has she slept at all?" Willie asked.

"I've got nothing to give her." She left the kitchen and went slowly back to the bedroom.

Ruth's face was blotchy and red and it stared accusingly at Hannah. "Why didn't you tell me?" she screamed out. "Why?"

Hannah went very pale; so it was over at last. She moved her hands helplessly. "I left it too long," she said. "It became impossible. I wanted to save you from it."

"I didn't sleep with a kaffir," Ruth said savagely, "so it doesn't take much to work it out, does it? *Does* it?"

Hannah said nothing.

"So it means that my father was a kaffir, doesn't it? That's what it means." She began to shake. "And that means—that means that I'm black, I'm *black*," her voice shuddered. "I'm *black*! Aren't I? Tell me, tell me now."

Hannah moved the chair nearer to the bed. She knew that she must pick the words with the care and precision of a hand reaching into broken glass. "Your father was not black," she said. "Your father is Zelda's brother, Dawie. And I, of course, am your mother."

How simply the words came now.

"You?"

Hannah nodded.

"So then, you could have told me—years"—she screamed out the word—"*Years* ago!"

"Yes."

"Well, why didn't you? Why the bloody hell didn't you?" Her anger faltered. "I asked and asked and asked. I asked *you*."

"I was afraid, I didn't know how you'd take it."

"But you couldn't hide it forever."

"I thought I could." Her head dropped. "I wanted to. I didn't want you to live as I did, belonging nowhere. I wanted"—she was pleading now—"I wanted you to be white." She whispered, "You *were* white, you were perfect, you were white and perfect." She looked up. "You still are."

"No," the girl yelled, "I'm not. I'm a colored girl like you and I have a black baby. That's the truth, that's the truth, admit it now."

"You can be what you like," Hannah said desperately.

"No," the girl said scornfully. "That was your mistake. You can only be what you are—what you really are."

And with this she was calm. Like an overwound toy, she came to a stop.

Hannah went on talking quietly. "You were so perfect," she breathed, "just that little birthmark. And at first you could barely see it. At the beginning, I thought your skin would darken, the way your baby's did. But it didn't. Then I thought your second hair would come and be crinkled, but it stayed smooth. Every day I waited for things to change, and they didn't. So I thought God had spared you. I thought He'd forgiven me by sparing you. So I let it be. I thought I could save you if I kept you away from everyone, here. I thought you'd be safe if we never went to live in the city, if no one knew that I was your mother, if you never knew who you really were."

"And if I wanted to marry?" the girl asked dully, "would you have told me then?"

"I don't know. I made a bargain with God. I thought . . . ." Ruth couldn't bear to look at her. "I thought if I denied myself all that I wanted, if I never complained, never did wrong, if I stayed here in isolation, never married or took a lover, never tried to see Dawie, refused to go with him when he came back"—her voice was fading—"I thought that if I did all these things and more, that He would always spare you."

Hannah's head fell forward but she wasn't crying—because that, too, was something she had always denied herself.

Slowly, Ruth turned her face toward Hannah, looked at her calmly and said, "I only wanted to know, that's all, to be told the truth. All my life I sensed that something was wrong, that there was something bad about my parents." She watched as Hannah flinched. "But I never thought this, I just never thought it. I thought everything else—all sorts of things, awful things. I thought the worst things."

"Is anything worse than this?"

"Oh ja," Ruth lifted her head, "there's worse. The worst is to have no father, to have no mother, all your life."

Hannah's head fell forward and she began to cry. She cried with her face in her hands and her body quite rigid. Her daughter watched her. Then slowly and deliberately, Ruth turned her back, pushed her face into the pillows, and closed her eyes tightly.

"You buried me alive," she said.

Twenty-Four

DAWIE DROVE TO THE OLD FARM, ONLY STOPPING ONCE. HE'D asked at the Post Office to find out where the present owner, van Niekerk, lived. The old boy was relieved to get rid of it—spooks, he said, full of spooks, no one had been near it for years.

Now it was his. He felt an extraordinary sense of relief. He wanted the walls pulled down quickly, and all the rubble removed, as soon as it could be arranged. The house must be rebuilt, be made beautiful again—not a shrine to the past but a home for the future.

When he reached the farm, all that was left of it was the gaunt ribs of the old farmhouse and the slightly more intact out-buildings. Where the sheep couldn't reach, the veld grass had grown high among the broken walls. They were still black, and when the wind blew he seemed to smell those fumes again, saw Zelda coughing and retching again, trying to run into the burning building. Her face came back to him, distraught and screaming as she ran back and forth, crying out, "The smell, the smell. I can't bear the smell!" And Hannah, dragging her away to sit near the water.

He sat down on a pile of bricks, near where the cellar had once been—the cellar where his mother kept her gin, where all the big jars of peaches and apricots were stored and which they'd raided as children. Dislodging a stone with his foot, he found, lying there on the ground, a ring—a gold ring, two hands with fingers interlocking. He picked it up, his face very pale. It was the Australian's ring: Zelda's lover's ring. Here it lay, where his body must have lain when the fire had started so mysteriously. "The smell"—oh my God, the smell: that's what she'd meant!

He sat there a long time. Then he drove up into the mountains. Here it was cool and the air in the early morning had an astringent quality. He looked down, down, over the austere country to the low hills beyond. Nothing had touched it yet. Could it, too, end up like the shattered cities, the corpse-strewn roads? Maybe he was looking at it for the last time.

Earlier he had gone back to all the old haunts he'd known intimately as a boy: sat under the willows by the dam, walked the overgrown paths where he had played and whispered with Mannah, found an old camp of theirs hidden in the bush.

This was the only place in the world where he felt this sense of belonging. It was vast beyond the reach of the imagination, and so still—not even the shadow of a cloud to relieve the glare. On the rocky mountains, the baboons sat with their young, surveying the sheep as they moved slowly along the paths in the long grass, the goats on the flat plains moving restlessly between the trees.

Across this emptiness, running over a nek and down into a low valley, wound the dusty white road. It made a turn to skirt the mealie fields and the sprawling white farms with their dams and their trees. It was the same as it had ever been. Inside those houses sat dour farmers with their heavy wives, leading lives shuttered and repetitive. Could it really change? Could it all be swept away? Would he live to see it gone?

But maybe it wouldn't happen? Maybe it could be stopped, even something done to make it right. As he continued to watch, the wide scope of the land returned his old sense of possibility. But he knew that what he had to do first was to get back to his first responsibility: Hannah. Deep in the bosom of this place, in a farm he'd seen only once, Hannah was waiting.

SHE WAS SITTING QUIETLY BY THE STOVE. SHE HELD THE BOY in her arms. He slept as deeply as his mother did. She stared hard into his face, at the widely spaced eyes, the button nose, the beautifully etched mouth. He was lovely; she felt she knew his nature, the kind of child he would be. And then, with a burst of happiness, she thought: he can be whatever he wishes. He's free, or very soon will be. Nothing can stop him. He was peaceful, as if he knew his timing was right: he had entered the world at the right moment. She held him closer. The house was quiet. She was tired, drained. Once or twice she looked into the little face and whispered "Just hold on, a little longer. Then it will all be ready for you." Then her eyes filled and tears ran slowly down her cheeks.

SHE REMEMBERED IT. HOW SHE HAD CREPT AWAY WITH HER pain, as a young girl no older than Ruth; crept into the bush in the middle of the night and knelt on the ground as she had seen her own mother do when her children came. She was not afraid, because that would not help anything. The pain gripped her until her body was numb with it. When at last she heard the cry, she wanted to laugh. It was such a mighty cry—a cry of triumph: the shout of a human being determined to be born, to be heard, to enter the earth from the sea and survive there.

She had hidden in the bush for two long days, rocking the child. She had nowhere to go, no one to help her. She hid herself, she hid the child. She had no milk, nothing to give it. Soon she began to feel sick and feverish, her mind playing with her, sending her sometimes to the big house, sometimes to the kraal.

Later, the child weak and unwilling to suck, her own body hot and faint, she walked to the dam and sat under the willows with the small bundle held close to her. Moonlight shone on the water and the frogs croaked; they filled her with sadness because she knew they were mating. Her head was light, and once, seeing so much blood, she put the child down and went to the bushes and vomited. When she returned, the child was sleeping so soundly that she imagined for a moment it was dead.

"If the child is dead," she whispered to the water, "she won't suffer. No one will hurt her. If she's dead, I will always know where she is. God will take her and keep her for me."

A picture she'd once seen in a magazine came back to her: a

photograph of an English garden, hollyhocks and roses, ivy scrambling up the walls, green grass like a pasture, and a cradle basking in sunlight. Surely this was heaven? And surely this was where her baby would go? She held the tiny body against her cheek, against her throat, and then moved it down to her arm. She was radiant, preparing to give what she loved best to God.

How long did she crouch there beside the dark water, dreaming of heaven? She thought, in her delirium, that Dawie stood with his hand upon her shoulder and urged her on. Dawie, so far away at college, ignorant of his fatherhood. As he must always be, she vowed; and, stooping to the water, she placed the baby in it, pushed its head down under the water and held it there. The tiny face looked up as though blinded and still she held it there. Until an arm from behind yanked violently at her, pulling her backward until she fell.

Later, they walked together down the road; it was white, and shone like satin in the moonlight. The stars seemed to be watching them as they went on in silence to the farm. Zelda was carrying the child.

Twenty-Five

NEVER HAD A DAY BEEN SO LONG; LOOKING AT THE GLEAMING
kitchen shelves, Hannah found it hard to believe that she'd cleaned
them that same morning. It was late, very late for Zelda not to
be home, but it felt like a blessing. Hannah dreaded her arrival,
having no resources left for a scene. She had even considered hiding the baby, but knew, this time, that she couldn't. Then the
phone rang. She let it ring, and finally went reluctantly to answer
it.

It was Zelda. She was ringing to say that she wouldn't be coming home that night.

Hannah forced herself to sound quite normal—Zelda would
swoop like a harpie on any tremor of fear or relief or hesitation.

But Zelda detected nothing: her spirits were low. She'd gone out
early that morning to recruit men from the other farm. Even with
very high unemployment, it was more difficult than she'd antici-
pated. Everything was so uncertain. People came and went; when
they were hungry they came, when they got paid they went. That's
the way it was now, and she knew she had to accept it. She was
going to try again in the morning.

Knowing she wasn't coming back, Hannah felt almost light-
hearted. She went to the cupboards and got out the softest sheets
and some old muslin squares that had lasted from Ruth's baby-
hood. There was so much to do. She had been sitting, for hours,
like a person marooned, but now she must get busy. She bathed

the baby in the kitchen sink. One of the maids brought her an orange box to turn into a crib, and between the two of them they found enough ribbon and quilting to bed it out.

Hannah was excited by the preparations. She hadn't been able to do these things when her own child was born and she made up for it by showering all her attention and time on Ruth's.

Ruth slept for hours and hours without once moving. Her face was so pale that the birthmark stood out dark and prominent. It reminded Hannah how, at Ruth's birth, it had been small as the bruise from a needle, and how she had watched it as obsessively as, later, Ruth came to do.

But now as the orange box was padded out—every rough plank bandaged with muslin, the sheets hemmed, the blankets cut into squares—at last Hannah's emotions began to stabilize: joy and grief settled. It would be all right, they could make it so. Ruth would get better, she would change toward the baby. She had always loved children. She needed to be nursed and cosseted; she must be put before all other considerations so that she could adjust and get better. So Hannah thought as she tucked the baby into its crib beside her bed. She would guard it with the same devotion that Willie had shown, returning every hour to sit beside Ruth's bed in case she woke up.

In the morning, when she went in to see Ruth, she found Willie sitting in the chair beside her bed, fast asleep, his head on the covers. He was holding Ruth's hand and neither stirred as she entered the room and stood there watching them. Ruth turned her face into the pillow slightly, and from that angle she wore her father's chin.

In that moment all Dawie's strength and sweetness returned to Hannah in a way she had never allowed before. It was as if for the first time she had him: he was her husband and this was their child.

It was still very early and the air smelled good; the doves were cooing in the trees and the maids had arrived. They stood about the kitchen, clucking with pleasure at the sight of the small baby: brown eyes wide and alert, skin beginning to unfold from its wrinkles, his mouth beginning to explore the immensity of his hand. They were looking for a woman to feed it.

Miriam said, "What will he be called, then?"

"His mother will have to decide," Hannah said.

It was touching, almost bewildering to her, to see their easy acceptance of this child. He was a new life, a warrior born. They greeted him with songs, clapping their hands together; they brought beads and fruit, eggs for Ruth, and little clothes for her baby. He was a child—no more, no less.

As the morning got hotter, Ruth woke, ate a little, but did not ask for her child. She was listless, but not desolate. Hannah sat beside her bed, sewing, waiting to see if she would talk at all.

Finally, pulling at the hem of the sheet, Ruth asked, "What will become of me now? What happens when Zelda comes back?"

"Don't worry about that—and don't worry about the baby."

Ruth turned her head away. "We're taking care of him and he's fine, taking some milk," Hannah said, hearing the glow in her voice.

"Who's feeding it?"

"Joseph's wife."

"Great—just like a proper piccanin."

Hannah smiled and said lightly, "He's not black you know, more the color of sand."

"Darker than you," Ruth said in a level voice.

"Yes," Hannah said calmly, "darker than me; sometimes it happens like that."

"I don't want to talk about it, I don't want to see it again."

"That's all right."

"No"—her head swung round—"you don't get it. I mean never, I never want it. I *never* want to see it again." Her jaw was stiff and her mouth did not tremble.

"That's all right," Hannah repeated.

Suddenly, Ruth sat bolt upright, her eyes wide with fear. "What was that?" she said.

"What?"

"That," she snapped. "It sounded like Zelda's jeep." She was a frightened child again, all her steeliness gone.

Hannah leaned forward and restrained her. "Look, don't worry. It'll be all right, I promise. Just let me talk to her. She's not an ogre, you know."

"I want to go. I've got to get away from here." Ruth kicked off the covers.

"*Ruth!*"

Hannah's voice ordered in such a way that the girl looked up, startled. She was going to say something unpleasant, but stopped.

"I want you to stay in this room and rest. I'm going to speak to Zelda, and if there's any trouble, any at all, we'll leave. Is that okay?"

Ruth nodded. "You've changed," she said. "Something's changed you."

"Yes," Hannah said.

In the kitchen, Zelda stood by the table. As she was about to yell for Hannah, Hannah walked in, her eyes darting to the place where the baby had been lying. She saw that it had vanished. She smiled to hear Miriam's clear voice singing a lullaby in the corridor.

"How did it go?" Hannah said, moving to the sink so that her face couldn't be scrutinized.

"Oh, not bad. But they'll be unreliable, none have worked for us before. They were surly too, knew I needed them more than they needed me."

"Oh, I don't know. They have to eat. We need each other."

"Is it as simple as that?" Zelda asked wearily.

"No. How many did you sign on?"

Hannah was listening with one tenth of her concentration, trying to work out some form of words, some way of saying it. But the child took his destiny into his own hands: he let out one loud yell.

"What the hell's that?" Zelda said.

"It's a baby."

"I can hear that. I'm not deficient. What's it dong here?" The sound of the crying was deeply disconcerting to her.

Hannah sat at the table, opposite Zelda, and said, "It's Ruth's baby. She came back last night. It was born soon after."

"Ruth's? What do you mean, Ruth's?" Her face twisted.

"I mean, it's Ruth's baby."

"But how did it happen?"

[219]

"The usual way, I imagine."

"Jesus, Hannah, I'm going to hit you one, sitting there like that!" Then her face changed. "Who's the father?"

"I'm not sure."

Zelda's face cleared with a sudden comprehension. "My God," she said breathlessly. "Where is it? I want to see it."

Hannah hated her. Hated her quite vehemently. "If you want to see it" she said furiously, "then I'll bring it to you. Wait here."

Miriam was trying to hush the child when Hannah came in. "He wants to eat," she whispered. "What could I do? Suddenly he screams." She handed him over reluctantly. "Will there be trouble now?" Her face was downcast.

"No," Hannah said firmly, "no trouble. You do your work. When will Angie come to feed him?"

"Now. She's coming any minute."

"I'll bring him back in a minute, then."

She walked back down the corridor like a woman embarking on a crusade.

Zelda was sitting with her hand over her mouth, looking down at the table. When Hannah entered, she looked up, feigning indifference, taken aback by Hannah's anger. Hannah walked up to her and held the baby so that it could be seen. It was quiet, watching Zelda, or so it seemed to Hannah.

No word from Zelda, just a blank wide stare. And then she looked away.

After a long silence, Hannah asked, "Well?"

Zelda looked at her, very long, very slowly. "We'll just have to get rid of it," she said.

Twenty-Six

RUTH STOOD IN THE DOORWAY, SHIVERING. THEN SHE YELLED out, "I heard that, you fucking bitch. Why don't you just kill off everything and everyone that doesn't turn out the way you want it, hey? Why don't you put a bullet through me, right now?" Her voice rose higher and louder. "You're mad, I'm telling you, you're sick in the head. You invent stories about my father—and he's your *brother*. You kick me out of the house with a pack of lies about where he is—you think you can get rid of my baby and that we're all going to stand back and let you. Well, fuck you, fuck you and all your revolting little plans. You're never going to do anything to me, or anything of mine, ever again, you hear?"

The baby began to wail; Miriam sped in like a shadow, took the child from Hannah, and went quickly out of the back door without looking at any of them.

Hannah took Ruth over to a chair and tried to calm her. The girl was red in the face and veins were pressing through the fine skin of her temples. Zelda stood impassive as a monument.

"This must stop," Hannah said. "We're not animals, we must just do what's right."

"Did *you*?" Zelda snapped, losing control. "Did *you* do what was right?" Her face murderous, she stormed out of the kitchen and into the yard.

"I wish she'd have an accident," Ruth said as the jeep revved up. "I wish she'd do us all a favor and die."

Once, Hannah thought sadly, once she saved your life. And once I saw her carry her dog for two miles when it had been hit by a car—a big dog, a big bloodied dog with its legs broken.

All day they waited for her to return and she didn't. All day the hours seemed more full of the menace of her absence. Ruth was sleeping again. The baby had been fed and it too slept on. Hannah felt that her nerves would give if she didn't shut out everything for a while. She tried to sleep in the late morning, but couldn't. She lay on her bed watching the sun make streaks on the floor through the closed shutters. Her ears were constantly alert, waiting for the sound of the jeep.

The afternoon drew on, the house closed in around her; the heat deadened her energy to think. She slept. When she woke, she wasn't sure that she had slept, except that her mouth was dry and her body damp with sweat from lying in one place on the sheet. Then she knew with a shock that there was someone in the house, in the kitchen. She could sense it more than hear it. She sat quite still and in a moment she heard footsteps coming down the corridor, footsteps slowing outside the room the baby was sleeping in.

She rushed to prevent Zelda from hurting the baby. She ran into the corridor and saw that it wasn't Zelda at all.

It was Dawie. She saw him standing there, like a stranger, nervous about entering someone else's house. That was the way he looked: apologetic and ill at ease.

Then he smiled. He walked slowly toward her, noticing the pale blue dress, crumpled from sleep, her long arms, the hair swept up with little strands falling over her forehead, the sleepiness in her face that now turned pink, that now smiled, then pulled back the smile, hesitated, as she moved toward him too, shyly, slowly, like an awkward child entering a room where the reception might be uncertain: that girl walking into the classroom and waiting for Meneer's reaction. Years swept away. He smiled again. She ran to him and he caught her.

Twenty-Seven

AT THE DOORWAY, WATCHING THEM, ZELDA FELT BEREFT, AN
appalling sense of her own loneliness swept over her. When she'd
seen the car, even before she noticed the Cape Town number plate,
she'd known he was there, in her house, wielding his power over
Hannah. Entering the house, just for a moment it had seemed like
returning home from school and finding he'd got there before
her, seen Hannah before she did: the same sense of disappointment. She was weakened. It occurred to her that she might lose
everything she held vital. It was possible; it had never seemed so
before.

It was their attitude that was so painful to her. Not that they
touched, not that. They sat close together on the old sofa under
the bookshelves in the dining room, their backs facing her. They
spoke quietly and earnestly, but their absorption was so complete
that they had not heard her and were still unaware of her presence.
They seemed, in this short space of time, to have joined forces
again. There was something inviolable about their two bodies,
the way their heads inclined toward each other. They were allies
against the world again. And she, as always, was excluded.

It had happened—and she smiled scornfully to think of it—so
much earlier than either of them realized. But she had known it,
from the minute it happened. That time, they had been building a
reservoir in the mud by the dam, their hands working so fast,
building up the banks, holding back the water, their heads touch-

ing as they spoke, Hannah laughing up at him and saying, "No, no. Not that way." And he, with that smile—his smile for Hannah, Hannah's smile—he had given way to her. "What are you doing?" she'd asked harshly. Hannah's face lifted as if drugged, her peaceful possession of him needing no reply. Dawie's head had not even raised. Hating them both, she'd wanted to kick the walls to pieces and laugh as the water rushed back and spoiled all their work.

Now Hannah's face dropped, as if what Dawie was saying was hard for her to hear. In the relaxation of the closeness between them, Zelda felt her own strength revive. Like a spider in another's web, she watched and waited for her moment. Like a little hard-baked girl, she stood outside her brother's door in the early morning and heard him tell Hannah his dreams—things he never told *her*. She had stored all these treacheries, waiting for a time to get even, to claim what was hers.

Look at Hannah now, how she agitated her fingers. It was almost as if she was crying, but Hannah did not cry. Yet all the same, she moved toward him; her body had lost its own fixity, it was in motion again and the motion was his. Her adolescence had returned to her, all her beauty was springing back; it was as if she had never been broken. And he sat there, her brother, his arms open to receive it, his voice low and compelling, urging her, promising her, taking her away.

Hannah shook her head. He moved toward her urgently, taking her by the arms and seeming to lift her. For a moment Hannah let her head fall forward onto his shoulder, as if the stem support-ing her face was just too weary, or to heavy, to offer any great resistance anymore.

Now was the moment to smash down the dam walls, to stamp all over the delicate constructions. To pull them apart, to stop the tenderness in the hand that moved to Hannah's hair. To end this for once and for all.

Like a rock, she hurled her voice at them. "You have no right," she said savagely. But to whom? To Dawie, who had entered her house, or to Hannah, who betrayed her by being so moved by him?

Hannah's face lifted quickly, but she did not turn. Dawie looked up and around at his sister, but his hand remained where it was, then moved slowly down to Hannah's shoulder.

"Hello, Zelda," he said, feeling for her, feeling her deep unhappiness.

"I won't have you here," she snapped. "You can't change anything now." But her voice wavered sadly because she could see that they had not disengaged. Her threat had only locked them closer together. She was deserted.

He looked at her and all he could think of was the ring in his pocket. The ugly gold ring that the Australian had worn and could not take off; the ring signifying his engagement to Pauline. The ring was the key to Zelda, unlocking all her secrets. He knew that every time he looked at her, he would think of it. He could walk up to her now, open his hand and show it to her, proving that he knew. But it would be like shooting her in the back. He knew he could never do it, never say anything about it to either of them.

"Come and sit down, Zelda," he said.

She would not move. She was thinking about Ruth, Ruth and that—that creature of hers, and the whole disgusting business going on under her roof.

"I hope you've come to take your brat away," she snarled. "It's about bloody time. Take them both away and good riddance."

"Why are you like this, Zelda? Why can't you stop?" he asked angrily. "Why can't you discipline your emotions a bit?"

"Me?" she scoffed. "*My* emotions? Don't make me laugh." She tried to mock him but saw he would not bend.

"Ja, your emotions and your tongue. You have to help us now. It's about time."

Her face shifted and became childlike. "Don't try and order me about, Dawie."

"Either help, or stay out of it altogether."

Zelda watched as Hannah's face turned to look at her. Both of them, seated, watched her, waited for her to make a move.

What was it about them that made her feel so forlorn? His head, her head, his arm about her; Hannah's look of compassion, underlined with determination. Oh, it wasn't that she hated them. It was just that, just that . . .

She moved backward, and, in changing her physical position, changed her attack. "Have you seen it yet?"

"What?" he asked. "Have I seen what?"

"Ruth's . . ." she hesitated, unable to choose a word.

"Yes, I've seen him," he said calmly.

"Well, what will you do now?" It was a small singing chord. "What will you do about it? Have it bleached? Re-classified? Hide it away all it's life?"

"No." He shook his head mildly, with pity. "Those days are over now. Hannah and I will look after him until we see what Ruth wants to do."

"Why do you always . . . ?" she breathed out sharply, feeling anger take its toll inside her guts. "Why must you always . . . ?" She stopped again.

She would get rid of all of it, whatever it cost her. She began wildly, "It was all right, I could take it, everything, even the way you shut me out, hid things from me, played those games, ran into the bush without me whenever you could, kept secrets from me—it was all right." Small specks of purple appeared high along her cheekbones. "Until you, until you went too far—"

"In what way, Zelda?" he asked, wanting to make her say it.

She looked at him and laughed and laughed and laughed. "You think I cared a damn about that?" she raved. "You really think *I* cared?"

"Well, then," he asked quietly, "what *did* you care about so much?"

"Nothing" she said stiffly. "Nothing, nothing at all. Niks."

A small figure in a nightgown appeared behind her, walked past her into the room, and up to the sofa, where she stared down at Dawie. Zelda felt her breath go, as if someone had turned it off with a switch. She watched, transfixed, as Ruth looked from Dawie to her mother and then back to Dawie—where her attention stopped. He too stared at her. She stood quite still, her face very white and strained, the birthmark almost gone, her blue eyes enormous and the bones of her face as prominent as a woman's after long illness.

"I've seen you before," she said.

"Yes." His heart went out to her; she was trying so hard to be adult, to be brave.

"You came over once," she said.

"Yes." He saw that she did not recognize him from the road-block.

"I was swinging on the gate when you came."

He smiled. "Ja, you were. And I said to you, 'Whose little girl are you?' And you said, 'No one's. I'm no one's little girl.'"

"Did I say that?" she asked dreamily.

"Ja, you did. That's when I knew who you were."

Zelda's eyes went dead. Her mouth was a line thin as a knife cut.

"Was that the first you knew about me?" Ruth asked, checking her mother's story.

"Yes."

"And it was after that that the money went to the Post Office?"

He nodded.

"Why didn't you come again?"

"I was asked not to. I came the first time to ask your mother to come with me, to bring you and come with me out of the country, somewhere we could live together."

"And?"

"And she refused."

Ruth flung round at Hannah. "Is that true—that you refused to go?"

Hannah nodded.

"Why?" Ruth snarled. "Why wouldn't you go?"

Hannah smiled. "Perhaps one day I'll tell you."

"I have just one question for you, Ruth," Dawie said.

"Ja?"

"Who is the baby's father? Was it Andries?"

She hesitated, then she smiled. "Perhaps one day I'll tell you," she said.

Twenty-Eight

THEY HAD GONE. THE ROOM WAS EMPTY, APART FROM A FLY, which, trapped between the gauze and the window pane, fought to escape to what was out there: heat, dust, emptiness—and, far in the distance, a woman with something shorn about her, walking her lands with a quiet fury.

As the car slowed to take the bend, she did not turn her head, and when it disappeared in a haze of dust, she merely put her hand down for an instant to touch the dog's head and quiet its savage bark. In the car, Hannah was crying, as if, once she had let herself do so, she could not stop.

Over the blue koppies, where the village had once nestled, the car slowed down. Ruth got out and stood there. She talked for a while with Willie; then Hannah and Dawie joined her. In a little while the car drove off again.

Willie, standing alone among the broken bricks and rubble, watched the car as it gathered speed on the white road and went on toward the horizon.

Then he raised his hand and waved.

192463

F Sla